"I am I and greater than you," said Sheen. "You will be my first conquest."

"I don't want to die," whimpered the tare.

"You won't die. You'll live."

"It will be a living death. No one but you could do such a thing."

The tare's eyes rolled back in his head and his body convulsed. "Somebody tell me what to do!"

"Come," said Sheen, and reached.

"No!" screamed the tare. Even as he said it, he was surrendering.

Frederik Pohl, four-time Hugo Award-winner, editor of some thirty science fiction anthologies and author of more than forty books, is an acknowledged master of his field.

Each book that bears the crest "A Frederik Pohl Selection" reflects the taste, integrity and discrimination that have made his own works so highly respected by critics and enjoyed by millions of readers.

Bantam Science Fiction
Ask your bookseller for the books you have missed

a billion days of earth

by doris piserchia

BANTAM BOOKS
TORONTO   NEW YORK   LONDON

RLI: $\dfrac{\text{VLM 8 (VLR 6–9)}}{\text{IL 8–adult}}$

A BILLION DAYS OF EARTH
A Bantam Book / November 1976

ISBN 0-553-08805-X

Published simultaneously in the United States and Canada

Bantam Books are published by Bantam Books, Inc. Its trade-
mark, consisting of the words "Bantam Books" and the por-
trayal of a bantam, is registered in the United States Patent
Office and in other countries. Marca Registrada. Bantam
Books, Inc., 666 Fifth Avenue, New York, New York 10019.

PRINTED IN THE UNITED STATES OF AMERICA

to
Joe

a
billion
days
of
earth

prologue

Had it just then been born? The creature didn't know. It crawled up out of the volcanic crater, hung there on the lip and stared about. It saw a small thing hopping in the tumbleweeds at the foot of the mountain.

"Help!" it cried.

The animal in the tumbleweeds came to a halt with its short, broad ears perked. It was a tare and it was a descendant of an animal called a rabbit that had been extinct for a billion days. Long-legged, brown-furred, it weighed approximately twenty-five pounds. It was subnormal in intelligence because it wanted to find sense in this world of Three Million, A.D.

"Who calls?" The tare had sufficient intelligence to speak, but he had never before communicated with anything but another tare.

"Who calls?"

The tare was puzzled. "This isn't Echo Valley so why do my words come back to me?"

"Me?"

"You're a silly echo, wherever you come from."

"You?"

"I, you, he, we, you, they," said the tare. "I'm here, you're there, we're both somewhere. Are you up in that dead volcano? Who are you?"

There was a pause, then, "I am I. I want. I am in need."

Grinning up at the mountain, the tare said, "Ask and receive, ignorant child."

"Take my heart that we shall be one."

"Certainly. Would it be to your liking if I trundled up the side of your happy home and flung myself over?"

"That will not be necessary. I will come to you."

The tare saw a thin length of silver slide over the high lip of the mountain and flow downward, and his amusement at the situation changed to uneasiness. "Good Lord, you really do live in that hole. I think I'll get out of here."

"You would abandon me, then, a babe in the woods?"

Pausing to look back, the tare saw more of the strange material edge over the mountain. He gasped and threw his paws over his eyes. "The sheen! I can't see!" For only a moment was he blinded. "Now I'm all right," he said in relief. "But you're still too bright. You look exactly like a stream of mercury."

There was a great deal of the creature. Its front end was already in the grass, but still it poured from the volcano in a steady flow.

"I like that word of yours," it said, as it advanced. Wherever its words originated, they came from no mouth or any other opening. All of it seemed to be speaking and the words were real sounds. It talked without a voice box, it thought without experience, it existed without purpose. Or so the tare assumed.

"I like that word of yours," the creature said again. "It touches an inner chord within me. I will make it my name. From this moment onward, I am Sheen."

"Don't come any closer," said the tare. "To what genus do you belong?"

"The genus of Sheen. I have love for you."

The tare was flattered in spite of his fright. "What a crazy thing you are. We're not the same, so how can you love me?"

"I don't know. You came and your coming inspired me to wakefulness. My thoughts are directed toward you."

Again the tare was amused. This creature was naive, behaved as if it had just been born. "You can't focus your affections on me. You have to set your sights on something like yourself. By the way, what are you besides Sheen?"

"I am I."

"What kind of answer is that?"

"There is much to learn, but I am quick. I love you."

"There you go again. I'm a tare while you're a liquid-solid thing, the likes of which I never saw before, and you can't love me."

"Why?"

"It's against the rules. Gods love Gods, men love men, tares love tares. That's the way it is."

The front portion of Sheen rose in the air and seemed to look about. Earth appeared peaceful. The sky was blue, the sun was orange, the grass was richly green. Without eyes, Sheen saw. His mind touched everything. A mile away, a family of tares made a new burrow in the side of a hill. The mother and father took turns guarding the young and widening the excavation. They would remain together all their lives and have many children. In a few days they would gather with all the mature tares in their area and confer with one another. They would discuss the weather, food, enemies, life. Five miles away, the grass ended and desert began. Sheen looked no further. He was too busy now.

"Do you love nothing in all infinity but tares?" he said.

"Yes, of course, but that isn't the same thing."

Sheen swayed. He no longer came down the mountain but lay across the valley in a thin coil. His head, which had no features, was raised several feet straight up in the air. "I don't understand."

"It's confusing no matter what you are, I guess," said the tare. "One way you can tell what you love is by eliminating everything repulsive to you. You love what's left."

"Nothing is repulsive to me."

"Then you must be very inexperienced. As you go along you'll find plenty to turn your stomach. In fact, most of your life will be spent avoiding those things."

The head and neck of Sheen lowered and coiled at the tare's feet for a moment and then quickly shot into the air like an alert snake. "Enough. Take my heart that we shall be one."

"You said that before." The little tare trembled. "I'm trying to move. There's something wrong with my damned legs. Don't come any closer."

"I think we will merge."

"I don't know what that means, but I don't like the sound of it. I don't want to."

"Yes, you do."

"No!"

Sheen stopped. "Why do you stand there if you want to run?"

"You know why. Release me."

"I'm not in contact with you."

The little beast opened frightened eyes and saw it was true. "You hold me with invisible hands. They're in my mind, pulling at me like magnets."

"Have these hands a voice?"

"A confounding one. No lover ever sounded more alluring. You can't keep so many promises. You lie."

"I've said nothing."

"Lord, lover, companion, tutor, haven! You lie, Sheen! Why do you lie? And why pick on me? See there in the grass, the creature with the shell? It's a jare. Take it and let me go."

"Ah, well, go, if you insist. I choose the lesser creature."

The tare bit himself. "You're holding me!"

"I swear I'm not."

"Don't you know yourself? Take away the picture you've planted in my mind. How can I think straight with that dangling in front of me?"

"Describe the picture, please."

"I don't believe it. Nothing could be that beautiful. This is still the same damned dirty world around us."

Sheen swayed gracefully. "Is life so full of disillusionment?"

"Nothing is the way it should be. Even the elements conspire against me. It's a terrible world full of cruelty."

"Sad, sad."

The furry face twisted, the mouth drooped. "Tares are stupid and hard. No wonder men regard us as nonentities. Poverty, misery, ignorance; what do tares care as long as they have their carrots and their tail every night? Animal comforts are all they're concerned with."

"You have my sympathy," said Sheen.

"The way they behave isn't as bad as the way they

4

think! A person could go mad trying to make sense of that. The world of reason is a terrifying place."

"I can see you're worried."

"Anyone would be. You never know what they're thinking. You knock yourself out trying to please them and they treat you like dirt."

"I know what you mean."

"They never give you a chance! Everything is geared to the almighty carrot. Goddamn it, there are other things worth living for. Just because a fellow has had a few hard knocks and is having trouble getting onto his feet is no reason to consider him inferior."

"I agree," said the shiny one.

"If they would only tell me what they want! If they'd just sit down with me and make a list of do's and don't's. I'd work my ass off learning the rules. By God, they'd have to go a million miles to find somebody willing to work harder."

Sheen glittered, swayed in the air. "Come to me, tare, and I will give you peace."

"No."

"Then give me back my picture. I didn't offer it. You took it."

The tare spoke to the picture in his mind. "Go, before you become my downfall." At once it began to fade. The tare felt a pang of sorrow. The picture contained every fragment of his dreams. Now he knew reality was as drab as he had suspected. As the picture drifted farther from him, he experienced panic. Terror at life's grayness captured him.

He snatched the picture close again, glared at Sheen. "It's mine! Give it to me with no strings attached. I need it."

"I am I and greater than you," said Sheen. "I see the difference between having my cake and eating it, too. You will be my first conquest."

"I don't want to die," whimpered the tare.

"You won't die. You'll live."

"It will be a living death. No one but you could do such a thing."

"I repeat, you are free to go."

"I can't give it up." The words came through chattering teeth. The tare's eyes rolled back in his head and his body convulsed. "Somebody tell me what to do!"

"Come," said Sheen, and reached.

"No!" screamed the tare. Even as he said it, he was surrendering.

The gleaming figure hovered in the air. "Poor little bunny; a living, breathing conflict. The living and the breathing will continue but the conflict will cease."

The tare's face was a rigid mask. "Come closer," he moaned, and Sheen touched his shoulder, flowed. "Draw nearer that I might feel the sheen of you. How cold, how glorious. Know me as no long-lashed lover could ever know me. Fill my body with pleasure and my mind with joy." He gave a weak scream as the silver covered him. "No, I can't give that up! You didn't explain! Take me, but don't take that!"

Sheen consumed the tare's will.

"How could I possess one without the other?" he said, and his tone was puzzled. "Didn't it know they were one and the same?"

There was no response to his remarks. He was alone.

Presently the tare began to walk; or so it seemed. Actually it was Sheen who moved and left the large remainder of his self in the field of grass. Inside an exterior of silver, the tare dwelt in a dream of his own making.

By and by, Sheen approached the jare. It was the descendant of a turtle. Nearly three million years of evolving had given it the ability to open or close its thick shell whenever it pleased. Large and black and intelligent, it lay with its bare back exposed to the sun. Like the tare, this creature had never, until today, conversed with anyone other than its own kind.

"I love you," said Sheen.

"Oh, go on with you," said the embarrassed jare. It slowly closed its shell, just in case. "I'm not that attractive. Besides, you're a tare and we don't fraternize with your kind. By the way, what kind of tare are you with that fancy coat of silver? I've never seen anything like you."

"I am Sheen. Take my heart that we shall be one."

Such a simple conquest it was. The ego-eater quickly conned the jare and consumed his will. Figuratively smacking his lips, Sheen then looked about for something else of the planet to sample.

Over his head, a cloud in the sky began a lazy descent to

the ground, moved toward a spread of soft grass. A large brown creature stepped foot to earth and gestured for the cloud to ascend to its former place in the sky. Sheen observed with interest as the big creature stretched out on the ground. His curiosity increased when the brown one did nothing more than begin a casual search through the high clover.

He approached to within feet of the dark head. All at once he knew. Here was the offspring of Homo Sapiens, a species that long lay moldering in the grave. Was this brown personage Homo Superior? Obviously the brown one considered himself at least that, since he and his kind called themselves Gods.

"Come no closer," said the God, not lifting his attention from the grass. "Stand off or you'll burn yourself on my protective energy shield."

"What are you doing?" said Sheen.

"Looking for four-leaf clovers."

"Good Lord, why?"

"It amuses me."

"I love you."

The God raised his head. His eyes were dark and fathomless. "Not today, Sheen. You're in your infancy and haven't the power to beguile me."

"It's only the energy that separates us. I'll learn how to penetrate it and show your mind a vision of perfection."

The God's eyes were still. "I have lowered the shield. Assault me at once."

It was no assault at all. A fleck of down couldn't pierce steel. The astute Sheen learned his lesson. "You are not yet for me. Sheen would starve with only Gods to feed upon."

He went away and left the brown monarch to his clover hunting. There were degrees of greatness. A novice shouldn't set his sights too high. That which reigned directly beneath the Gods would be fair game.

Sheen turned back toward his birthplace, the Valley of the Dead, and by and by he drew near his mountain. To his surprise he saw a figure busily chopping off pieces of his volcano. The silver being knew things without understanding how he knew them. His mind was like a tightly rolled scroll. Confrontations with reality caused it to loosen, to play out a bit. Knowledge was there in his mind, startling and irrefutable. One day the scroll would be completely unwound. Until then, he would learn himself and the world a little at a time.

He knew something about the creature who was hacking at his mountain. Without ever having seen one, he knew what the thing was. It called itself Homo Sapiens. In this, it was mistaken. The Gods were the descendants of man. The creature with the ax looked a good deal like Homo Sapiens: It had hair on its head, in its armpits and groin; it had two arms and legs, a nose, two eyes, a mouth, a small jaw and a large cranium. It was cunning, omnivorous, and it built cities. It possessed a conscience. But it had no hands. Instead it had paws. Attached to its wrists were metal appendages which it used as hands.

"Hail!" said Sheen. He expected no response, but the creature surprised him by dropping the ax and whirling.

"Upon my soul! What an incredible day. What an incredible fossil."

"Who, me?"

"Indeed! You bear a remarkable resemblance to the Effu."

"The what?"

"An extinct serpent. It required uranium to survive, and there simply wasn't enough of it around."

"I am Sheen. Who might you be?"

The creature bowed. "Professor Blok, Archeological Institute at Osfar, at your service, sir."

"I'm glad to hear it."

"What are you?"

"I told you. Sheen. New genus."

"If I might have a piece of you to take away with me? I'd love to examine you under a scope."

Sheen shrugged. "We'll see. But first, pray tell, you're an inferior type of your species, are you not?"

Blok's eyebrows rose. "As a matter of fact, I'm not an inferior man. My health is only fair, but I'm above average in intelligence and I hold an important position in my society."

"Oh, hell, I have such rotten luck these days."

"What seems to be the trouble?"

"I can't do my thing."

"What is your thing?"

"It's difficult to explain."

His expression slightly impatient, Blok picked up the ax and attacked the volcanic wall.

"I've an uncanny nature," said Sheen. "I can't come into physical contact with a thing unless it grants me permission. You can see that this would be a lonely position for one to be in. I'm a very gregarious person, must have a pal or I go mad."

Blok was beginning to perspire. The rock was hard, barely yielding to the sharp blade. "I'll be your pal," he said, over his shoulder.

"What a wonderful thing for you to say. Just for that I'll do something wonderful in return." Sheen showed the Professor a picture of perfection.

Blok dropped the ax. "Good Lord!" he yelped.

"Ecstatic, eh?"

"How did you do that? How did you put that picture in my mind?"

"Does it matter?" said Sheen.

"Are you a telepath?"

"I haven't the slightest idea of what goes on in your mind. But I'm wasting my time here. I don't want to fool around with a superior person. What I need is a dumb one, somebody who can't discern a guileful remark. I'm afraid you would be too quick for me."

Said Blok, "See here, what are you up to? What are you going to do if you find yourself a dumb man?"

"Invite him to live in that world you see in your mind."

"Is that all?"

"That's really and truly all."

Blok thought it over. "It's such an attractive place, you might not be doing him an injustice. What would he have to give as payment?"

"His ego. That part of him won't fit in paradise. Botches up the works."

"Uncanny. What do you do with his ego?"

"Preserve it."

"Hmm," said Blok.

Sheen snorted grumpily. "Give me my picture. I must be off in search of someone who needs blessed peace."

"I sort of hate to part with it."

"Hand it over. You won't do. You have too developed a brain to tolerate true pleasure."

Blok looked displeased. "The best things in life are appreciated most by the most intelligent."

"Pshaw."

"The more awareness there is, the more there is to be aware of."

Sheen grew a hand on his tare-forearm and scratched his head. "I don't think so. I think you may be in error."

Laughing, Blok said, "For a second there you sounded like old Trop, a colleague of mine."

"Trop? Oh, yes, I know the man. Very sound fellow."

This time it was the Professor's turn to doubt. "How can you know him? You didn't even know I was a man."

"Who said that? I never said that."

"You did."

Again Sheen scratched his head. "Somebody around here is mixed up. But you may take my word for it, Trop is an old acquaintance of mine, and it is my humble opinion that he's a stout fellow."

Blok glared. "He's a buffoon and you know it. He has the gall to attempt a dissertation on the Effu. I mean, how silly can you get? No one knows a thing about it but me."

"I know about it, and Trop will, too, shortly."

"What do you mean?"

"He and I made a deal. He's going to give me his ego and in return I'm giving him the lowdown on the Effu. He'll be famous once he gets that paper finished."

"You can't!" Blok's face was red. "I've been hunting the Effu's geneology for ten years. That snake is mine!"

"How can something extinct for ten thousand years be yours? Don't be a hog."

"But not Trop! He's insufferable!"

"You have to admit he has a lot of courage. Imagine someone handing over his ego in exchange for the geneology of every snake that every lived? And I mean every snake. Trop will be omniscient. But, still, the ego is a very personal thing and shouldn't be given to everyone who comes along."

"Omniscient!" Horror was in every line of Blok's face.

"Yes. Incidentally, the Effu didn't pass away because he ran out of uranium and starved to death."

"He did!"

"He lived too homogenously, dropped the eggs in the same old places. By and by, the area became volcanic and Effu didn't have sense enough to move."

Blok's jaw was slack but his eyes were hot. "What does that mean?"

Sheen grew nails on his tare-paws, examined them. "Those eggs had extremely thin shells."

"Go on."

"Suppose you laid a thin-shelled egg on a slice of shale, and then suppose you hammered gently on its bottom side?"

"Good God, they cracked! The rumbling broke them!"

"Elementary."

Cried Blok, "Ha, that damned Trop can climb a tree! My paper will beat his into print by at least a week."

"Shame on you. But then it doesn't matter if you cheat. The Effu wasn't much compared to the Kubu."

"The Kubu!" Blok stamped his feet. "You can't do it. You can't tell Trop about the Kubu."

"That's more significant than measly old Effu."

"Wait, wait, just hold on a goddamn minute." Blok wiped his dripping brow, groaned and rolled his eyes skyward. "You can't do it. He'd be a hero."

The Professor was his own special kind of fool. After shivering and trembling and giving the situation some thought, he calmed down and even managed to sound casual. "Keep your blamed picture and your paradise. I don't care if you make Trop famous. I know what he is, and if others don't realize it, they deserve whatever they get."

"I wasn't trying to hurt you," said Sheen.

"Well, once he gives you his ego he won't do any more interfering. He'll be out of my hair. I can relax and indulge myself in interesting hobbies."

"You have hobbies?"

Blok waved a careless arm. His breathing was almost back to normal. "I go in for geneology of a very personal type. What I really want to do is trace my lineage back four or five hundred years. I've made a small contribution to the world. Somewhere back in time were unique people who made me what I am. I want to find proof . . . well, I just want to know who they were. I take pride in them."

Sheen writhed in anticipation. "How will you begin your research?"

"I already have. I'm a sixth-generation Easterner. My great, great, great-grandfather was one of the pioneers who came over on the *Chaos Queen*. It was the first train to run out here from the West."

"Hmm, yes, I know of the *Chaos Queen*."

Blok smiled. "What a geneologist does is tramp through graveyards and read headstones. Mostly, that's what he does. There are courthouse records, but too many times you're told the place burned down with all the records destroyed. The graveyards are the best bet, and they aren't bad spots. I take my lunch and spend the day."

"Sounds like a picnic."

"Not exactly. Unfortunately, I'm running out of graveyards. In fact, I'm just marking time. The graves I need are fifteen thousand miles across the desert, and I haven't a hope of making the trip. I'd need at least two months and I have a job that allows me twenty days off a year."

"You don't need to make the trip. I can show you your geneology back to Adam."

"Who's he?"

"Mythical father of the human race. Of which you ain't a member."

"Ain't what? I mean, isn't? I mean, what are you talking about?"

"What makes you think you're human?"

Blok's face was a portrait of puzzlement and increasing pique. "What do you think you are, a prophet? Are you trying to say something profound?"

Sheen laughed in good humor. "I like you, Doc, I really do. Do you want me to show you your primeval pappy?"

Alarm flared in Blok's eyes. He backed away and crouched low with the claw on his metal hands menacing. "Don't show me anything."

"Calm down. I won't do a thing without your permission. Come here and I'll tell you about your fourth great-granddaddy who's buried in Chin."

"Chin!"

"I can see him in my mind right now; tall and fearless, a

giant of a fellow in intellect and body. No wonder you're the man you are."

Blok came closer. "Really?"

"He was a bit of a hell-raiser, though; spent a few nights in jail."

The Professor grinned.

"Womanizer, too."

The Professor blushed.

"As a matter of fact, your ancestress wasn't his wife."

Blok blanched in horror.

Sheen grinned. "Practically everyone in Osfar is descended from a whore. What kind of women do you think those trailblazers fraternized with? What kind do you think came out here on the *Chaos Queen?*"

Blok's eyes were stark.

Sheen showed him a picture. "See there. That's your grandpappy who's buried in Chin."

The disgust in Blok's expression changed to admiration. "He was big."

Sheen showed a second picture. "And there is his father."

"Oh, he's so small."

"Not everyone can be a giant. The height came from the females in that case. And here is his father."

Blok stood enthralled as Sheen revealed to him the faces and figures of his ancestors, one by one. They flashed through his head like a motion picture. At times he laughed aloud or groaned at the ridiculous poses or modes of dress.

Then, subtly, the facial expressions of the strangers began to change. Or was it the features themselves that were altering?

"They're getting uglier," he whispered.

"You haven't seen anything yet." Sheen continued to show pictures, and it wasn't long before Blok was on his knees with his paws over his face.

"No more," he begged.

"Heck, they're still wearing clothes. I thought you were an intellectual. I'm showing you the ascendancy backward, and you're moaning."

Another picture flashed in Blok's head. There were two

figures in this one. He cried out, "What's that? Oh, my God, what is that?"

"It's a man drawing a bead on your grandpappy. Obviously, he missed."

"A man?" Blok gasped. "It looks like a God. It is a God! And that other thing! That isn't my ancestor!"

"I'm afraid it is. But don't give up now. The best is yet to come. To the devil with all these in-betweens, I'm going to show you a specimen of your primeval, primeval ancestors. Ready?"

The picture appeared, and a moment later Blok crumpled to the ground. He lay on his back, staring at the sky, and when Sheen bent over him he saw the surrender in the eyes.

Poor Blok couldn't take too much knowledge. Almost hungrily he reached for his savior. "Blank it out," he pleaded. "Take it from my mind. Take me and make me omniscient but never show me that picture again. It makes me want to vomit. I could never hold up my head again."

Sheen took him from the feet upward. "What does it matter if you descended from a rat? Nobody ever began from himself, except me."

"It matters," said Blok, tranquil now and ready for his destiny. "The mind is no good once it rejects itself as I've done. It was an instinctive reaction, but I went too far. I can't go back. I don't want to go back. I want peace and forgetfulness."

Sheen had reached his shoulders. "I'll be gentle with you," he said. The silver being experienced a twinge of shame. Blok hadn't been so bad. The man had some very good sides to his character.

"I will forget?" said Blok, as he was completely covered.

"Not exactly. I'm afraid you can't be omniscient with a memory block."

Blok saw and was shaken. "Oh, Sheen, you lied. No, you didn't lie. I lied to myself. Man is an I-want, an I-value, and an I-will. He is a hunger, a conscience, and a power. Now I'm an I-want and an I-value. Too late I see that man's I-will is his most vital part. With it he puts himself onto the path of mobility, makes it possible for his three parts to coexist. Now I have no peace, nor can I ever have it. The I-want is an appetite that has no boundaries or saturation point. It is a mouth that demands everything in sight. I want, and you provide it for me, but there is no way for me to choose between my wants, no way for me to say, 'No, not this one,' 'Yes, that one.' Though I know the good and the evil because of my I-value, there is no I-will to state the choice. My I-value can only sit there and judge this hell. A hog of an appetite and a Freudian guilt complex are the best description of what Blok is and will remain. Shame on Sheen. He survives on the agony of others."

The silver creature winced. "Be still. I say be silent. Chide me no more. I have consumed it all."

Blok was still. Blok was totally imprisoned. Blok was not.

"How do I do it?" murmured Sheen. "Born in ignorance, I have knowledge unheard of. It is there, a well of it, beneath the surface of my consciousness. A word, phrase or gesture taps that well, and I have all the answers. Nice. But what am I for? Why and who am I?"

He considered the history of Earth: Homo Sapiens disappeared somewhere around the year Two Million. His children, Homo Superior, the Gods, became the dominant species. Sapiens had enjoyed experimenting with the genes of other organisms. So did the Gods. Strange crossbreeds came into being. The sparrow and the honeybee were mated and became a fuzzy little creature that made its home in the rotted trunks of trees. Eventually the Gods crossbred it with the housecat. The zizzy was born: a furred, winged, four-legged animal with a stinger on its tail and a high order of intelligence in its complex brain.

While the Gods played with the anatomies of many lesser creatures, one of the least of all creatures began a rapid evolution on its own. The rat gained in stature and intellect. The Gods grew interested, watched and waited and soon saw that the rat was assuming human qualities. This amused them. They taught the rats to be like Homo Sapiens of old.

Perhaps evolution always followed the same pattern, or perhaps the interference of the Gods caused the rat species to produce individuals who closely resembled men of olden times. At any rate, it amused the Gods to teach the newly rising species to be men, and when some "rat" reminded the monarchs of a human in their own history, they gave the "rat" the same name. So the rats had their Khans, Lord, Hitler, Freud, et cetera, and never knew the difference.

Eventually the strength of the Gods increased and they lost interest in ordinary events. They had almost total command over matter. They were telepathic and could even move their bodies through the air.

In the year Three Million, Sheen came. He didn't know his destiny. He would when he began to dream. He was an ego. For the present the Gods were above him, while lower organisms would soon be beneath him. He came to accost and his targets were the evolved descendants of rats; new man; Homo Sapiens in nearly every aspect.

Sheen: a creature of conscience and increasing power.

chapter 1: the new men of earth

Rik was sitting in his living room reading the paper when a racket came at the window. It intensified until Aril threw it open. Into the room came her pet zizzy. As usual, it flew over Rik with its stinger pointed at him.

"Damn it!" he said, hunching down in the chair. "The next time that thing gets close to me, I'll hook it with my claw."

Aril grabbed the zizzy out of the air and held it close. "It doesn't mean any harm."

Rik eyed the animal warily. One stab of its stinger in his carotid and he would have no troubles left. "Put it in its cage," he said. He looked away before she kissed it.

The zizzy nuzzled Aril's neck with its woolly head and she giggled. She made little crooning sounds and squeezed it so hard it should have popped. It buzzed and snorted and tried to hug her with its puny forearms. Aril had found it in the street, half-dead, and brought it home.

Rik had already tried to get rid of it. Once when Aril was away he drove a hundred miles and dumped it out near an oasis. The zizzy was back home before him, tearing up the new roof gutters and screaming to get in.

He considered it a good-for-nothing. It wouldn't even gather nectar like a normal zizzy. Probably it had some brain damage. But it was bright enough to recognize a good situation. It was loose almost every night, chasing female zizzys or stealing desserts from window sills, and it conned Aril into reserving big portions of sweets for it. All day it snored in its cage, and in between times it terrorized the man of the house. It had no use for Rik. If he touched its cage door, it buzzed for Aril at the top of its lungs.

Zizzys had a three-foot wingspread. A man couldn't outrun one in flight. They had long sucker-tongues that could drain a tare dry in a matter of minutes, but they generally didn't eat meat, preferring fruits or nectar.

Pug was a fair example of his species, except for the intelligence part. He wouldn't have done a good job of providing for himself. It took cunning to build a pouch in a tree and then weave a handle and fasten it over a limb so that the pouch swung freely. It required brains to compartmentalize the inside of a pouch so that the food and water, the hatching pad and the sleeping quarters didn't fall in on each other. Pug had no need for a pouch. He ate what Aril fed him, or what he could pilfer, he grounded his females wherever he caught them, he slept in his cage and the tribal calls of his kind didn't seem to affect him.

Pug weighed close to thirty pounds. Built in three segments, he was black with wide orange stripes that crisscrossed his body. His face was furry, his eyes green, nose very blunt, mouth almost invisible until he opened it, and then there was the red hole full of sucker. He had a long striped tail that ended in a vicious-looking stinger. His arms and legs were too weak to support his weight for long. He had no feet or paws, just big sharp claws that could close about a tree limb and leave indentations in the bark.

A little mane of hair grew down Pug's neck, and whenever he became excited it stood erect. His wings were gray and nearly transparent, with five tough bones in each. They grew just behind his shoulder blades. When he took off from the ground, he tucked his tail under his belly and bent his arms and legs in tight. In repose, his wings lay on him like a double blanket.

Aril put him in his cage and stood stroking him through the bars. All at once she turned to Rik. "I'm going back to the fold," she said.

He didn't react outwardly.

"I need it," she said, and he knew better than to give her an argument. She hadn't been to church since she was fif-

18

teen years old, but she had forgotten that, along with all the other things.

"I can't stay away any longer," she said. "The Lord calls me night and day."

"Go ahead. It might do you some good." Right away he knew he had said the wrong thing.

"I'm not going because it will do me good."

"If you want to join again, go ahead. I hope they take you back, and I hope you do a world of good."

"You're pacifying me."

"No, I'm not. But if you want my advice, stay away from Brog and his pack of nuts." He knew he shouldn't have said it. Before she could react, he grabbed his hat and left the house in a hurry.

A few blocks away, a crowd gathered, and he spotted his adopted brother, Jak, in the middle of it. He pushed his way in and grabbed Jak's arm. "Come out of here," he said.

Jak pulled free. "I want to go with them. I'll never learn if I stay out of everything."

"You know all about zizzys that you need to know."

"They're raiding the Gods' silos."

Rik made a sound of disgust as he saw a group of policemen hurrying up the street. It was too late. He and Jak were about to be conscripted.

The officer with the loudest voice and the biggest badge climbed onto a box. "Everybody in this bunch is deputized!" he shouted. "Dissenters will be escorted to the courthouse where their names will be recorded in the Book of Cowards."

Rik stood still while a badge was pinned to his shirt.

"You ready to do your duty?" said the officer, suspicious because this man hadn't joined in the cheering. When Rik nodded, he said, "Get to the arsenal and pick up your weapon."

Yelling good-naturedly, the mob shoved its way across a boulevard to the red brick arsenal. Uniformed men threw guns out the door and metal hands snatched them from the air.

They went in big trucks that ground across the desert like sluggish bugs. There were six vehicles with twenty men in each. They all knew what to do, whether or not they had gone after zizzys before.

Everyone knew the psychology of King Bebe. Bebe was some kind of nut. Fifty years ago it had been a dog-eat-dog world, but now it was civilized. Every so often Bebe decided to ignore the armistice. Attacks on the silos weren't a declaration of war against men, but the treaty specifically stated that the property of Gods was to be left alone. People were liable to get killed if the Gods became perturbed. It didn't matter if a person had two legs or a pair of wings; the Gods became emotional when their silos were raided. They had to eat three-dimensional food and they didn't like spending time growing and harvesting it just to have men or zizzys steal it.

When zizzys went on a silo raid, men went out and attacked them. If the attack was successful, if the zizzys were driven back into the desert before the Gods came, everyone could go home and tell about their war experiences and not worry about Godly retribution. The fact that Gods never wreaked vengeance on those not actually at the scene of the crime was irrelevant. There was always the possibility the Gods would grow incensed enough to wipe out a whole city, maybe the entire race. Who understood anything about Gods; who could predict their reactions? Besides, war was hell.

If the danger from man had been confined to his ability to shoot at and hit a moving target, the zizzys never would have pressed for an armistice. But man was cruel and crafty. He was good at setting traps, his poisons were virulent and his fire was intolerable. An armistice was the only solution.

Men hadn't sat at a table with zizzys and talked over the situation. The two couldn't communicate. There existed no piece of paper, no legal document. The armistice was an understanding that had been reached through trial, error and bloodshed on both sides. Men learned how to behave in the presence of zizzys and vice versa. Both knew what was expected of them if there was to be peace. If one side broke the rules, the other side retaliated, so neither side broke the rules and hadn't for fifty years. Except, that is, during the occasional little wars. The treaty didn't apply to individual encounters. If a zizzy caught a man alone, he was liable to try and kill him. But groups of men left groups of zizzys alone. The armistice was never called off because of battles over the Gods' silos. Bebe would take his troops home and behave himself for a while after this fracas was finished.

Back to the war:

"It's too late to stop them!" someone yelled.

Everybody in the truck glared at the man.

"Rik!" Jak breathed the name and shrank down in his seat.

"You wanna quit?" growled an officer.

"Yeah, I wanna quit. I don't wanna get clobbered."

"What's your name, mister?"

"Turn your stiff neck and see how far those striped bellies have gone. How long do you think it takes a God to get the word? We'll be caught with our pants down."

All heads turned to the battlefield.

The striped bellies were having a hell of a time. Every window in the silo had been shattered and zizzys flew in and out of the openings. The building was a spear of bronze. From its twenty-foot-diameter base, it reared eighty feet to a pointed roof. It was difficult to believe it had been constructed by the mind of some God, yet it was a known fact that the monarchs didn't use machines. They had no cities, no factories, no smelting plants. All they had was an uncanny talent.

The zizzys coming out of the shattered windows carried honey and grain while those who entered were going back for another load. They ate as they flew. Thirty feet above the roof, a hundred zizzys made a train of their bodies, and into the carts on their backs went the stolen food. At ground level a dozen or so fat females lay on their backs while males hung from the silo windows and squeezed honey from tubes into their mouths. There were personal squabbles taking place here and there. Zizzys crawled up and down the walls in pursuit of companions who had snatched their food. Some rolled on the ground, clawing each other or trying to strike with their stingers. A few romances progressed in the high grass, and two females were making good headway toward dismembering a male they both claimed.

High in the sky above them all flew King Bebe. He kept watch for Gods and man, and he expressed his delight that man was there first by doing some fancy calisthenics in the air. It had been a long time since he had done any fighting, and he longed to draw the battle's first blood.

He had his wish. As the lead truck ground to a stop,

Bebe soared into the clouds until he was invisible. Folding his wings, he dropped like a rock, straight at the twenty heads in the truck. He was a missile in flight, his appendages tucked in and his stinger aimed like a spear. He made no sound as he dropped, and his stinger was two inches into a man's temple before anyone knew of his presence. The target died without complaint and Bebe was zooming skyward in the next instant, buzzing over his victory as he climbed. A bullet came perilously close as he ascended, and he slowed long enough to cast a startled glance below. Men were notoriously bad shots but the figure calmly drawing another bead on him was an exception. The fool had hunter in him. Bebe shouted with laughter and began some diversive flying that soon had the man bobbing helplessly. Quickly the zizzy leader forgot his skillful enemy. The other trucks had arrived and his troops were preparing to advance to the front.

The second truck lost a wheel and overturned in a ditch. A man with a weapon was a fair match for a zizzy directly in front of him but two coming at him from the sides made him vulnerable. Bebe signaled for a roundabout and sent a squadron pelting eastward. They circled sharply to the south and in minutes were positioned behind the scattered trucks.

Most of the men were still scrambling for solid footing. Where they intended to make their stand remained a secret, since the ranking officer had been killed by Bebe. Listening for orders that never came, they ran for tall grass while the first squadron of zizzys zoomed in from the southeast. The zizzys had no better aim with their stingers than men had with guns, so there was only one casualty from this assault. A man grew alarmed by the sound of wings behind him and whirled in time to take a stinger in the eye. The rest of the winged soldiers stabbed backs, rumps and skulls and did no real damage other than to numb the perforated areas for a few minutes.

Meanwhile, Bebe sent another squadron southward to catch the men with their backs turned again.

The men used their rifles as clubs. Now and then a lucky swing sent a zizzy crashing to the ground. A man could then ram his gun barrel into the soft belly and blast away. More often than not, excitement caused the shot to go awry. Only three zizzys died before the squadron from the rear arrived.

The last truck carried the flamethrowers, and it was toward this vehicle that Rik ran, dragging Jak with him. Ever since the man beside him had died with the stinger in his temple, Jak had been in a state of shock. Rik would have preferred to stay in his own truck but the zizzys had driven him out. The men were outnumbered and their commanding officer was dead. The other officers were too busy fending off the enemy to plot strategy.

Four zizzys attacked. Steadily cursing, Rik put one foot on the cringing body of his brother and used his rifle as a battering ram. Sure of a victory, the zizzys dodged the blows and three of them charged. Rik dropped the rifle and flexed his elbow at the proper angle so that the hook in his mechanical hand shot out about four inches. This was done in a split second and even as the hook was emerging he swung his arm in a circle and whirled. The hook caught the nearest zizzy in the abdomen. Immediately Rik fell on his back and held his arm up. The two enemies who were plunging at him collided while the one overhead stabbed its stinger into its dead comrade. A savage downward thrust of Rik's arm broke the impaled stinger at its base.

The crippled zizzy screamed and flapped skyward. It wept bitterly. For it, the fight was over. War was over. Everything was over. It would never grow another stinger, never be able to forage alone, never be allowed to participate in the mating games. The joy of life was finished. Now all that remained was the peace of death. The zizzy climbed high into the sky and plummeted headfirst toward the ground.

Rik didn't watch the suicide. He continued to drag Jak toward the truck that contained the flamethrowers. He wasn't thinking of waging war with the enemy. Someone was bound to go for the flamethrowers sooner or later, and he didn't want to be a target when some maniac began tossing fire around.

Zizzys came at him. He dumped Jak on the ground. "Yell if one comes at me from your direction!" he cried. He shot a zizzy from the air.

Jak screamed and Rik whirled in time to see a man haul a flamethrower from the truck. "Not at me!" he roared, and dropped flat before a stream of yellow fire blasted above him.

"I want to go home," moaned Jak, on his belly and trying to crawl.

"Get up and run," said Rik.

The man with the flamethrower staggered away from the truck. His face was white with fear. He veered to the right, stopped and looked about.

"I'll be branded a coward," whined Jak.

"Shut up!" said Rik.

The flamethrower was aimed at the silo and its operator was laughing hysterically. Every time he pulled the trigger, he screamed. All the warriors had gotten out of his way and were now running or flying to get beyond his range. A sensible zizzy began to descend over his head. Another man raised a rifle. Rik groaned and shot him in the arm. The zizzy finished his dive, stung the firethrower in the shoulder and put him out of action.

As soon as the danger of fire was gone, Bebe's troops returned to battle. They gathered in force behind the silo, about two hundred strong. To the appalled men they looked like a solid wall of stingers. Not a soldier held his ground. More than a hundred men tried to find protection beneath the trucks, in trees or shrubbery or under the bodies of their comrades.

Rik sat on a tree limb and picked off zizzys as fast as he could pull the trigger of his rifle. Behind him, Jak cringed and whimpered. Several zizzys flew at the tree, found it too time-consuming to crawl through the foliage and gave up to find easier targets.

A boy came running across the grass, his mouth open in a silent scream. He had no weapon. Behind him came two zizzys. They were in no great hurry. Their tails were curled in under their bellies and their stingers were out and on a level with the boy's back.

Rik shot the one in the rear and then took slower aim at the second. There came an ominous click that told him he was out of shells. The zizzy flew under the tree and as it passed below he left his perch and dropped onto its back. They crashed to the ground. Knowing the creature was either dead or stunned, Rik rolled clear.

"Get down out of there!" he called to Jak.

"No!"

"Come down. We have to get away."

"They'll get us!"

"You silly slob, come down."

Jak's head emerged from the leaves. "We can stay here. They can't get at us."

"Hurry. There's no time."

"Look out!"

Rik grasped the tree trunk and whirled around it. There was a thudding sound and a zizzy rammed its stinger in the wood. It buzzed and lunged and tried to pull free.

High in the air, King Bebe gave a shriek. Rik heard it because he had been listening for just that sound.

"Jak, I'm leaving you to the zizzys," he said.

Again Jak's head popped out of the leaves. When he saw that he was being abandoned, he came down the tree trunk in a flash. "You can't leave me!"

"Watch your back," Rik said. He kept walking away. The zizzys watched him, but their real attention was on their king who continued to circle in the sky and sound a warning.

Jak turned and saw a zizzy flying toward him. "Damn you," he said. "Damn you, Rik." With a swipe of the hook on his artificial hand, he drove the zizzy away.

"Come on," called Rik. He had paused beside a clump of brush. "Run, you jackass!"

"No."

"Stay, then, and when those Gods get done with you, write me a letter."

Jak gasped and looked at the sky. He saw the cloud at about the same time everyone else saw it. Luckily he didn't allow himself to be awed enough to linger. Running after Rik, he didn't see the black cloud again until it halted a few feet above the silo. A God stepped to the roof, then another God, and another.

The three monarchs stood on the glittering spires and surveyed the scene below. Their expressions were cold and austere. All at once they lifted their arms high. Anticipation held the armies stationary.

Things happened. The grass on the ground swayed. The earth rumbled. A tree was uprooted, elevated to fifteen feet. It remained in the air and thrashed furiously. Zizzys were overcome with fear and lost their power of flight. Men stood frozen with their eyes stark.

The low grass at the base of the silo began to stir. Dark

green vines that normally hugged the ground writhed and flowed outward from the building. They flowed slowly at first, spread out thinly and then they thickened and gathered speed.

"Run like you never ran before!" said Rik.

The vines flowed until they reached the first living creatures. Languidly they wrapped themselves about feet or wings, climbed upward to wind around heads and throats, clung gently. Mouths opened to shriek as the green matter came in contact with bare skin.

Outward flowed the vines like a river that ran over running men and crawling zizzys until there were only a few at the fringes of the battlefield who remained untouched.

Jak matched Rik's strides and together they sped away with the vines mere yards behind them. They ran with the soft rustling in their ears, and no one had to tell them which way to go. They went wherever the rustling sound was not.

The plants traveled in a wide circle that would close somewhere in front of them. Rik raced toward a line of crawling green on his right, gradually caught up with the foremost edge, and when the carpet suddenly surged toward him, he leaped across the slender strip and rushed into open space. Immediately the vines veered and plummeted ahead to try and cut him off again.

He saw a dark splotch in front of him, an independent patch of vines that waited for the larger growths to come to it. As his feet pounded against the ground, the patch came to life and slid outward in a wide rectangle. He ran faster. If the patch had kept its original shape, he would have been forced right or left where the greater masses crept all around him, but the rectangle was narrow on one end and he jumped across it. Without pausing, he crashed into the brush on the other side of the patch, fell to his knees and was up and running with the next motion.

Jak was the better sprinter because his legs were longer between knee and thigh. A few yards in the lead, he suddenly gave a cry as the vines swerved and licked his heel. He grasped the limb of a tree and hauled himself into it. The vines took to the tree trunk with fluid grace.

"Jump!" yelled Rik.

Jak stared in horror at the growths coming up after

him, stared in greater horror at what lay on the ground all around the tree.

"Jump!" Rik yelled.

Jak jumped. His feet were on the vines long enough for them to lash his ankles and then he hurtled out of them to freedom. He cried out and staggered.

"Don't stop!" Rik shouted, and Jak was on the move again.

A man came plunging through the undergrowth. He howled in agony and tried to yank a tangle of vines from his upper body. Those around his legs were uprooted by his savage thrusts. One by one they dropped from him, but he blindly staggered into another thick patch that took his feet and hobbled him. Falling, he lay thrashing and shrieking as the vines bound him tightly. He was still struggling as Jak and Rik passed out of sight.

Only a culvert lay between them and the edge of the desert, and as Rik approached it he saw the green carpet of vines already flowing over the lip. They were now moving faster than he, and they would either catch him in the culvert or on the other side.

He flexed his elbows and the metal hands withdrew up his arms. Without breaking stride, he kicked off his shoes and dropped onto his paws. The joint in the middle of each foot flexed and bent until only half his feet touched the ground. His body stretched out, his chest arched, and with his head held high into the breeze, he leaped out over the culvert with almost as much agility as his early ancestors had possessed. He and his brother cleared the farthest side and let momentum carry them skidding onto the desert.

Jak started to run again but Rik caught him by the leg. "It's all right! The vines can't come onto the sand!"

The boy he had saved from the zizzys came plowing toward them, a foot or so ahead of the green carpet. It looked as if he were going to make it but then a vine flashed into the air and struck his arm. He howled and dodged as it swung toward his throat. Another vine came at him from the left, tossed a tendril across his chest, curled around his back and tied itself in a knot. Seconds later, dozens of tendrils were wrapped around him. He dug in with his toes. His body bent forward, he strained with all his might and walked the last few inches over the grass with a hundred tendrils trying to hold him back. He touched the sand with a foot and continued to inch forward. The vines went with him until their length ran out. Giving a vicious wrench, the boy pulled free. He ran wildly across the desert and didn't look back.

The vines crawled to the edge of grass and stopped. Those behind the front fringes also halted. For the first time in many minutes, all was calm. Movement ceased. The green stretches of oasis once again lay quiet.

"Oh, God, I hurt!" wept Jak. "Why did so many of them have to die?"

Rik lay on his back and breathed deeply. "They aren't dead. They'll wish they were, though, for a couple of weeks. Then they'll be as good as new."

"What do you mean?"

"Anyone with no sense at all could fight his way out of that green stuff."

"What is it?"

"Kru. The more you struggle, the harder it rubs on you. Gives you one hell of an itch."

Jak hauled up his pants legs. His ankles were pink and glistening, already swelling, and they were spotted with a dark rash. As he scratched, he stared at the oasis. His face was pale. "Like a baby who needed a spanking," he said huskily. "Goddamn them. The superior bastards. I hate them."

chapter ii

Rik laid a gloved forearm across his mouth to stifle sudden mirth and faded back into the foliage in case some small sound had carried across the clearing. The figure leaning against the golden dais didn't turn.

As always, Rik marveled and snickered at the nakedness of Tontondely. The Brain, the Five-Fingered, the Great, yet for all this, the God looked ridiculous with his bare rump glaring in the sunlight like twin moons. Tontondely was a fine representative of his breed. What a head, what shoulders, what a rear!

Rik risked a wary step into the clearing. The old sun turned the hair on his head to amber. Sluggish wind ruffled it, chilled his neck. Tension dried his throat and nostrils. He knew he was asking for a hot bolt between the eyes. All Tontondely had to do was will it, and his energy shield could become a killing spear.

But Gods weren't perfect. Tontondely's formidable mental powers were concentrated on a game of creation. An enemy could now approach with stealth, even draw near if he dared, and, if he were foolish, he might hope to leap swiftly enough to evade the monarch's shaft of wrath when he was perceived.

The Gods seldom missed a trick, and Rik expected to be perceived. But there remained the tantalizing gamble that the youth wouldn't immediately destroy what he had made but would lay it down and turn to something else.

Above Tontondely's head, Andromeda lay suspended in

space like a miniature plate of jewels. The boy destroyed a meteor swarm and a solar system grew in its place. Rik knew what was being built. He had always been interested in astronomy. He also wondered why a young God should be so interested in a particular solar system in another galaxy.

The system was huge, or the distance between bodies was great. The bodies themselves were few. There were the sun and three immense planets, one the color of an emerald and cloaked with snowy atmosphere. This was the thing Tontondely seemed to love.

Like one of the petrified corpses in the forest, Rik stood without making a sound and watched as the young God made his toy in the air. The face of Tontondely was frozen in concentration. Not a line marred his brow, no expression touched his eyes or mouth. He was the great grandson of Luvon who had once walked down the main street of Osfar and stopped to lay his hand on a child's head.

Tontondely was seven feet tall and wouldn't reach his full height of eight feet for two decades. Sixteen years old, he would be mature at thirty-six and begin to age a century after that. Unlike the beasts and ratmen scattered over the earth, Tontondely had no body hair. His skull was covered by a dark brown layer of calse which was neither protoplasm nor metal. Calse was a combination of the two and grew naturally from the boy's head. The top edges of his fingers and toes were fortified with calse. His teeth were hard and small, twenty-eight of them, and the inner pulp was so solidly encased in white calse that no bacteria could bore through. His ears were small and round, nose short, eyes large and dark; the lips were thin and brownish-red. The facial skin was taut while the neck was soft but firm. Tontondely had no waspish waist. Heavy-shouldered and thighed, his powerful trunk tapered slightly at the belly, yet his body was supple.

This was Tontondely, great grandson of Luvon whose solidified corpse stood ankle-deep in the loam of Echo Valley.

The boy looked at the tiny galaxy he had made and suddenly gave a sigh. With a flick of his finger, he erased a corner of stars. Shifting his weight from the dais, he reached behind him and gestured it into oblivion. He called a low-lying cloud to him, braced it with thin netting and lay upon it. He picked the toy from the air and gently lowered it to the ground. Then he began to make himself a make-believe lover.

His new creation was less real than the galaxy. Tenuous in outline, she hadn't a fraction of the substance of the little worlds that rested beneath him. She would never lie in his arms or touch his lips with hers or perceive his thoughts and desires. She would never be as beautiful as Vennavora whom he loved.

In the meantime, Rik was running swiftly and silently across the clearing. Every nerve in his body flinched in anticipation of a hot bolt as he grabbed the toy cluster of stars. Turning, he raced back toward the foliage. He ran with his prize held close, and had Tontondely killed him on the spot he would have died smiling. Anyone with a grain of courage would choose to go down resisting a God. The big brown lump named Tontondely was no deity. He and his kind were not omnipotent, omnipresent, omni-anything. They were evolved creatures, the same as ordinary people, and people would realize it if they weren't so stupid.

Rik cried out his triumph as he sped through the sheltering trees, but he did it softly because the Gods could fly on wings of their own making. He didn't slow down even after he knew he had escaped. Across a wide flat rock he ran; down he slid into a gully and scrambled up the other side. Suddenly realizing that he was on top of a living hill, he came to a quick halt.

The wrinkled brown hill didn't slope upward to a peak. Three feet high and many yards in diameter, it had an uneven surface peppered with fat round pores from which grass blades sprouted. The surface rippled and bulged as the hill moved stones and pebbles toward its edges to be discarded. Now and then a pore stuck up in the air as the organism attempted to squeeze out a grass blade. No one knew what the living hill would become. It spent its long life eating and clearing debris from its flat top.

The living hill couldn't know what Rik was, having no brain to speak of, but it responded to his weight by forming two prongs that sought to grasp him and draw him to its center where its mouth yawned and hungered. It ate copper, phosphorous, protein and a variety of other elements, and

Rik met some of the requirements. It would suck him into its internals, absorb what it needed and pass out the rest.

It tried to grab hold of him. He sidestepped the sluggish prongs, retraced his steps across the heaving slab and went hurrying down an ordinary incline that hadn't yet decided to evolve into something else.

The breeze was more brisk and moisture from the morning rain blew from trees and sprayed his face. His shoes sank into soft soil. The sun dragged in its orbit. The earth was hot and peaceful. Reluctantly he started to leave the oasis and step onto the desert. Heat thrust him backward. Though he wasn't thirsty, he drank from the flask on his belt. His eyes slitted as he put one foot onto the cracked ground.

He withdrew the foot. It was too hot. He wasn't ready to go back. Finding a shady spot beneath a rock, he threw himself down on the grass. Carefully he laid the toy aside.

By and by, a silver ball rolled from the shrubbery to pause by his dusty feet.

"I'm a failure and afraid in a world of sin," said the silver thing.

Rik took a grass blade out of his teeth. With a frown of annoyance he kicked at the shiny ball. It flowed around his sock and rolled away, leaving no trace of itself there. Having it on him for those few seconds had been like wearing a plaster cast that never came in contact with the skin. It was an uncanny sensation.

"My name is Sheen," said the glittering ball. "How do you do?"

"Beat it, whatever you are," said Rik. He slumped against the rock and stared up at a dark cloud. His head ached and there was a bad taste in his mouth. Sport with the Gods was no cure for what ailed him.

It would be some time before he took real note of Sheen. At the moment, he saw with only part of his mind. The larger reality was blocked off. It might have been a defense mechanism. Whatever, the weird phenomenon of the silver creature's existence was now only a half-realized annoyance.

He groaned, kicked the ground, showered the silver ball with clods. Absently he noted how it moved from beneath them in a fluid motion that left no dirt clinging to it.

32

"Wish me a happy birthday," said Sheen. "I was born mere days ago in the bowels of a volcano."

Rik renewed his interest in the dark cloud overhead. It would probably rain. He would get wet. He would shiver and be generally miserable, maybe even catch a cold. He was too lazy to move.

"Are you so stupid you don't know I'm here?" said Sheen. He became a two-pronged stalk of brightness that rose several feet into the air. "See me and know that I am Sheen."

Rik had a sudden hallucination. He thought he saw a tare skulking in the nearby brush. His mouth watering, he leaped to his feet with a stone in his metal hand. Rushing through the body of Sheen and nearly dividing it, he charged into a patch of foliage and stood looking about. There was no tare and there were no tracks. Satisfying himself that the animal wasn't hiding behind a tree, he crossed a clearing and stood staring out across the oasis. Nothing moved wherever he looked. He must have been mistaken. There hadn't been a tare in the bushes. There was nothing living here. And that was damned strange. This place was usually teeming with small life. Now there was nothing.

"I am obtuse," murmured Sheen, behind him. "I am inferior, a no-account. Don't be offended but I love you."

Rik returned to his former place and picked up the toy galaxy. He walked away in search of some animal life.

Sheen watched him go. A little pulse throbbed somewhere in him. "For this cause was I born?" he said softly. "This is an interesting situation if I ever saw one. That man is either an idiot or blind or ... how shall I say it? Tasty? Yes, I think he may have good taste."

Like a raised blister on a parched slab, the city of Osfar humped in the desert and baked white under the sun. Even colored stone tended to fade so that newer parts of the city assumed the same dessicated look as the old. Osfar had been laid out piecemeal in a sprawling oasis of green grass, orchards and cool streams. Almost as soon as the last patch of mortar had been slapped smooth, the first underground rumblings were felt. Then came an earthquake. When the air cleared, it was seen that nature had played a cruel trick. The streams had been diverted and Osfar was a desert city.

There was no rain where there was no grass. Torrents could fall on one spot while only yards away the ground was cracked and arid. Men perspired and wiped their necks with big handkerchiefs and wished for another earthquake to come and turn back the waters. They couldn't abandon so much and start over again. Osfar was too big, too important. The entire eastern industrial complex depended upon this one city. Within its walls throbbed a thousand different commercial organs without which the east would have reverted to barbarism. Among the essential things made in Osfar were artificial hands. A man with only a pair of paws was scarcely a man, and the old city could have justified its existence with just the one product.

It was common knowledge that early man wore a loin-cloth and ate like an animal. As his intelligence increased, he learned to manipulate ropes and pulleys with his teeth. From those crude beginnings he progressed to machines and artificial hands. No one wanted to go back to pulleys or loincloths, and so Osfar must live, desert or not. A great water system had been built beneath the city and deep reservoirs were tapped.

Outside Osfar lay thousands of miles of the hottest land on earth. There were two seasons, summer and winter, the former lasting three-fourths of a year which numbered 365 days. In summer, a man wore insulated shoes and carried a water flask wherever he went, whether on foot or in a vehicle.

Perhaps this part of the world had been a verdant plain millions of years ago. It made no difference now. A man relied on his senses to tell him if it was safe to travel. He was prepared for hail or flood. Old Sol was master. If he dried up the biggest stream before it could lunge underground, the rain might not come, and if the rain failed, the ground died. If a man liked things cold he had to wait for winter or go across the desert beyond the oases to the Horny Mountains, weird stalks of granite that seemed to march down the world forever. Cold places lay on the other side and trains journeyed through them, carrying men and trade goods to the big cities thousands of miles away. A man's body temperature was 102 degrees and he liked warm weather.

The one sea provided the world's moisture. It was large and reached from the shore of Enjy, a hundred miles east of Osfar, to Alf and Nisa, the earth's western shoreline. Legend had it that the world was once mostly water with several separate land masses. Now there was one great piece of land and one sea. The area along the shore was mapped but most of the hinterland was unknown. Aside from the huge coastal cities—Osfar, Enjy, Alf, Nisa, Chin—the world was unexplored desert. Probably nothing lived inland but the Gods who didn't care what the weather was like because of their powers. They rode on clouds, wore no clothes, had no place to call home. They seemed to be the only creatures who didn't live with conflict or claw their way, inch by inch, up the evolutionary ladder.

Everyone had seen Luvon. He was a dead God who once walked down Osfar's main street and paused to pat a child's head. Now he stood in the oasis called Echo Valley that lay three miles south of the city. An underground spring surfaced there. Everyone had journeyed to see Luvon. They had touched his metallic skin and tried to pull his eyelids down over his staring eyes.

They hadn't seen him die, but his death had been ordinary. A century and a half after he reached maturity, Luvon sensed a stiffening in his joints and spine. There was little pain since vital parts of his brain were hardening. His powers continued to diminish until creating the simplest objects was impossible. Increasing rigidity soon rendered him helpless and then one day he was unable to blink his eyes. The end came swiftly. Luvon became a stiff and silent statue. His friends placed him in Echo Valley and he stood there staring blindly at the white walls. The winds of the kingdom came to play with his petrified parts. Rain painted him hoary while the sun tried to burn him. Nothing could touch him. He was a dead monarch who would stand where he had been placed and go on standing forever. In time, his condensing mass would sink into the earth. The burial might require centuries but eventually Luvon would be one with the nations underground.

The people in Osfar liked dead Gods better than mobile ones. Sometimes men suffered from the wrath of the living Gods, though not often. A petrified God could be admired without fear. He never contradicted, never objected, never tried to make rules. Summer picnics were inspired by Luvon's presence in the oasis.

The Valley of the Dead, where Sheen first entered the world, had been given the name because it stank. Likely, some of the deep openings between rocks led down into old burial grounds or mineral springs. No one went there but archeologists or hikers passing through.

The Valley crawled with small game, and while Rik wasn't much for killing, he liked to do as much of his own providing as he could.

Society didn't want him to do things they couldn't understand. Why would a man in his right mind spend hours wandering around looking at things? Meditation was fine, but it shouldn't be overdone. If a man went into the wilds with a gun, no one asked questions. So Rik carried a gun when he took his walks. He probably knew the Valley of the Dead better than anybody and he realized that if all the animals had disappeared, it meant something cataclysmic had happened. People would want to know about it and since no one ever went into the Valley they would never learn of it unless he told them.

Noise grew as he approached Osfar's suburbs. Women were stringing laundry on lines in their yards. Their artificial hands clicked rhythmically as steel fingers snatched up shirts and trousers and hung them to dry.

He caught a cross-town bus that let him off a block from his house. Even before he reached the sidewalk, he saw Aril. She stood on the hill beyond the back yard of their home, her head bent as she looked down at a gravestone. There was no body in the grave. Behind her reared another gravestone, and this plot had a body in it. Aril paid no attention to it.

Rik paused on the sidewalk and stared up the hill. Aril gave a sudden jerk, as if something had startled her.

"Look at the other grave," thought Rik. "Just give it one glance, and I'll love you for the rest of my life. I'll forgive you for all of it if you'll only look at that other grave."

Aril raised her head, looked at the sky, turned and started down the hill.

He went into the house and hid Tontondely's toy in the

back of his closet. As silently and as quickly as he had entered, he went back out to the street and walked to the bus stop.

His intentions were matter-of-fact when he went into the police station.

"Why would anyone want to go into that valley?" said the officer behind the desk. "I never been there myself but I hear it's real ripe."

Rik was patient. "Yes, but getting back to the animals—"

"You didn't answer me."

"What?"

"Why would anyone want to go out there?"

"Sergeant, I—"

"You a stranger? I don't recall seeing you before."

"I was born here. About the animals—"

"I'll tell you one thing; you evade questions if anybody ever did. On this form you filled out, you left a lot of blank spaces. The first one, the addresses of family members, why didn't you fill in the space after your son's name?"

Rik backed from the desk. The room was hot and he wished he had gone fishing. "There are no animals out there."

"Never mind that right now. First things first. This form comes first. If I don't get it all filled out I get chewed by the Chief."

"I came in here to make a report, not fill out a form."

The sergeant sat back in his chair and worried a fat cigar. He had big black eyes that looked empty. "No form, no report."

Rik started to walk away.

"Get back here," said the man.

Pausing, Rik said, "Why?"

"You want to make a report?"

"Not if I have to spend thirty minutes discussing my vital statistics with you."

"You in a hurry?"

"My time is my own."

The cigar aimed at him like a gun and the growl was practiced. "It's hot, I got six hours before I go off duty, there are such things as rules and regulations, your skin is thin, I got sandpaper for a throat. You're worried about the Valley of the Dead where nobody but nuts go. What kind of fellow are you?"

a billion days of earth   37

"A harassed citizen, but I asked for it." Rik hiked up his pants and walked out.

He decided to forget it, and then found himself flagging a bus that went the University route.

"Maybe you want the Archeology Department." She was the first woman at the first desk in the first building he came to.

"Why?" said Rik.

The woman's nose wrinkled. "They're the only ones with an interest in the Valley."

"This is an institution of brains. Something out there is killing every living thing that moves, and I should think even the janitors would be interested."

The woman left her chair and disappeared through a door. A few moments later she came out again. "The Valley of the Dead is strictly the archeologists' domain. Professor Kine will give you all the information you need. He's in Building Seventeen."

Professor Kine was out to lunch.

"He won't be back today," said a man named Trop. "He's busy."

"So am I," said Rik. "Are you an archeologist?"

Trop's nose wrinkled. "Yes, but I don't work in the Valley of the Dead."

"I know the place stinks, but that has nothing to do with it."

"Nobody but Professor Blok would be caught dead out there, but you can't see him because he's disappeared. As a matter of fact, he went out to the Valley last week and hasn't been seen since."

"Did anyone look for him?"

Trop seemed amused. "He knows that place like he knows his own face. He'll show up."

"About those animals—"

"Not my domain. Nor Kine's. If I were you I'd see the local authorities."

Rik started to walk away and then turned back. "Do me a favor."

Trop's eyes were bright. "If I can."

"Why doesn't anybody hear me when I say something?"

"You're too intense. You have to learn to relax. If you

want to be a carrier of bad news, you'd better overhaul your image. Make like the message was the least important thing in the world."

"What if it was really important?"

"Irrelevant."

"Pretend for a second that I have all the necessary qualities for striking up a conversation. Pretend that I'm relaxed. We've gotten the preliminaries out of the way. Then suppose I tell you something is killing all the wild life in the Valley of the Dead? What is your automatic reaction?"

Trop spread his paws. "There isn't a thing I can do about it."

"But you're curious about it. You're going to think about it and maybe go out there and have a look for yourself."

"Whatever for? It isn't my area of responsibility."

"There's such a thing as public domain."

"Then let the public handle it."

"Who is the public?" said Rik, and as Trop only stood there smiling at him, he did something he had been doing all his life. He resigned from the human race.

chapter iii

On a handsome piece of property at the north edge of Osfar sat the estate of the Fillys. There were four others like it in different parts of the world. A man could stand beside the electrified fence and admire the estate's green miles. On a clear day he might see the tops of the five manors, and if the thought came to him that it would require a pile of money ten feet high and ten feet across merely to run all those buildings, he immediately realized that every one of the Fillys inside those buildings had a million dollars. And when he figured that all those people represented maybe fifty million, all told, he knew this was enough to run the place and have some left over for groceries.

A few centuries before, the rich of the world were philanthropic. Their descendants monopolized wealth, eliminated all but the very elite, took the family name of Filly, stopped giving money away and knew no fear of anyone but the Gods. They needn't have worried. The Gods didn't care what rat-men did, rich or poor.

If looking over that electrified fence at the estate made an observer sick because he suddenly began to think about a hundred piles of money as high as a hundred hills, and that those Fillys in their manors were sitting on more dollars than he could count in his lifetime—if this was what the observer thought—he looked over his shoulder to make sure he was alone, after which he let it all out in one loud, crazy scream and then he went home and tried to forget he had those thoughts.

It would be unendurable to live in a world where ninety-nine percent of it were serfs, while the remaining one percent silently manipulated them. The philosophy of the sacrifice of the one for the many wasn't perfect, but it had served man for all of his existence. Hadn't it? Philosophies were suspect and humanity must be cautious in his choices. For instance, consider the philosophy of the sacrifice of the many for the one: that was just too goddamn . . .

Filly One strolled in the garden while his fourth child was being born. He knew he should return to the house at once. Arda hadn't screamed for an hour, which meant the physician had anesthetized her. The child must be large and difficult to bring.

One shivered, and a ghostly pallor crept across his aristocratic features. A thin paw hovered over a flower, descended to stroke it, quickly removed itself lest the fragile blossom be damaged. He loved the gardens at this time of day. The sun was to the west and the arbors were in shadow. Coolness reached out to him like balm. His anguished spirit sought once again to rise from the despair into which it had plunged. If only she would cry out! With reproach, he stared at the sun. The source of life winked at him in good humor but he knew it lied. This was a day of mourning.

His step became more brisk. Pessimism was unlike him. Statistically speaking, he had almost every chance of terminating this day with delighted laughter. The sun struck him on the cheek and he frowned. It was unpleasant to be reminded that he was subject to something. Through narrowed eyes, he viewed the orb in the sky, laughed at himself. There was a limit to control, after all. (But he didn't believe it.)

It was then that he saw the physician standing on the porch. His heart gave a single violent flutter before he was calmed. So controlled was he that he could pause on the path to examine a blue bud. These marvels would be the most beautiful in his gardens. They needed only the rain, the sun and the gardener. Wasn't it true that those three things were all any living being required, even his child which Arda had borne, else why would Flur be standing there? The child had known an abundance of sun and rain in his wife's body. The unknown quantity was the skill of the gardener: himself. He had planted four seeds, and, judging from the fruit of the first three, his thumb wasn't any too green.

As he always did when his thoughts were common, Filly One winced.

Flur leaned against the porch pillar and struggled to contain his contempt. Mingled with the contempt was a tinge of satisfaction. He was thinking of his own son, born a month before. Had Flur known how starkly his hatred shone on his face, he would have bleated a terrified denial, but he didn't know, because the features of the man who stepped onto the porch betrayed no emotion.

"I'm sorry, sir." For an instant, the physician expected some reaction to his remark, but then he remembered. It was a block of ice standing there, not a human. Three times Flur had stabbed this man with a sword of doom and it would be no different this time. The face would be a cold tomb. In about three seconds, the mouth would open and the stalk of ice would speak. It would say, "How is my wife?"

Filly One said it.

"Very well, sir, no problem at all," said Flur. "I've left her asleep."

"I will see the child."

In spite of his hatred, Flur was jolted. The fourth time! A part of his mind burned with pity. "Must you, sir? It isn't a good thing."

"I will see the child," said Filly One.

Flur followed the master into the house. He shivered as the smell of richness struck him. God, it was worth all those years of study just to get a look at this place. To know that such a house existed made the torment of living bearable. His eyes evaded the gleaming walls of the foyer, misted as they dropped to the rug. It was like walking in the warm fur of a living animal.

They entered a room that soared high and still higher to a silver ceiling. Voluptuousness and fastidiousness were here, combined with such an overwhelming aura of sublimity that Flur was momentarily blinded and stumbled on the first step of the stairs. His cold paw clutched the bannister, greedily gripped. If he could carry away one of the statues on the landing, one of the vases or portraits, he would never have to do another day's work for the rest of his life. Hell, one of the drapes was worth a fortune! Or the marble tiles on the floor; or the band of gold on the bannister he clutched; or the rug on the steps he climbed, so soft he wanted to bury his face in it and weep.

They reached the upper landing and went down a wide hall. Flur thought of the woman they would see. Pity squeezed at his vitals for a moment before rage took its place. It was justice, by God. He hadn't a thing he could call his own, but at least he had his son. What were all the objects in this unbelievable house compared to his little babe? The cold fish who walked beside him like a zombie thought he was so damned precious because he was rich, but he couldn't even shell out a normal kid, something the lowest wretch in the worst slum could do. No man would trade places with him.

The last thought beat at the shambles that was Flur's brain. He felt like crying. He knew. He would gladly give up everything he had to trade places for a year with the zombie beside him.

He opened the door of the bedroom with a quiet paw and a sympathetic expression, but he was conscious of nothing but his terror at himself.

A gray-haired nurse stood beside the bed in which the wife of Filly One lay sleeping. For ten years she had been the body servant of the mistress of this wing of the house. A younger nurse stood beside a basket at the foot of the bed. Her artificial hand lay protectingly on the edge of the basket, but there was a kind of revulsion in the manner in which she rocked it. Steadfastly, she avoided looking at the infant she guarded.

Arda lay like a candle of wax. If her dreams distressed her, there was no outward evidence of it. Exhaustion drew the flesh of her cheeks into hollows. Her lashes were bird tracks on splashes of gray snow.

Filly One moved to the basket and looked at his son.

I'm better than he is! thought Flur. At least I have the good sense to know that thing ought to be destroyed. The physician gave a start when he realized Filly One was staring at him.

"You'll see to it that he is taken where he belongs," said the master of this grand house, this city, this country, this . . .

"Yes, sir, there will be no delay. The nurse will go with me." Flur cast a grim eye at the girl who was regarding them with an expression of horror and disbelief. No doubt she had been expecting him to prepare a needle and put an end to the blasphemy.

"Do it now," said Filly One.

Flur and the girl took up the basket and bore away the product of their master's passion. The girl would return, forced back to the estate by the man who drove them to their destination. Flur would be allowed to stay abroad. Of all the servants of the Fillys, he was the only one who retained his freedom.

Filly One sat beside his wife for a time, and then he went to the room where his brother waited. His first thought: Damn him, why did he bring the child?

"Hello, Two," he said, and patted the curls of his niece who rushed at him and grappled with his legs. He picked her up and sat down.

"I heard," said Filly Two. "I can't tell you how sorry I am."

"Thank you."

"There will be more. Arda is young."

Thought One: My God, he has two sons and he also has this precious creature in my lap while I have none.

Thought Two: The hell she'll have more, and even if she does they'll be no good, like the rest. My brother's seed is rotten; as is mine.

There was a marked resemblance between the two men, or perhaps it wasn't so remarkable, considering that their ancestors, for several generations back, had been close relatives. They had the same fine heads and sharp ears, identical jawlines, long noses, small gray eyes. Both seemed to have been pried from the same mold, until a closer examination was made. Then subtle differences were discernible. The equanimity of Filly One remained static while Two's occasionally wavered and threatened to shatter. About Two was an air of pent-up loudness, repressed, but there beneath the surface.

Said Filly One: "We will survive this as we always survive calamity."

Thought Two privately: I'll survive, but you won't.

It may have been that Two fully comprehended the meaning of his words as soon as he thought them. His body jerked and victory gleamed on his face. "You don't have to rely on Arda, you know," he blurted, and then he sat mute and frightened.

Filly One held the wriggling child still. "What does that mean?"

"Nothing. It's just that . . . I hate to see you childless!"

"This isn't the first time you've said such a thing."

"I'm concerned for you! I don't like to think that Arda will give you no heirs." Two's fright quickly ebbed and changed to sullenness. "What a tragedy, and only me to help you. Three, Four and Five won't be back for three weeks. But brothers are useless at a time like this."

"Yes. How is business?"

Two seemed relieved to get to another subject. "Terrible."

"Explain."

"You know I occasionally dress in commoner's clothes and go into town. I do it to keep in contact with public feeling. Dissatisfaction is everywhere. The members of the Luvonite sect are all over the place, preaching on soapboxes, holding large gatherings. Too, I've received many reports of people disappearing. I know nothing about it. Probably it isn't significant. But the combination is getting on my nerves."

"The ticker tapes show no change in buying trends."

"I think it should be investigated. If nothing is happening, all well and good."

Filly One looked at his niece, touched a bright curl with his paw. "I'll call Redo," he said, with a smile for the baby. He didn't see his brother suddenly give a shudder.

After casual talk, One left and went to his office. Soon he had a visitor, a little brown man of indefinite features who slid quietly into the room.

"You have news?"

"I have." The man sat beside the desk. His voice came like the rustling of dry leaves. "The single atavism that has gone unaccounted for has at last been traced."

"It lives?"

"Probably forever, since he possesses the constitution of a mountain."

"Why? What makes them so strong?"

The man shrugged. "It is not to be borne and yet it remains a fact."

"Get on with it."

"He has been there twelve years. The caretaker has a safe where his mouth should be, and no bribe will crack the seal of that safe. He believes his charges to be the seed of Satan who are destined to overwhelm the world. The man is mad. He won't talk. He cares only for his work. He has no wife, no family, nothing but the . . . personages he oversees."

Filly One's eyes were marbles of snow. "You are in love with your own verbosity."

The brown man coughed. "This one went unnoticed for too long. Tracing him was difficult. I finally decided to become a regular visitor there. I'm gratified to say the idea paid off. A man came, a gentleman from the suburbs. He returned two weeks later, and two weeks after that. Twice a month, without fail, he comes and gives the caretaker money."

"His name?"

"He lives on Ujan Street and goes by the name of Cadam Rik."

"That means nothing to me," said Filly One.

The brown man regarded him sadly. "His wife's name is Aril."

"Ah, yes, and there we have it."

"A family name. Filly Thirty-Two of Chin produced one named Aril by a woman he picked up in the streets. The child was sent here and placed in an orphanage. She was adopted by a young couple who had no children."

The expression of Filly One was blank. "And Aril grew and married and continued the Filly heritage."

"Her child is the seed of Filly Thirty-Two, watered down, but nevertheless a son of Satan."

"You're so very eloquent."

"I'm a geneticist, sir, not a priest. If you recall, I was against this research from the beginning. I had no wish to work for a man bent on self-destruction."

"You are courageous. Or are you a fool?"

The little man squared his shoulders. "Your line is finished. Not in the next generation, but now. The mixture of bad seeds has run its course and from now to eternity the family of Filly will produce monsters. It was written in the beginning that cousins shouldn't marry. When men compound this error by marrying aunts and nephews, brothers and sisters, for generations upon generations, they reap the consequences."

Filly One sat, relaxed but watchful.

The visitor trembled. "Do you think I don't notice the men you've set to follow me? Confidences such as I have accumulated against the Filly family must be cut off at the source, because men like yourself can't understand that another man might care nothing for what his knowledge was worth." Again the visitor trembled. "I have a thing growing in my head. It's going to kill me. It may happen quickly, but probably not before your men get to me, once you give them the word. I'd like to finish the life God gave me but that's up to you. I care nothing for what I've learned, other than that it's knowledge of a kind I've always sought. Genetics is my work and my passion. I know the Filly family has spawned each and every atavism on Earth. My disgust at this is impersonal."

"I have no wish for your death," said Filly One.

The little man's expression remained grave. "I have nothing but my life, and I desire to continue it. The decision is in your hands. I believe you will decide against me. Still, I see no virtue in accepting death as if it were destiny. I'm asking you to let me live. Your secret is safe with me. It will never go from me to another living soul."

chapter iv

Aril's mind cracked the day the boy was born.

He was still their son, she said to Rik. He was so small, so harmless, so innocent and helpless. Rik had to build a cage for their son before he was two years old.

They adopted a little girl and named her Tene. Aril refused to put Sten away. He was so small, she said; so innocent and helpless, so harmless. Rik took him away where he belonged, and Aril tore up the house and screamed until he told her. She went after the boy and brought him back. She accused Rik of loving the wrong child. Tene had everything while poor Sten had nothing but her love.

He could never decide how she really felt about the two, whether she loved Sten and hated Tene, whether she hated them all, whether she could differentiate between the two emotions.

When Sten was six, he got out of his cage and killed his sister. Too late, Rik stopped listening to Aril. Too late, he took Sten to his rightful place. He buried his daughter and stood blankly, silently, and watched Aril make another grave for her lost son, watched her put his toys in it. Only when she turned her back on the real grave did he begin to give her up. She had forgotten the wrong child and he would never forgive her.

That was all in yesterday. Today was now, and today he was going to the zoo.

It covered two hundred acres. The grounds looked green and attractive from a distance, but before one drew near the entrance strong odors assaulted the senses. Curiosity stood fast against almost anything, so the zoo was rarely empty of visitors. There were plenty of sidewalks between the cages. Nobody walked on the grass. It had been ruined by animals who roamed around after closing hours. Outhouses were a common fixture, but the animals preferred to drop their britches wherever the inspiration found them, and visitors never sunbathed or had picnic lunches at the zoo.

Nose filters were on sale at the admission stand. They cost a dollar apiece and were effective for about three hours. On a long weekend there were never enough filters to go around, so it wasn't unusual to see a visitor suddenly drop everything and make a desperate dash for the exit.

The first thing a visitor saw after stepping past the admission stand was a large pond. It stank, but it was necessary. A direct hosing had bad effects on some animals. The temperamental ones were taken from their cages after hours and tossed into the pond. The shock of hitting the water after baking all day took some of the starch out of them. Once in a while one or two went berserk and ran speeding through the grass, in which case they had to be chased down with a net and thrown back in the pond.

A few yards farther were long rows of open cages. They were occupied by young animals of mixed genders. The older an inmate became, the more his savagery increased, so that by the time he reached puberty he lived alone. Infants or cripples who couldn't feed themselves were cared for in a nursery which was not open to the public.

Rik went to the zoo twice a month. He didn't buy nose filters, didn't stroll around the pond, didn't stand by the cages and observe the animals at their play. His course was always the same: past the pond, by the open cages, through shade trees to a sandy path that led between closed cages and onward beyond the sight and sound of humanity.

Today, as always, he headed for the maximum-security section. This building was wooden on the outside but the inside walls were of solid steel. Security wouldn't have been so tight if an escaping animal could be depended upon to head for the desert and freedom. They never did this. Always they headed for the heart of the city where they holed up and preyed on night walkers and children.

Animals seldom escaped from the maximum-security section. They weren't taken from their cells. The floors were hosed once a day and the debris washed into wall gutters. Securing food was a problem. The zoo supervisor bought from anybody, and he usually received carcasses too ripe for the human market.

The caretaker of maximum-security knew Rik by sight and didn't ask for a pass. He stepped aside and watched as Rik walked into hell.

Huge fans blew overhead but they couldn't make the place cool. No recorded music could drown out the sounds, no nose filters could cope with the smell of maximum-security. The public couldn't have coped with this section of the zoo. No one wanted to experience real hell, nobody had a desire to know real horror. In the raw, these were intolerable. Only the taste of them was needed. It was all right to approach and observe from a safe distance. Reality wasn't a safe distance.

The cages were large. Most were bare of furnishings. The straw ticks were ripped apart. There were exercise bars in some cages, some held rubber balls, some had unrecognizable objects in them. Rik walked down the aisle and stayed in the center of the passage. Something hurtled at him from the right. It loomed enormous in his peripheral vision, crashed against the bars with a terrible thud. A long arc of urine came from the cage to his left, spattered in front of him. He stopped and backed up, swerved and then froze as something touched his back. He knew it was the nail of a paw.

He didn't look at anything but the paw as he turned. Carefully he backed away a pace, turned again and oriented himself in the aisle. He walked ahead.

An animal on the right leaned heavily against the bars of his cage. His body was plastered so snugly on them that there seemed to be no dividing line between metal and protoplasm. The animal yearned not for freedom but for the female in the cage across the aisle. Had they cut off his vision or put someone else in the cage that held his viscera and his mind transfixed, he would have died. This was how he lived, in a constant state of excitation or agony, his madness focused, his motive singular: he must dissolve the metal bars

a billion days of earth   51

with his will, arrive at his destiny and take and consume, first with his body and then with his long sharp teeth.

Rik kept walking, and the light became dimmer until the things hurtling at him from every side were only shadowy shapes. Hell had different levels. The deeper a visitor descended, or the farther he went down the aisle, the more lost became the souls imprisoned there. Gloom was enhanced as shadows thickened. Sounds already sinister and tainted with despair became merely despairing. Here there was nothing that was known. Evil was a shadow within a shadow, weakened and tenuous when no light probed inward.

Dimness flooded the aisle now, likewise silence, save for faint rustlings, furtive movement, watchful seeking, savage anticipation, cunning chuckling. Came the rasping of paws, and suddenly there was a cage in which there was only metal. Everywhere there was metal. Fat round pipes formed mazes that created an environment for a creature born millions of years ahead of its time.

Furry hind, sleek and obese, backed out of a high tube, paws clutched and impaled steel surfaces with ease, long body emerged, barely discernible in the dimness but seen with dreadful clarity when observed by a stricken soul. Down the pipes, out of the hole, then emergence from pit-like night into half-day, paws touching the floor, head cocked, ears perked, nose twitching, eyes seeking, teeth bared, ferocity curdled in the throat like a dammed torrent. All at once came the quick sensing of a throbbing heart beyond the bars of home.

Crouching on all fours, belly touching the floor, the thing's two eyes blazed into two other eyes that blanched, flinched, cringed. Head cocked, the thing's paws reached out and the body scaled the bars until it seemed to be standing at normal height. Light entered the eyes, penetrated the brain for a split second and incredibly the mouth opened to cut like a sword.

"Da da da da da."

Rik stumbled back against another cage, stood listening to the howling in his mind, and all the while a strange tongue hungrily traced the outlines of his neck and head. Eager paws fumbled at his chest and tried to draw him closer. He pulled free.

"He hasn't done that in years," said the caretaker, at the exit. "Hasn't tried to speak, I mean."

"No," said Rik.

"He's young, strong as a mountain. He'll live a long time."

Rik gave him money and left.

A dusty boulevard, a cobblestoned alley, shadows, a straight course for two blocks—these led to a lot filled with junk. A glittering step stuck out of the ground in one corner of the lot. No one but a God could have made such a step, so children stayed away from it. There were six more steps below the first and at the bottom was a piece of shiny metal. Pressure on the piece caused it to sink away out of sight, leaving a black opening. By descending another set of stairs, a visitor could enter the hidden room. The field was Rik's property and the underground room was important to him. In it was his cache of hidden treasures, his collection of Godly material. The toy he had stolen from Tontondely was deposited in the room.

Jak, the adopted brother of Rik, was a Leng. His kind lived far away, near Big Sulphur Lake, and he had left them because they were too backward and uncivilized. They had no artificial hands, they couldn't make machines and they lived like animals.

The Leng's constitution was strong, otherwise he would have died before Rik found him. Lengs couldn't tolerate temperatures below 60 and he had laid for hours out in the Bleaks where it was never more than that and sometimes went down to 50. The climate was hot around Big Sulphur Lake and Jak had never experienced anything like the Bleaks. But Rik found him, took him home and cared for him and later adopted him, even found a job for him at the factory. They made artificial hands.

When Jak received his own metal appendages, he became a changed man. Now he lived in a civilized world. No more would he use paws to pick up his food. He would learn to write with a pen, dress himself, tie his shoes, shave the hair from his chin. He had a pair of hands. The thoughts made him dizzy with exultation. He was like the Gods now. What did they have that he didn't have?

To Rik, who walked beside him that day, Jak said, "Why do you always wear gloves?"

Rik whirled on him, snarled, "None of your damned business!"

The response startled Jak and put him in a bad mood. The next day he was still in a bad mood. He sat in Rik's underground room with a book pinched between his metal fingers. He had been looking at the book for a long time.

"I know how old this book is," he said suddenly. "I've subjected it to a dozen tests. Its age is approximately two million years. The Gods preserved it by spraying it with something. Handled carefully, it will never wear out. They left it in one of their libraries when they took to the clouds and abandoned everything." Looking at Rik, he said, "Do you know what this book is?"

"Plato's philosophy."

Jak laid the book aside, reached out and took another book from a table. "But *this* is Plato's philosophy."

"It will take you a long time to understand."

"Try me."

"Read any book in this room and history is what you'll be reading. Whether it's a book written by a man or a God, the history will be the same, with only minor variations."

"Go on," said Jak.

"We've mimicked the Gods, copied them. It's almost as if we're reliving their early experiences. Our origin is shrouded in mysticism, as was theirs. Our development was slow for millennia, and then we suddenly leaped ahead, the same as they did a billion days ago. They had the Greeks and the Romans, the Renaissance, the industrial revolution, Hitler and a population explosion, as we did."

"But not the same names!"

"Yes."

"Not the same people!"

"People with the same qualities."

Jak struggled to sit straighter in his chair. "A man named Freud was born three million years ago?"

"And a man with the same name was born a hundred and fifty years ago."

"Christ lived three million years ago?"

"And two millennia ago."

"I won't accept it," said Jak, shaking his head doggedly. "It doesn't make sense. It's illogical, impossible and indecent."

"Too coincidental?"

"No, that's accident. This sounds like deliberate design."

"None of our historical figures were given the names they used later. The names their parents gave them were changed by someone."

"Themselves?" said Jak.

"*That* would be too coincidental. They didn't know the Gods' history."

"Then who?"

"Who else but the Gods?"

"But why?" Jak said in surprise.

Rik shrugged. "It amused them. They recognized that those men had the same qualities as their own historical figures. They gave new names to our individuals and forced us to accept them."

"But how could two separate species have people with the exact same qualities?"

"I don't know. They probably weren't really exact. Maybe evolution always follows the same pattern."

Jak drummed his steel fingers on his knees. For several minutes he was silent. Finally he said, "History being relived. We're doing what the Gods did."

"Why are you smiling?"

"Well, I don't feel like crying over it."

"You should," said Rik. "We didn't have to do it all over again. We could have done it differently. We could have been better."

"That's just theory."

"Tell me a more substantial way to commit suicide."

Jak grinned. "Some day men will be riding on clouds. Their worries will be over. I wish I'd been born a million years later."

"You'd like to be as they are?"

"Sure."

"Why?"

Jak frowned. "What do you mean?"

"Just answer me."

"Damn it, wouldn't you like to be riding around on a cloud?"

"What for?" said Rik.

"For heaven's sake, what a silly question!"

"If it's so silly, let me hear you answer it."

"I thought you admired the Gods."

"I haven't made up my mind what I think about them."

"What's wrong with them? Put it in a nutshell for me."

"They make mistakes."

Jak burst out laughing. "You know what's wrong with you? You want perfection. That's illogical."

"Why? Who says so?"

Ignoring the question, Jak said, "I don't understand how history continues. I don't see how people and Gods can keep going the way they do."

"I don't either."

The Leng pounced on the statement. "Don't tell me you agree with me about something?"

"I can't see how idiocy continues forever. That isn't what you meant."

"What do you want? An avenger? Some omnipotent wrath that will give us all what we deserve?"

Rik chuckled. "That one word: deserve. There's something to it, you know."

"Justice?"

"Maybe."

"Now is no time for men to receive justice."

"Why?"

"It only functions where there's sanity and morality," said Jak. "If men were given justice today, there wouldn't be anyone left alive."

"Is that a confession?"

"Of my own evil? No, I simply classify myself with the rest of humanity."

"That may be one of your problems," said Rik.

Jak didn't respond to the remark. He was lost in his imagination. "Do you suppose the Gods were the first species to evolve to real intelligence on the earth?"

"I don't know."

"Why didn't they tell us we were doing the same things they used to do?"

"Because they didn't care," said Rik.

56

"They may simply think a species has the right to make mistakes if they want to."

"Isn't that what I just said?"

"You said they don't care. That isn't what I said. They aren't morally obligated to tell us when we're bitching things up."

"If they had lifted a finger fifty thousand years ago, we'd be a lot better off."

"They're not our keepers."

"No, they aren't."

Jak flushed. "They have their own problems. They're Gods. Why should they care what happens to us?"

"They shouldn't."

"That's the truth. They shouldn't and they don't—" The Leng broke off. "That's what you said." His eyes slitted in annoyance. "Did you do that on purpose?"

"If you saw someone racing blindfolded down a road you knew was washed out, would you be morally obligated to warn him?"

Instead of replying, Jak jumped to his feet and angrily stalked from the cache.

Aril had difficulty accepting the Leng.

"Why don't you two get married?" she said sweetly one day when Rik was trying to read the paper and Jak was taking a walk. "I've never seen two men as thick as you are."

"He won't be here much longer. Just until he can find himself a place to live."

"I suppose that won't be the end of it," she said.

"He's my friend."

"He's weird. Why doesn't he get a girl?"

Rik rattled the paper. "He's shy and they haven't gotten used to him yet."

"They'll never get used to him. He isn't like us."

"He's not so bad. He's young, he's intelligent and he has more manners than most of the hooligans in this city. Soon enough some girl will come along."

Aril stood with her hands on her hips. "What kind of children would come of a match with him? He's like the bugs in the cupboards. A good stiff wind comes along and he goes into hibernation like a jare. Do you know how many blankets he uses at night?"

"I haven't heard you complain about those damned living hills that block the roads everywhere."

"They're the Lord's creatures."

"What's Jak? Do you think he popped out from under a cabbage?"

Had she intended to answer? Whatever Aril was going to do, she didn't. Instead, she forgot. As quickly as steel fingers could snap, the memories of the moment fled. Rik could see comprehension fade in her eyes. She looked at him as if she didn't know who he was. Her head tilted to one side. She seemed to hear a call from somewhere.

"I'm going to Brog," she said, and left the house.

So did Rik. He sat on the front curb, whittled on a stick and thought about the shepherd of the flock.

His parents had dedicated him to Luvon when he was born. At age five, he was taken to Brog who led him into the oasis where the corpse of Luvon stood.

"This is the Lord," Brog had said.

"How?" said Rik.

"This is the Lord," said Brog, and gave him a pinch.

"Hello, Lord."

"Bow down. Ask the Lord to hurry up and return to life and take us all to paradise. Every night before you go to bed get down on your knees and ask the same thing. If you miss three times in a row, you'll get a disease that eats out your eyes."

Brog was old and smelled ripe. He might have made a temporary convert if he had been more impressive in looks or style. He wasn't and he didn't. Rik became an atheist that day. He made his annual pilgrimage to the corpse of Luvon until he grew bigger than his father.

Eventually, old Brog died and his son took his place as shepherd. The new Brog was an epileptic and schizophrenic, and because his behavior was often interesting he had a large following. His people were all hardy and strong. It was Brog's contention that Luvon demanded human suffering, and the unconverted in Osfar often saw Brog and his friends walking naked through snowdrifts that piled up by the roads in winter. The nudists were forbidden to accept rides or gifts of food during their sacrificial periods, so they were naturally healthy types. Strangely or not, they were the first to notice when the periods between sacrifices grew shorter. Some decided that Brog's behavior wasn't interesting, after all. Others discovered that while they could go without food for two or three days, freezing as they were doing it, they couldn't take a full week of the same treatment. They dropped out and returned to their homes and jobs.

Those who remained with Brog were Luvonites to the core. No snowdrift was too deep to wade through, no hunger pain was too intense to bear. It actually wasn't all bad. Summer always came and life could be pleasant. There were long evenings with plenty of trysting places where one met with a friendly fanatic of the opposite gender, and cornfields were spaced abundantly throughout the oases. It didn't matter if eating and loving sometimes kept them from the Lord. With all due respect, He wasn't going anywhere. He could and He would come the second time, but go He wouldn't, for his feet were already up to the ankles in the hardest dirt this side of the Horny Mountains.

Thoughts of his dead father, of Aril, of Brog, of life, were in Rik's mind as he sat on the curb and whittled on his stick.

"I love you," said Sheen, lurking behind a shrub. He was a small silver tare with a turned-up nose and a bow-mouth.

There was no response to the remark.

Sheen's sweet mouth pouted. "The truth is actually the opposite. What I really feel for you is hatred."

No response.

"Indifference?" The shiny creature frowned. Suddenly he smiled in triumph. "Tolerance!" he bellowed.

"Beat it," said Rik.

"Heaven goes wanting for lack of your peaceful spirit."

Rik examined his wood carving with a critical eye. Maybe if he practiced for a decade he might whittle a decent figure. It wasn't coming along as he wanted.

"I'm ignoring you," said Sheen. "I hope you're taking note of it."

Wood shavings began to adorn his beautiful head. "I suppose the boot comes soon," he predicted somberly. "I must have conditioned your leg since it flashes out every time we meet. Can't you control yourself better than that? You aren't fooling anyone. Violence is always precipitated by fear."

Rik accidentally dropped the stick. He shoved the silver tare out of the way in order to retrieve it. Sheen went rolling down the sloped street. Once again Rik examined his work of art. It was no good. He had no talent. With no regrets he tossed the piece aside and stuck his knife in his pocket.

A child picked up the figure and wandered away with it. It was an odd and interesting thing. Of course it was supposed to be a God, but it was very strange to look at. Hair grew from the head while the body was too slender. Also, the little nails on the tips of the toes and fingers were not Godly.

The child ran to his little cubbyhole in a wall behind the iceman's wagon, where he removed a board. Into the small space there he crammed the wooden figure. There were other things in the hole, odd bits and pieces he had found or stolen. Later he would take them all out and look at them. He would speculate and dream, pretend his toys were time machines capable of taking him into the past. His hand lingered on the pile of objects and a smile grew on his face.

He gasped as a shadow suddenly fell upon him. His steel fingers automatically tightened on the things in his cache. With a quick movement he slammed the board across his treasures and sealed it with his back.

It wasn't a neighborhood bully standing there ready to taunt him. It wasn't a wino, nor was it the iceman who usually threw rocks at him. It was only an ordinary man.

A closer look told the boy he was wrong. This was a particular man, the one who had thrown away the wooden God. For some reason he had followed him here, and now he stood staring down with a strange expression on his face.

Prepared to lie as soon as the first question was put to him, the child's face assumed its normal coldness. A moment later, it registered puzzlement. The man had said nothing. After the one curious look, he turned and walked away.

The child watched the dwindling figure and his thoughts spoke to him. "He knows." There was no quick answer to the next idea: "What?" The child was only conscious of the fact that the man who had made the carving knew. "Everything?" he asked himself in a whisper.

60

Immediately he was on his feet and running down the street. Driven by intense excitement, he rounded the corner and stood searching the sidewalks. The man was gone. But there was nothing to worry about. The man's image was burned onto the young retinas, and no matter how far or how fast he traveled with his secrets, he wouldn't be able to hide forever. They would meet again.

chapter v

The sweet voice of Sheen was music in the morning air. "Jak, Jak, long have I yearned to meet thee face to face. The sun has risen and shone many times upon the mass of me, caused the ground to yield blossoms and all kinds of growing things, yet wherever I looked I beheld an ugly desert because Jak was not there."

"My God," said the Leng, his melancholia fleeing. Open-mouthed, he stared into the culvert at a large mound of silvery material. As he watched, the mound became a slender stalk that swayed with grace for a few moments before rolling to the ground again and forming itself into a star. Almost at once it changed to a long trickle of flowing fluid that broke into a dozen smooth spheres. They converged to build a pyramid of glittering loveliness.

"I believe you're trying to entertain me!" said Jak.

"As a craven lapdog!" yelped Sheen. "A drooling slave, a mindless lackey, a nincompoop who subsists on the nectar of obeisance, I kneel at your feet." The pyramid changed to the form of a man. Kneeling, the man assumed a humble pose.

Jak clapped his steel hands. "I've never seen anything like you! Excitement, bewilderment, incredulity—my emotions are impossible to contain. But before we go any further, I have to know one thing. What in hell are you?"

The silver head bent. "I am Sheen."

"That's only a name. It tells me nothing. What are you?"

"What does it matter?"

The longer the Leng stared, the greater grew his astonishment. He knew this was no ordinary creature. Everything about it cried of alienness. A serpentine length of fluid one moment, it could become a perfectly-formed man in the next. Unlike mercury, it didn't sag beneath its own weight, which meant that somewhere within that smooth body was a musculature. But whoever heard of muscle tissue that could stretch until it was thread-thin? This thing called Sheen was intelligent, it could communicate, it could reason. Obviously it was a protoplasm-mineral organism, but it wasn't like the calse which Gods wore on their heads nor was it similar to living hills. They were primarily protoplasm. Sheen seemed to be mostly mineral. The whole idea was impossible. The things of Earth begat their own kind. There was nothing on this planet that could have begotten Sheen, yet here he rested, a weird spawn that confounded reason.

"You came from space!"

"I did no such thing," said Sheen. "This is as much my world as it is yours. In fact, it's more mine. That you got here first constitutes nothing."

"What is your origin?"

"I was born in the bowels of a volcano in the Valley of the Dead."

The Leng shivered. "That inspires me with sinister thoughts. I see toadstools and hear wails of anguish. I think of shade, cold wind and stealthy creeping."

"Cataclysm exists in the eye of the beholder. Evil coexists with threat, but aren't they within one entity?"

"By God, I'll say one thing for you; you speak in riddles."

Making a purring sound, Sheen said, "Do I?"

"So help me, I don't know what to think."

"No matter. But for your information, I think I had another origin and that I was placed in the pit."

"How? By whom?"

Sheen sat down and began hunting for four-leaf clovers in the grass of the oasis. "To be frank, and I'm not often, what I just said is probably only my imagination. It tries to get out of hand now and then. What do you think of dreams?"

"Dreams?"

"There are times when I dream." Sheen gave a delicate shrug. "Always it is the same dream. Would you care to hear it?"

"I would," said Jak.

"There is an amphitheatre of vast dimensions, so vast I tell myself it must be the core of space. In this great cavern rests a throne of unbelievable size, and on the throne sits the green and barnacled Earth. I see your eyes widening in incredulity. Nevertheless, the dream figure in that chair is the old Queen of us all, ensconced in majesty and beetle-browed in Her ferocity. From Her throne, Earth calls me forth to life."

Jak stared at the human figure at his feet, gazed into the eyes fixed so calmly on him. All at once his throat tightened and he shuddered. He was afraid, and he didn't know why. "Let's pretend for a moment that your dream is reality and not symbolism," he said. "For what purpose did Earth call you to life? If she called you to her, she surely had words to give you."

Sheen snickered. The sound held a nervous quality. The sober expression on his face became something else. He lowered his head. "To be a garbage collector," he said in a low voice. "For this cause was I born." Suddenly his head jerked up and his look was arrogant. He gave a human snort of derision. "It's only a dream. I am so beautiful, so intelligent, so fine in my every facet. An infinity of spiritual distance lies between myself and the offal littering this world."

Jak had begun to pace about. His arms were locked behind his back and he was frowning. All at once he stopped pacing, turned. "What definition did Earth give you for garbage? The word must have been explained."

"Only obscurely. And yet ... strange how one knows. Weakness is my destiny, Leng." Sheen laughed uneasily. "I am to consume all that which is weak on the earth."

The two creatures stared across the short distance into each other's eyes. The wind plunged through the trees overhead and gave gleeful chortles that sounded eerily lifelike. Far below them, in some cavern, a low rumbling began.

In a faint and horrified whisper, Sheen said, "I think the Queen has decided to bathe herself. I'm the water."

Jak was staring in mounting fear at a vision his mind opened before him. He saw the wellsprings of life shoot upward from Earth in a splattering fountain. With a roar, the water showered out of a gigantic hole and in the midst of it he saw a towering figure take form. Master, God, Earth, Kismet—what mattered which name a mind gave it? The figure was the Maker, the Life-giver, and on her face was a frown.

Insignificant thing, a frown; except on that face. There it assumed monumental importance. Man might be displeased, yes, but this one never. Please, no, I'll be good, I won't do it again. Smile, please smile. Show me you don't mean it. You can't mean it. You can't have had enough of it. Your patience is eternal. Who said that? I can't remember. All I know is you can't do what that frown implies. Who are you to judge what you've made? If we're your best product, you have to be satisfied with us. Why? I don't know why, I only know you're responsible for our existence. That's why you're going to destroy us? Stop putting words in my mouth; don't you know I'm not perfect? No, no, I don't mean to offend. Yes, I know, you gave us the seeds of perfection, but it's too difficult, can't you see that? Have you no mercy? Do you want to see your best work destroyed? Please don't say that! It can't be your answer. It's terrible to have the ability to make something wonderful and then destroy it because it has a few faults. Goddamn you, who do you think you are?

The Leng opened his eyes and saw that he was on his knees. He hadn't been aware of kneeling. His mouth was dry and his heart had slowed to a dangerously weak throb. He felt his body surrounding him and he didn't want to get too close to the thing that was himself. It was threatening, that thing residing in his brain. Careful!

He looked at the sky. Some kind of spell had captured him. The clay was the final answer and it would deliver him from truth. His knees hurt, his stomach complained of hunger. The wind turned chill on his back. He looked at Sheen and experienced rage. The rage altered, became derision. His scorn was heavy and relieving, almost blanked out the murky fear.

"You've taken that fantasy to heart!" he said, too loudly.

Sheen had been watching him. The silver, human mask was now serene. All traces of his earlier distress were gone.

"Not so, and neither must you. I am I, alone and unafraid. I'm no servant commissioned by a hunk of brainless sod. I am without beginning or end. Admittedly, my subconscious bothers me now and then, but my power grows daily and will continue to grow until I am omnipotent. A silly dream won't confine me."

Jak climbed shakily to his feet. "A thing without beginning doesn't come to life, but you were born in a dead volcano. You swear you aren't a commissioned servant but I think you believe you are. Omnipotence? Granted, such a state could exist for you if you consumed all weakness. It depends. What stimulates your appetite?"

Sheen grinned. "The I-will."

"And there you have it. Kill ego and what's left to oppose you?"

"I was, before I consumed anything. And I'm no killer. Nothing will ever die because of me."

"What a ridiculous argument! You're mortal, after all. I've never heard of a truly evil mortal who didn't wear a mask of benevolence."

"Ah, well, if you're going to fantasize. By the way, did I mention that I give my victims their choice?"

The Leng shivered. "Don't say that!"

"Why?"

"If you gave them their choice, it would imply that the evil connected with your acts was in the minds of your victims. That's a contradiction. It makes no sense. I can't stand it. Your very existence means you have to be evil."

"As an open window serving a suicide has to be evil?"

"You're mixing me up. Shut up. I have to figure this out." Jak spent several minutes pacing. Finally he turned back to Sheen. "Your dream means nothing. None of what you said is true. Life goes on whether we like it or not. Evil, like the poor, is always with us. It's a fact of nature, a state of affairs, a statistical absolute. Nothing will cancel it, and certainly not you."

Sheen climbed onto a nearby mound of dirt. His human shape seemed to flow, and all at once he became a silver Leng with a dunce cap on its head. "You're missing something pretty obvious, it seems to me."

Jak said coolly, "You mean that by destroying all other

evil you'll become evil incarnate? No, Sheen. By your own words, you weren't commissioned to destroy everything. Only the weak."

Sheen laughed and clapped his paws. "But what if that word describes everything mortal?"

"You're wrong. There's strength in the world. People haven't endured by chance."

"Achilles was a God brought down because of one vulnerable spot on his foot. The heel is such a small part of the anatomy. Do a good job of protecting it and your chances of survival are good. But beware the enemy who dedicates himself to locking his sights onto this spot and aiming his arrows at it. You can't keep dodging forever."

The last sentence had been spoken so strangely, so emphatically, that Jak took a backward step. "You're speaking of me."

"It is my intent to seduce you."

"You crave my I-will?"

"You will be my second greatest conquest."

Jak smiled frigidly. "Only the second greatest? Who comes before me?"

"A fool of a creature whom I'll have if it takes me till doomsday."

"But I'm not a fool. You can't have me without my permission. You said so."

"I ask you, in your case, so what?"

"You must have a very low opinion of my character if you think possessing me will be such an easy task."

"On the contrary," said Sheen. "It won't be easy. You're obsessed with morality and justice. But it is my suspicion that these qualities can be used as your Achilles' heel."

Jak spoke gravely. "I have the feeling you're giving me a warning. Are you always so forthright with your victims?"

"Always. No one comes to Sheen reluctantly. The feet may lag a bit but the ego flies on wings to my bosom."

"I'm not afraid of you."

"Good. If there's one thing I can't stomach, it's a sniveler."

"I think you're suffering from an oversized ego."

With a laugh, the silver Leng said, "It grows daily. To

this date I've conquered three thousand, one hundred and fifty-one life-forms."

"That many!"

"Sometimes I tell the truth. I just did."

"You said life-forms. Not all human?"

"I've only just discovered the species."

Grimly, Jak said, "You won't be allowed to continue killing things."

"I'm not a killer. Who or what is to stop me?"

"The brain of man."

"I'll do you a favor by telling you something important: I'm indestructible."

"How do you know?"

"The Queen told me."

Jak sneered. "Earth? A brainless hunk of sod?"

"That brainless hunk of sod created you, my friend."

"A minute ago you said you didn't believe your dream."

Capricious Sheen. Foolish Sheen. Silly Sheen. He gave up his Leng-form, flowed, became a pretty girl who did a graceful little dance around Jak. "I may or I may not," he said lightly. "What I say may be truth or lies. But one thing you can depend on is my prediction: In a hundred years you'll all be gone."

"You like solitude," Jak said quickly.

"I'll mourn to high heaven. I'm gregarious, and the sound of a voice is pleasant to my mind."

"Which resides in what part of you?"

"Now the scientist speaks. You wish to find my Achilles' heel. I have none."

Jak made marks in the dirt with his shoe and without looking up, he said, "Tempt me, Satan."

A picture flashed into his mind so abruptly that it seemed to strike his brain. He stiffened and recoiled. "Don't tell me you lure your victims with that!"

"Or its equivalent. It is this planet in a state of perfection; your notion of perfection. Notice how everyone is kind. No one is suffering. All are happy."

A world I made. The thought leaked through the Leng's brain. But—wasn't that what kept people from jumping off cliffs—the idea that, though the world was rotten, it wasn't that way because of them? They hadn't made it. But what if they had?

The place in his head was Utopia. It was also Hell. Everyone was happy. Because of him. His inspiration was theirs, his joy theirs—his wants, his desires; all his. The millions of people in this glowing world had nothing he hadn't instilled in them. Which meant, of course, that they didn't exist. No one lived here but himself.

"How will I bear the loneliness?"

His cry brought him back to reality. He stood with his arms up to ward off the creature who threatened him. But the silver menace was gone. Sheen was no longer there. He hadn't taken his picture away but had left it in the Leng's charge, to be kept or discarded, whichever Jak desired.

Vennavora was about to bear a child. It would live and so would the mother. They were Gods and this fact explained all why's and wherefore's.

The living hill wasn't in agreement or disagreement with those self-evident truths. Having no real brain, it survived by responding to any stimulus that brought direct pressure upon it. Its guts took care of the rest, accepting practically anything. It had no way of knowing that the pregnant Vennavora was in a high bracket of desirability. The hill neither knew nor cared. It lived only to eat and roam about.

Vennavora groaned. Her mind fought pain and simultaneously attempted to energize her protective shield that would save her from this creeping horror. She had known she couldn't have a baby on a cloud because if her concentration was broken by that curious thing called pain, the braces supporting the cloud would disappear. However, she could remain airborne until the first warnings sent her to the ground.

That first warning had been too much for Vennavora. She had expected to be surprised by pain, but she hadn't anticipated blinding agony. It had been so severe that she crashed to earth, and the only reason she hadn't been killed was because she had been quite low and had landed on the spongy surface of the living hill. Now the thing was preparing to eat her. She screamed for help.

Living hills meant nothing to Gods. Though Vennavora had seen this one earlier, she hadn't been frightened. Nothing that moved on the face of the world could frighten her. As a God she was an entity that existed beyond or above her environment.

She was suddenly and terribly one with her environment. She screamed again. The pain was unbelievable, and she regretted having hidden from her friends. They could have annihilated her discomfort by sending her mind into a place of pleasant dreams. But she had blanked out her thoughts, had flown far from familiar territory, and now she couldn't call anyone because of the fire inside her.

To endure this experience alone had been her wish. To know pain had been her intent. A great mind could comprehend agony, but only a body could know it. The Elders had experienced it, but they had tried it in small doses. Vennavora had wanted to beat them all. Curiosity was another name for the thing that had been in her mind. She hadn't been thinking about cats. They had been extinct for millennia.

"My unconquerable will!" she gasped.

The living hill behaved in its usual manner. It deduced in its weird way that the mass upon it might be tasty. The hill formed a depression beneath Vennavora and flattened one side so that she rolled a few inches toward its hungry mouth. Then it formed a new depression, flattened an edge, and again the large mass moved in the proper direction.

"Energy shield!" commanded the monarch, but the order was burned to death in fiery agony.

This was no ordinary contest of mind against matter. Once upon a time, when Gods were men, they had some things better. A courageous woman could squat over a hole in the ground, give a gusty yelp and hold her baby in her hands a minute later. But men were always in the grip of evolution. Their bodies grew larger and the head which contained the big brain swelled out of proportion. It wasn't easy for a God to pass her offspring's head. The use of machinery by the monarchs had ended when they discovered the mind could do almost anything. Babies were born from their mothers because it wasn't inconvenient. Only a thought was needed to support the bulge, and the birthing meant a trip to dreamland, which was a familiar place. Gods found most of their entertainment there.

The head of Vennavora's baby pressed at her pelvis as it

attempted to escape its cramping environment. Its father was Tontondely, who had a swelled head, and the baby was like the father.

The mother screamed. Her fine mind had taken a vacation. Her behavior had much in common with that of her ancestors of three million years past.

She expected no help. So well had she isolated herself, and so frantic were her thoughts, that her cries could never raise anyone. Nobody but her own kind could help her. None could assist a God but another God. Still, she screamed.

By and by, two inferior figures appeared on the scene. They came from a far distance, slowly at first and then more rapidly as the sounds of the God increased in intensity and volume.

The living hill was a mature one, a thousand feet square. Not much grass grew on it so that most of its dirty gray surface lay in plain view. Its pores were large and clogged and its skin was wrinkled and pitted with scars. Here and there clods of earth grew, but their edges were loosening and they would soon be rolled aside and dropped to the ground. In the center was the mouth, a series of small gullies that ran to a common source and sank from sight. It was engaged in violent sucking, as if in anticipation of the coming meal. Vennavora lay to the left, a big and writhing brown body.

"Pain has killed her power," said Rik. "She's helpless. Let's haul her off that thing."

Together they crawled upon the heaving surface. Each took an ankle and pulled. Getting her down onto the ground was the most difficult part, as she weighed nearly three hundred pounds.

Rik looked down at her. "There is a God at my feet."

"Something's wrong with me," said Jak through chattering teeth. "I don't believe this."

"I'm actually stronger than she is," said Rik.

Jak shivered. "What's the matter with me? I always thought they were so great. I don't feel that way at all. I hate them." He poked Vennavora in the ribs with the toe of his shoe. "I can't stand to look at her!" He wet his lips with a nervous tongue and glanced at Rik. "Let's kill her."

Rik didn't hear. The God woman was young, no more than fifteen, and her tawny skin glowed like the coat of a zomba. Not a bone jutted from her flesh. She was warm gold lifted from a mold, with neither scratch nor blemish.

"She's beautiful," he said.

Heedlessly, Jak continued. "Since the minute I saw her, I knew. They don't have the right to treat us like animals. I'll kill them all."

The chest of Vennavora rose and fell. Rik's eyes lingered on the rose tips of her breasts.

"I can hook her in the throat with my claw," said Jak. "They bleed like we do. They'll die like we do."

Rik stared at the brown body. "There are no Gods. I've been saying that for years. Why didn't I believe it?" He came out of his mental fog in time to see Jak lean down with the hook on his steel hand aimed at the soft throat. "What are you doing?" he yelled. "Get away from her, you son of a bitch!" He leaped across the brown legs and slammed his arm down on Jak's wrist.

The Leng's eyes rolled back in his head. "What, what?" he gasped. At that moment the head of Tontondely's young burst forth with crimson cap. "Two of them!" Jak screamed and fell to the ground, and touched his claw to the infant's throat.

Rik stood over him like an avenging angel. "Don't move! Pinch that hook and I'll kill you. I'll scatter your bones in the Valley of the Dead for the birds to pick clean." He wasn't looking at Jak as he spoke. He looked into the pain-filled eyes of Vennavora.

"I don't care!"

"Don't move!"

"Rik, Rik, let me kill it!"

"Get out of the way. I'll bring it forth." Rik shoved the Leng aside.

Vennavora gasped as he reached for her. "Touch me not," she said and shrank from him. All at once her belly contracted. "Help me!" she cried and flinched as he knelt between her legs.

Jak lay on the ground and stared at the sky. "Why can't I kill it?"

"Because it's better than you are."

His face twisted with terror and hate, the Leng shrieked, "No!"

"This baby has more talent than both of us put together."

"We're as good as they are!"

Rik held up the baby and smacked its rump. The son of Tontondely opened his mouth to cry. Upside down, he could still cock his head, and his eyes darted to his mother. The cry never sounded.

Rik laid it at Vennavora's shoulder, saw it grope for the breast, saw it pause to stare at its mother's face. All at once it nodded its head and calmly began to eat.

"Did you see that?" said Rik. "Already she's his teacher. He's no sooner born than he's in the first grade. Tell me some more about how great we are."

The God lay quietly. Her chest no longer heaved with the pain of drawing breath. Calmness rested upon her now. She didn't move as she regarded the small man standing over her.

Jak was on his feet. "Why should you decide we aren't going to kill them?" he said belligerently to Rik. "Who gave you the decision?"

"I did. Watch what you say. She isn't vulnerable now." Conscious of the burning sun overhead and the perspiration on his back, Rik kept his gaze on the God. "Maybe you'll tell me, maybe you'll fry me, but do Gods appreciate it when men do them favors?"

"Go," said Vennavora.

Jak hastily backed away but Rik stayed where he was. The brown eyes were microscopes staring at everything he owned. Did he imagine it or was there a glint of curiosity in them?

"I thought I was mature but I wasn't," he said. "I don't feel like getting down on my knees to you and I suppose that's a step forward. But I feel like giving your rear a kick for shattering my last illusions."

Vennavora didn't smile. He only had the impression that she did. "You will survive the longest," she said. Her glance strayed to Jak. "Your curiosity is not always a virtue. Too often it is self-flagellation." More intently, her eyes fastened on the Leng. "You wanted to cause me pain. Listen to me, man, and know your own pain. Once you sat at my feet, licked my hand, laid before my hearth, worshipped me and lived for no other pleasure. Your devotion, your loyalty and your life were nothing without me."

Again she looked at Rik and again he caught the impression of a fleeting smile. "My bright-eyed savior, go in peace but approach me never again. The archetypes of my ancestry forbid it. The intellect can never completely interpret and direct emotion, never sort out that which lies at the bottom of the subconscious. You think we are friends? In the world of emotion we can never meet except as mortal enemies. I bow to my own heritage and know bemusement because of it. You have taught me something I didn't suspect. I, Vennavora, am not yet a God."

Jak knelt at her feet. "I'm sorry, I'm very sorry," he mumbled.

"Yes, you would have torn out my throat and been terribly sorry you did it. That is your way."

The little Leng cringed, and tears coursed down his cheeks. "What you say doesn't bring me pain. I don't understand. What do you mean when you say I worshipped you and lived for no other pleasure?"

"She's talking about your ancestors," said Rik.

Jak shivered in his fear. "What does it mean?"

Ignoring him, Rik faced Vennavora. "Why won't I survive in the long run?"

"Too much is being sent upon you. You cannot stand."

"Can you?"

Her eyes bored into his. "What do you know, man?"

"What are you talking about?" Jak demanded, but they paid him no attention.

"I know only what I suspect," said Rik.

Vennavora's reply was wintry. "Take care. Bring not the wrath of the Gods down upon you."

"I've lived under somebody's wrath all my life. I couldn't avoid it if I tried."

"Tontondely is a special kind of God. His mind is greater than all."

"I'm left out!" cried Jak.

"Your boyfriend made a mistake," Rik said to Vennavora. "He let me steal the toy. But, then, it really isn't a toy, is it?"

"And now you think you have bargaining power?"

"Yes."

"You don't know the Gods."

"I know them. They can kill me. Tontondely can hunt me down and burn me to a cinder. But I won't give it back; not for nothing."

Vennavora's gaze was relentless. "Nothing is what you want for it. If you can't have it, then it is nothing. You cannot resist what is beyond your power to resist."

Rik felt the trembling in his legs. "I hold the work of Tontondely in a safe place."

"You know too much."

"Then kill me."

"I never destroy anything valuable. But I can be cruel. Perhaps now is the time for cruelty, though it can be effective only when the response is proper. I wonder, are you capable of the proper response?"

"You mean, can you hurt my feelings? The answer is no."

"You're not that good."

"I want to show you something." Rik stripped off his gloves, held up his arms. "You know what this means. We won't be behind you forever."

The God looked at his hands with their ten fingers. "You wear gloves because humanity doesn't want you to have those fingers. Men are advancing at an extremely rapid rate. But your cultures are oppressive and your claim of strength may be premature. I think I'll test you." The large eyes narrowed. "From what species do you think you come?"

"I don't know and I don't care."

"No curiosity?"

"I didn't say that."

"I will have the toy. By cruelty, if necessary. Know this: Of all the things of Earth, you spring from the most despicable."

"In whose opinion?" Rik said.

This time the God looked faintly startled. "No denial, no belligerence, no spontaneous emotion. Why is that?"

"I told you I don't care."

"You have no feeling for your ancestors?"

"Why should I?"

"No sense of cringing at the thought that the creatures who bore you were the scourge of the Earth?"

"In whose opinion?" said Rik.

"Why do you repeat that?"

"I'd mind if I descended from some disease that plagued creatures who possessed good minds. I'd mind that, but not very much. But I know I didn't descend from such a thing. I came from some animal that scratched and scrambled to survive, while your ancestors shrank in disgust at the sight of him. He was a scourge because your people looked on him as a scourge. I can't help what they thought of him. He had the seeds of survival in him and he was capable of producing me. I'm grateful to him."

"I know you now, or I'm beginning to know you," said Vennavora. "Those ten fingers mean more than I thought."

"To hell with my fingers. All they mean is that I'm on the road to Godhood."

"And that doesn't please you?"

"*I* won't run," said Rik and watched her intently.

"You cannot stand against the creature. You will die."

"Only by external forces."

"You're not that good," she said with finality. Before he could speak again, she and her baby began to rise slowly into the air. More swiftly they went, and in moments they were specks in the sky.

"What I want to know is what you were talking about?" said Jak. "And why didn't you tell me you had hands?"

"If you don't know, I won't say it."

"I thought we were friends."

"Until you wish we weren't."

Confusion, doubt and envy vied in Jak's expression. His eyes grew round and glistened with tears. "What's happening to us?" he whispered. "Why do you talk like that? You know you're my friend."

"I know it. Do you?"

The Leng moved away. In a frail and weary voice, he said, "We really can't know anything. The world is worse than I thought."

"No, it isn't. It's much better." Rik looked at the sky and frowned. Vennavora had given him a warning. He had Tontondely's toy and he intended to keep it, but why was it so important that a God would demand to have it back? What creature had she been talking about? What could be powerful enough to frighten the Gods?

Mr. Kulp existed to feed fowl, stray tares, zizzies, zombas and jares. Doing it made his heart swell so that he could scarcely catch his breath. He never helped anyone or anything that wasn't on its last leg. It was the only way he could get the choking feeling which he interpreted as a sign of his soul touching nirvana.

He was too practical to want to attain the final state of nirvana. His dead wife had left him half a million dollars. He was content to graze holiness through good deeds. The real joy was that fate had granted him permission to define good, bad, ugly, pretty ... anything else? ... well, nothing that made any sense. Sometimes Mr. Kulp got the four words mixed up. For instance, he only ate pretty food. And dull-colored things were bad ... or was "ugly" the right word? The gentleman didn't give a damn. He could afford to buy whatever struck his fancy.

Today, a doll in the store on Ujan Street struck his fancy. It would make a nice toy for some deserving child. It was dressed in bridal gown and veil made of delicate white lace. Little red shoes stuck out from under the dress. The hair was long and sleek, yellow and of pure quality. The face was pink and pretty, the eyes clear blue. The doll cost 40 dollars.

Around the corner of Ujan Street toward a group of children, went Mr. Kulp with the doll under his arm. He passed the terrible man who lived at the end of his block, sniffed his disapproval with a soft sound. Whittling on a piece of wood, the man named Rik sat on the curb as if he owned the whole street. For an instant, Mr. Kulp had the urge to stop and talk about his half-million dollars. Rik couldn't know about it, otherwise he would have stood up and nodded.

Another man stood on the opposite side of the street, but Mr. Kulp didn't look at him. Loafers must be ignored, though that seldom got rid of them, as they were insensitive creatures. Voyeurs, that's what they were, always hanging around watching what people did.

Mr. Kulp stepped off the curb and hurried over to the

children. A fat little noisy group. His mouth thinned in censure. Fat children weren't hungry, noisy children weren't sad. But they were children and one instinctively loved them.

Most of them played marbles. Younger ones sat or stood watching. As Mr. Kulp approached, two or three pairs of eyes riveted on the doll under his arm. He walked around the group with the toy held high, so that all could get a good look at it. One little girl, about four, sat with her arms in her lap. She suddenly reached. The swift hunger in her eyes captured all of her as she looked at the doll. She was a leaning, groping spirit filled with desire. Her tiny mouth smiled, her snapping brown eyes acknowledged the fact that here was the thing for which she had searched all her life.

Mr. Kulp's gaze met the brown one, and he was repulsed. No child this age possessed enough intelligence to know exactly what she wanted. And it was indecent to want something so badly. In fact, it was dangerous.

A little smile on his lips, he circled the group faster and faster. His eyes flashed from face to face, and how satisfying it was to know the snapping brown eyes followed his every motion with so much hope. Nothing that he did went unobserved by those eyes. They were all-seeing, and the need in them fed Mr. Kulp's soul until he finally arrived at the brink of holiness.

He was in the act of handing over the doll when, lo and behold, it happened. He saw the face, that single significant countenance, and he froze so abruptly that he nearly stumbled. It was the perfect face; the face of nirvana.

The face belonged to a girl of seven, and it contained everything for which Mr. Kulp longed. It held nothing. The eyes were blank, the mouth was lax, the body shapeless. The head was cocked as if its owner pondered upon some profound mystery, but this mind would never ponder over much of anything. The girl was an idiot.

She didn't notice the doll until Mr. Kulp thrust it into her lap, didn't notice that the child beside her burst into tears. When her eyes finally focused on the doll, she awkwardly reached out and laid a paw on the pink cheek. She dug in with the paw. The child beside her screamed. She looked up at the man who smiled, and smiled. Her paw caught in the cheek. Fear made her hastily pull away. The screams coming from the child next to her began to frighten her. She gripped the fragile face of the doll. A nail caught in the veil, others became ensnared in the filmy dress. The yellow hair made a prisoner of one paw and freedom became paramount. Freedom wrought destruction. The hair, the veil and the dress came away with savage yanks that turned to strokes of rage. Anger was vented on the pretty face. A sharp elbow punched it beyond recognition, beyond beauty and confusion. Two infuriated feet flattened the soft body. Within moments the doll was garbage.

The idiot looked at what she had done, stared up at Mr. Kulp's smiling face, turned her head and saw the tear-streaked face of her companion. Something happened inside her brain; some spark of light filtered through cobwebs, stirred inert cells to wakefulness. This strange thing filled her with anger so acute that she launched her heavy body at the man in front of her. Her sharp claws impaled themselves in the flabby face, raked across the wrinkled neck, once again searched for the face.

Mr. Kulp staggered backward. His eyes were stark with horror and, as he saw his blood leak onto his shirt, he gave a high shriek, not of pain but of rage because an unfeeling world had turned on him like a ravening beast. Numb with stupefaction, he stood without flinching as the idiot hurled the ruined doll in his face and ran away.

There was such a loud roaring in his ears that he shouldn't have been able to hear anything, yet he clearly heard two sounds. They came simultaneously and he thought for a moment that they were one sound. His gaze flashed to the children. They were doing nothing but staring at him. Still the terrible sounds went on, wounding him, stripping him bare. Someone was laughing. Someone had seen and understood.

Long, echoing laughter split the noon air and Mr. Kulp knew that as long as he lived he would never feel clothed again. He was doomed to walk naked before humanity. He knew exactly how a condemned criminal felt when he was pronounced guilty. He marched down the middle of the street and looked neither at the man sitting on the curb nor the one who stood across the street. He was alone in the world while they had a common bond: their united condemnation; their laughter.

Sheen stared across the street at Rik, made an elaborate bow. He was a man, tall and slender and silver. His suit was made of the best flannel, his shoes were fine and shiny. He even wore a flower in his lapel. The hair on his head was short, curly and glittering.

"If I had known a simple laugh was all it would take to get you to notice me, I'd have laughed up a storm," he said.

Rik looked without smiling at the silver man. "You couldn't have planned something like that."

"You disapprove, don't you? You don't like to think there may be something between us."

"There isn't."

"Then why did we both respond the same way at the same time?"

"It isn't important."

"It might be everything. And here's another by-the-way for you: I'm going to come to mean a great deal to you."

Sheen walked away. Rik didn't watch him go, just sat and stared at the street and remembered the words of God.

chapter vi

Redo sat in the back of the limousine with one paw clamped around a fat cigar and the other resting on the gold knob of a cane. The cane was the only ostentatious thing about him. It hinted at things forbidden, such as pots at the end of the rainbow, or pirate's treasure.

Redo cared nothing that he was handsome. He had seen too many Apollos snoring in drunk tanks. Good looks were useful to youths bent on seduction. Redo seduced no one. He knew he was intelligent but considered the fact of little importance. He was acquainted with men of brilliance who kept their feet dry by stuffing layers of newspaper over the holes in their shoes. What Redo possessed which was worth coveting was his mental attitude, his outlook on life, his visceral state. His conscience was his own.

The long car left the fetid air of the city and plunged into the clean atmosphere of an oasis. A side road beckoned and the car turned into it, entered a forest, stopped at a gate. A sweet-faced old man came out of a booth to give the driver a look, transported the stare to the back seat, checked his mental roster and went back into the booth. He returned with a key, unlocked the gate, waved the car through with a sweet smile and stood watching it disappear between the trees. It was possible the car wouldn't be admitted through all of the next four gates in which case the occupants wouldn't live long enough to retreat to this point. But there was always a slim chance. After relocking the gate, the old man took his automatic weapon from the booth and stood waiting in the road; hopefully.

A servant opened the car door and Redo followed him up a marble walk to the entrance of Wing I. Inside and abandoned by the servant, the visitor sank to his ankles in the carpet. Soft, rich murmurings came to him from the ether as he followed another servant to the conference room. Air passing across an expensive portrait had a special sound to Redo's ears. He could spot a good original in a collection of junk simply by listening to it. The house smelled wealthy. He basked in its glow. For comfort was a man born and that was really all there was to it.

Filly One sat at a desk in the conference room. He didn't look up as Redo came in and seated himself.

"You are well?"

"Yes," said Redo.

"We meet rarely."

"There is always the thought."

"Quite so, and now to business."

Redo spoke rapidly. A door opened quietly as he talked, and a baby crawled into the room. It was old enough to walk but it wanted to investigate secrets in the carpet. With delight Redo let his gaze rest on it.

Said he, "My second son is reaching his maturity, and I've a mind to put him in Factor Seventeen. He shows promise and will make sure the pushers stay away from the very young."

He watched the child pull at tufts of the carpet. It scowled when the fibers proved to be strong. No doubt she belonged to one of the servants. Babies like this one mustn't be able to buy the pills when they were stuffed into the school system. The son of Redo would see to it. Factor Seventeen wasn't going to destroy infants like this.

The thoughts went through the mind of Redo in an instant. He continued with his report:

Factor Two—a sound success. The family of Elu were wise and understood that they weren't to encroach upon the suburbs or slums. The city of Osfar was Elu's territory and he knew it.

Redo watched the child on the floor. She was chewing a

table leg. Pray God this sweet one wouldn't find her way into Factor Two and its whoredom when she grew up.

"We've run into a snag with Factor Twelve, nothing we can't handle, but some politicians can be tenacious when it comes to enforcing laws that threaten us. Our vetoes aren't on vacation but we have to approach the scene with a delicate step. The mayor of Boro Three is a little nit picker who has no sense. He tried to carry out a raid on a Factor Seven unit after one of our people spent a week explaining the situation to him. We may have to veto him, in which case the Boro will be without law for a while. But of course this won't be a bad thing. The Boro will riot, they'll break into homes and tear up a lot of furniture, and after conditions quiet down they'll behave like good consumers and purchase merchandise to replace what was destroyed. Incidentally, there are several TV stores in that area, and I understand one of your factories is developing a new model. Business on your end will pick up. Yes, I definitely think the mayor of Boro Three is due for vetoing."

Redo paused, frowned. "That's it. Everything is running smoothly; rough edges minor as usual."

Said Filly One, "My brother Two believes otherwise."

"Oh? Was he specific?"

"No."

"It will take a day or two to investigate. I've heard nothing, noticed nothing, but then . . ."

"Quite right," said Filly One.

The baby on the floor was trying to climb Redo's leg, and he ignored it no longer, picked it up and tucked it in his lap. "You'll forgive me," he said over the curly head.

Filly One regarded the child with fondness. "She is my niece, the youngest of Two."

Redo had been about to tickle the baby's ear. Slowly his gaze lifted to meet the chill stare of his employer. Was it possible that One was a fool, after all? As if this rosy-cheeked morsel could have come from Two and his ghostly woman.

Like a bloodhound, Redo examined One's expression. Finally he relaxed and looked elsewhere. One had undone himself this time. He had demanded genuine pearls but his brother had sneaked a cultured specimen into the pack.

"She has siblings?"

"Twin brothers," said One.

"They are as handsome as she?"

"The image of my mother."

Three cultured pearls. Redo again searched with his perceptive sense. He was aware of gloom and quiet determination, sluggish happiness and satisfaction, all emanating from the dry stick seated behind the desk.

Filly Six lay dying. He had been dying since his conception 40 years before, but only of late had he put any real effort into it. Now his breath rang through the sumptuous apartment and it was with extreme force of will that he managed to reach the tassel hanging over his head. His voice was feeble and querulous as he questioned the male nurse who came in.

"My brother has been summoned?"

"He has." The nurse was old and weary of waiting for his employer to die. He had no love for anyone or anything in this mansion. Though he had been in the service of Filly Six for 25 years, there was no affection between the two men, just as there had been none between the nurse and Six's father, whom he had served for 30 years. Somewhere in the old man's mind was a small ball of memory. In it were a warm hearth, fat loaves of bread baking in an oven, and the cheerful face of a woman who cuddled him in her arms. The old man didn't care that the memory was probably false. The mind was a bulwark between the human soul and reality. Life was precarious enough without demanding logic. The old man knew he had been sold to the Fillys when he was little more than an infant, and people didn't sell children they loved. But there remained the memory, and circumstance was capricious. Possibly he had been stolen from the cheerful-faced woman.

The nurse had been well-treated by the Fillys. He received a good education in the science of nursing, he had his own cottage and a warm wife. There had never been children in the cottage. The old man blamed his wife, but he remembered when they had taken him to a white building and sterilized him. Some of the servants on the Estate had children. Evidently the quota hadn't left room for him.

He would live here until he died, cut off from hearths

and baking bread and the loving woman in his dreams. The Filly Estate was his prison. He would die as he had lived, grayly and wounded by the desire to be born again in another world where there were no Fillys.

Filly Six stared up into the face of the nurse who had been his companion most of his life. Tears rushed to his eyes. "Don't hate me!" he cried.

The old servant said, "What a silly thing to say." He fluffed the pillows around the sick man, straightened the cover, took up a thin paw and felt the pulse. "Did you have another bad dream, sir?"

Six whimpered. He couldn't take his eyes off the wrinkled face. With a sense of wonder, he realized he had never really looked at this man before. Why—he was so old!

"Poor Jub, what have we done to you?" he said weakly.

"Don't distress yourself, sir."

"I'm going to die."

"Not today. Your pulse is nice and steady."

"Goodhearted liar. What would I have done without you?"

"Found another to take my place."

"How cruel the truth!" wailed the Filly. "It's truth that makes the world what it is. We should have clung to lies and then our deathbeds wouldn't be full of maggots."

"It may be so, but then we can't bear to look at worms, so we'll have the truth. It paints a pretty picture, if you let it." The metal fingers hesitated on the fine coverlet. "You ought to let the brush stroke freely. Don't hold it back. A man deserves whatever beauty he can get."

Filly Six shrank back against the pillow. His eyelids fluttered and his mouth quivered. "Lies! I'm sick of them. All my life I've heard lies."

"Because you cling to the bed," said Jub. "Sometimes we have to force ourselves into the world, cut out our niche and jump in it. Staying in this bed makes it hard for you to find your niche."

"I can't get up! It's so ugly. My stomach hurts and I can't breathe. Somehow I know that if I get up I'll have to leave this room, leave this place altogether." Six began to weep. "I'll have to leave the Estate and I've never done that. I know there's an army of ghouls waiting for me to step off the property. They'll rip and tear at me till there's nothing left, if I go."

"Stay in your bed, then. There are no ghouls here."

"There are! I see them when I close my eyes, or I used to. Now I see them when I'm awake." Six squinted up at the old man. "You're one of them. You're one of the ghouls."

"Me, sir? Me who cleaned your nose and showed you your first living hill?"

The wasted paws of Six moved restlessly on the coverlet. "But that's it. That's what makes a ghoul. He's unique. You murder him and then you shoot something into his veins that makes him walk and talk." The paw groped for the servant. "Do you see?"

Jub's eyes were suddenly opaque and still. "Yes, I see. I always have."

Six shrank. "You wouldn't take your revenge? I'm a dying man, and besides I had nothing to do with it. I hate them all. You believe that, don't you?"

And lived like a king all the while you were hating—so thought Jub; immediately, he was surprised at himself. "Your imagination is haywire this morning and you're working yourself up over nothing. As if I'd ever harm you when we've been together all these years."

Six lay as if his body were boneless. The hollows around his eyes were black and more than ever his head resembled a skull with dirty skin stretched over it. Only his eyes were alive, the eyes of a fanatic who saw a new and strange road in the distance. The mind in the skull mewed like a sick zizzy.

"I've never been together with anyone or anything," he said. "Not you, not my brothers, not even my wife. She loathes me. Somehow I don't mind that. I think it's because she isn't a ghoul. She's like me—crushed against the wall by an army of maddened souls."

The door opened. Jub furtively laid his paw over the mouth of Filly Six. With lowered head he turned, nodded at Filly One, left the room.

Six tried to sit up but fell back with an exhausted sigh. His eyes blazed as he recognized the visitor. "Goddamn you!"

"For heaven's sake," said Filly One.

"Yes, for heaven's sake." Six looked at his brother.

"You're a mountain of a man, Filly One, but you're made of tinsel."

"I'm not, and you know it."

"Bullshit." Six grinned as the other frowned. "You never did like my vocabulary."

"You picked it up from the servants, though I've expressly forbidden them——"

"Expressly! You sound like a train, but a train speeds and is made of steel. You're all bullshit and you stand like a stupid animal."

Filly One fingered his brow. "Please——"

"Don't 'please' me, you stiff-necked turd. I'm a dying man and I can say anything I want, and I want to tell you I have no respect for you."

One pulled up a chair, sat down and crossed his legs, settled the crease in his pants with a pat. "I have the utmost respect for your opinions, or I did have until lately. You've the vapors these days, exactly like a silly woman——"

"That's all there are in this whorehouse!" yelled Six. "Silly women! Half of us have flies on our pants but there's not a damned thing behind them. The last Filly who had balls died a century ago."

"For God's sake——"

"Don't 'God' me. If he showed his face here, you'd sterilize him and put him to work pruning your blue roses."

Filly One sat quietly but his eyelids were white and gleaming.

Six puffed his pillow with surprising alacrity, slammed the coverlet with a paw, chuckled out loud. "Looking at your dead kisser puts piss and vinegar in my veins. Don't raise your eyebrows, bub. As far as I'm concerned, you're my kid brother whose ass I should have booted a long time ago." Six stared with open hatred. "Look at it," he said bluntly. "See it? Understand it? What do I think of you?"

"That has never been a secret to me or anyone else."

"Know why I despise you?"

"You were born to be Filly One. You were the first son of our father. Unfortunately your brains were addled. You decided you'd rather go to bed than be the leader. Every once in a while you become enraged at yourself for abdicating——"

"You silly asshole, I abdicated because the first time I stood up and took a good sniff with my nose I got a terrific whiff of shit."

One smiled. "If you didn't like it, why didn't you leave?"

"Where would I go to get rid of the smell? Is there any place on this planet that the stench of the Fillys doesn't reach?"

"I'm grateful to you for stepping down."

"Don't I know it? But I did it as no favor to you." Six leaned back and closed his eyes. "Never mind any more bullshit. Save it for Two; he's developed a taste for it." The burning eyes flicked open. "That interest I'm getting on the little wad in First National—I want it turned over to the organ-transplant foundation."

Filly One didn't wince. The interest represented nearly a quarter-million.

"If you don't want to do it, I'll hire myself another flunky," said Six.

"I'll do it. I always carry out your wishes."

"All except one. You still haven't shot yourself."

Standing, One said, "Is that all?"

"No, it ain't all. Sit down." One sat again and Six glared at him for a moment. "What have you been up to?"

"What—"

"I have people who are loyal to me!" Six gathered himself as if for an onslaught. His eyes narrowed and his teeth bared. "My goddamn mail is mine and I'm sick of your tampering with it." A skinny paw flapped. "No bullshit! I never said anything before because I didn't give a damn, but I'm beginning to take a new look at things. Lately the smell of shit is making me gag. I've had my mail diverted to keep it away from the mangy likes of you."

Filly One sat motionless.

"I got a very damned funny letter, so I ask you what you've been up to?"

"What kind of letter?"

"From an expert in the language, I'll tell you. No bullshit from him."

"Stop beating about the bush."

"The letter concerned a certain subject that has to do

with genes." The expression on the face of Six was watchful. "Does that ring a bell?"

"Should it?"

"You hired that man to do a job. You went over my head to do it. Family affairs are my business, even half-assed ones, and you had no right to do it without consulting me."

"You were ill. I didn't go over your head, and it wasn't a family matter. I'm not trying to relieve you of your responsibilities."

"Liar." The face of Six twisted in a scowl. "What's behind that letter?"

"The man was . . . is . . . an expert in . . . geneology."

"Took you long enough to get that out."

"I hired him to trace some obscure branches of the family tree. Does that sound important enough for me to have consulted you?"

"What obscure branches?" said Six.

"There are some, you know. The archives aren't perfect."

"You making it a hobby or something?"

"Why not?" said One.

"What about your blue roses?"

"There are twenty-four hours in the day. You can't expect me to spend all of them in the gardens."

"Only an idiot would spend any in those allergy nests."

Filly One stood up. "I'm being patient with you, more, I'll admit, out of respect for our father—"

"Who hated your white guts!" yelled Six.

One turned and walked swiftly from the room.

Filly Six glared at the closed door for a full minute before he looked at a dark corner to the right of his bed. "Papa," he said softly, and after a while he thought he saw a gray and misty cloud begin to appear. He waited until the cloud assumed the proportions he desired and then he spoke again.

"One is up to something, Papa. I think it's bad this time. I hope you'll stand by me. I have the feeling a great deal depends upon what I do. First, I'll have to investigate the letter. That won't be easy since the man who wrote it is dead. One had him killed. I wish the letter had been more specific. But we know a lot of things my brother doesn't. We know about loyalty, don't we, Papa? That's something I never told One, and I trust you aren't going to chastise me about it again. Poor brother. He doesn't know that whatever I set out to do, I get it done because this Estate is crawling with people who would die for me. As long as I hold onto that little medallion you gave me, I'm Filly One. Poor brother. He thinks he wears the crown because I told him he did."

Did the cloud seethe or was it only his imagination? Six shivered. "Forgive me, Papa, but I've always hated what we are. I can't bear cruelty. One has been a good leader because he can shut off his soul from the sounds around him. I never could do that. I could never bring myself to tell him about the medallion and the oath all of us took that night when you were dying. I wear it always. Did you know that? I've never forgotten my promise. You were always proud of me and you don't have to be afraid I'll betray our heritage. The Filly line will go on uncontaminated forever, I swear."

Papa had nothing to say.

Redo squeezed the gold knob of his cane. He was content. The wine was refreshing, the room was cool and comfortable, and his good friend Elu was going to ask a favor of him. Since he intended to receive a favor in return, perhaps soon, perhaps later, the day was a successful one. He never liked to see a day finished before a new piece of business had been transacted. This would probably be a little piece of business but mountains were only big mounds of little bits of granite.

"Health," said Elu, sipping his wine. "You are comfortable?"

"Very."

Elu's gaze slid around the room. "Ah, God, it has been a fine day, eh?"

"Indeed."

"Your family is well?"

"Extremely so. And yours?"

"Ah, God," said Elu. His seamed faced was a wreck. He had been born tired. Only his mind was alive. It had been said that he was the ugliest man in the world. His face was a series of blobs that resembled brown dough. He had a bulging chin, swollen cheeks, bags under his eyes and bulbous ears. His forehead hung over his face like a loaf of bread.

He looked across the table with an apologetic expression. "It is time to make the confession."

"I'm a priest?"

"Not that kind of confession." Elu waved a listless paw. "A little indiscretion I committed many years ago concerning you."

Redo sat and sipped his wine. The stillness in the room was good. Faint cooking odors lingered in the air. The wife of his friend was an excellent cook.

"It is my wife," said Elu, as if reading the other's mind. "It was to her I made the indiscretion."

"Your indiscretions are notoriously insignificant."

"Yet the mote is more worrisome than the beam."

"True."

"You are a man of distinction."

Redo smiled.

"So well-read," said Elu.

"Yes."

Elu sighed, sat back in his chair. "Many years ago my wife asked me how you made your living. My response to her was the indiscretion. I told her you were a detective."

Redo nodded.

"Is it not shameful that a grown man couldn't do better than that?" said Elu. "I should have poked her in the eye and told her to mind her own business."

Redo drank and said nothing.

Elu frowned. "I grieve because it sounds so stupid. Also I grieve because the mind of woman is like a clam. Nothing ever leaks out of it. Whatever she hears she stores away inside the two shells and they seal together for eternity. Woman forgets nothing."

"That is the way they are."

"They will be the death of us. We get away with nothing because they never forget the idlest word or gesture. We work ourselves into the grave, dying while we are still young men, and our wives sit on our coffins with their clam-minds full of enough memories to last them another lifetime."

"Perhaps that is why they outlive us," said Redo. "They always have something to think about."

Elu glared at his empty glass, took his time filling it

again. "The mountain of meat that is my wife was once a glorious creature with flesh like the white pearl. I could not love her enough. I adored her." Gloom shadowed Elu's face. "I still adore that mountain of meat as much as I did in my youth. It wasn't her body but her spirit that won me."

"You would do anything she asked."

"I would be loyal to her above all else in this world, save for one thing: my solemn oath to you and my kind. But this doesn't detract from my love for my wife, because my solemn oath is my soul and without my soul I am a dead man and of no use to any woman."

Redo thought it had been very well put.

Said Elu, "My youngest son, little Chik, is missing now for three days. The mountain of meat in this household is crying the rafters down. From her clam-brain she drags the memory of my words of two decades ago. She must have the best detective in the land to search for her son. Forgive me, my friend, I told her you were the best tracer in the universe. Forgive me, I ask you to become a cheap snooper. It is deplorable. I ask your pardon. You should refuse me and wipe your shoes clean of this house as you go out the door."

"Little Chik, eh? Where has he gone to?"

"Who knows? He isn't the best of my sons, but I've given my promise."

"He stays away often?"

"Never for three days. Something has happened to him and if you don't bring him back, his mother will slay us all with her grief. I could hire a hundred detectives but she wouldn't be satisfied. So it is to you I've come. All because women have clams where their brains should be."

Redo gripped his cane and stood. "I'll do it."

Elu turned red. "What can a man do but go to his friends when he is in need?"

"I suspect it won't be much of a task."

"These women, they make a farce of living."

"He's probably holed up somewhere with acquaintances."

"I should tell her to shut her mouth."

"You love your wife."

Elu slumped in the chair. "I love my wife. I also love her sons, but I'm going to beat the hell out of her baby when I see him. He is no good."

chapter vii

Rik loved Aril. He had always loved her. In spite of her illness, he hadn't stopped caring. The poor damned woman was being driven crazy by the same things that made maniacs of them all.

Today he was laughing with genuine humor. "You're kidding me, Aril," he said, laughing again. "Come on now, a joke is a joke, but don't carry the hilarity too far."

Aril looked at him in confusion. She fumbled at the scarf around her shoulders. Her mouth moved jerkily but no words came.

"What I mean to say is, cut out this crap you're telling me, because it really isn't funny!"

The mouth of Aril drooped, the face of Aril pinched with concentrated effort, the eyes of Aril narrowed as if the vision were too distant. At the moment she was mad as a hatter.

"Stop telling me that!" Rik's mind tried to recuperate from the punch she had delivered. He peered into the crimson fog in front of his eyes, attempted to find something sane and tangible. There was no logic anywhere but in reality, so reality must be hiding. All he had to do was find it.

The red fog became purple. Of course it was true. The thing of it was that it was fact. Aril never lied. She was too goddamn mean to lie.

"You stupid bitch, how the hell could you believe for one second that you were a virgin?" he yelled.

"The cleansing ritual. There were no virgins in the group. Someone had to sacrifice."

Wildly, Rik looked about. His gaze fell upon his own arm stretched out in the air. Maddened by the sight of it he sank his teeth in it. The pain felt good. He laughed, liked the sound, did it again. "So Brog did a little hocus pocus over your head and you were convinced!"

"That and the weed he gave us convinced me."

"Shut up! I want to understand this." He paced the room for a few minutes. Finally he went back to stand before her. "That pack of nuts decided they wanted Luvon to produce an heir, and they figured the only way to manage it was for some virgin to shack up with him, but since he isn't too randy they put his spirit into Brog and then they made you the virgin."

He gave a shriek that made the walls vibrate. "I've lost my mind! I just felt it drop away somewhere. And I'd just as soon not find it, because if and when I do I'm going to break you neck."

Without looking at her, he said, "Are you pregnant?"

"No."

The days following the confession weren't sane days, but he managed to find out whether he had become the laughing-stock of the neighborhood. Only two people knew about it besides the virgin and himself. There was Brog, who couldn't be located because he had suddenly gone off into the wilderness to meditate and feed birds with nectar Luvon dropped from the sky. Then there was Irn, the imbecile. She had prepared the virgin for the sacred rite, but believed she had merely helped Aril get ready to take a bath. Rik's reputation was spared, not that he gave a damn. The issue was one of those odd abstractions he felt compelled to investigate.

He thought of things he might do. He could kill Aril. He could kill them both. He could pack his things and move out of the house. He could stay home and torment Aril with his frozen silence.

He didn't do anything. He continued to go to work and spent weekends tramping through the deserts and oases beyond Osfar. He wasn't surly or broody. He wanted a logi-cal solution but knew it didn't exist. If he killed Aril, he wouldn't have her any more. Killing Brog would land him in jail. Trying to get even with Aril would be a waste of time because she had completely forgotten the incident.

They were in the cache—the underground room below the empty lot—and Jak was upset.

"What did she mean?" he said for the third time. "What the hell did she mean?"

"Something," Rik said.

"Or nothing!"

"They never say things meaninglessly. They don't talk to hear the sound of their own voices."

"By God, to hear you, you'd think they were omnipotent."

"Why are you sore?"

"I'm curious!"

"You're mad as hell. I don't see why. She gave us some clues we needed."

Jak sat down and pinched his eyes shut with the fingers of his metal hand. "She was insulting us."

"Why should it bother you? We had to come from something. Lengs are no different than anyone else."

Jak took another look at the picture on the table beside him. Encased in transparent material, the small portrait might yield to the cutting edge of a diamond, but to little else. "I'm not a dog," he said with soft vehemence.

"You're a Leng."

"I didn't evolve from a dog!"

"Vennavora said you did. What's the difference?"

The Leng sat rigidly with his eyes on the picture. "They were so stupid."

"You know you didn't evolve from Homo Sapiens. If you had a choice, you couldn't pick anything more dignified than a dog."

"Man's best friend. 'Lick my hand, pooch; step and fetch it.'"

"A dog was a fine animal," said Rik.

"Crap on the rug again, pooch, and it's off to the pound with you!"

"He was loyal and intelligent and he was capable of a great deal of love."

"He was a leech!"

"He was taken from the forests and domesticated because he was bright enough to be of use."

Jak looked at Rik with eyes that glittered. "Maybe you evolved from a pig. They ate pigs."

"Then at least I was useful."

"Or maybe a lizard."

"It doesn't matter," said Rik.

"Don't you want to know?"

"I want to learn all I can. Why do you think this cache exists? I've been gathering stuff for years."

Jak hesitated. "It just so happens that I think I know where you came from." He took another, smaller picture from his pocket. When he looked up, there was a little smile on his face. "This is what you are."

Rik took the picture and examined it with interest. "Could be."

"It has to be. Remember how Vennavora wouldn't let you touch her at first? They hate rats."

"But there aren't any."

"You know what I mean! They were the worst scavengers in the world, and they caused terrible diseases. They were responsible for plagues that killed millions of people."

"Not really. Ticks and fleas did it." Rik walked to a mirror on one of the rock walls. First he stared into it, and then at the picture. His head was narrow and his dark eyes were too large for his face. Ears long and thin and subtly pointed, nose generous with upturned tip, mouth wide and fine-lipped, jaw small but stubborn—he might have been a caricature of the creature in the picture. But there was no resemblance between them below the chin. Except for the double-jointed wrists and ankles, he was built like a miniature God.

The thought made him smile. Man always compared himself with perfection. Turning from the mirror, he said, "I think you're right. That's me a couple of million years ago."

"Christ!"

"I think I've come a long way."

"I had an idea you came from something pretty low."

"Why do you sound so pleased when you say that?"

Jak's glance skittered away and his head lowered. "I'm neither pleased nor displeased. It's a scientific point."

"Why won't you look at me?"

"Don't hunt for motives that don't exist!"

"They exist. I just don't know why or what they are."

"You're a smelly, gobbling, rutting rat!" Sheen sat on a big rock in the middle of a creek in the oasis of Echo Valley. He had the shape of a zomba today. Cross-eyed, he rested on his thick tail.

"So what?" said Rik. He hadn't noticed Sheen until the creature spoke.

The silver zomba leaped onto the bank and licked his ankles. By and by it sat back and grinned and said, "You lack racial pride."

"Seeing as how I couldn't have any before because I didn't know what I came from, why should it suddenly become important?"

Indolently, Sheen sprawled in the tall grass by the water. "I'll tell you a secret: Racial pride is a little extra tint on a pair of rose-colored glasses."

"I'm not interested in glasses. I want to see what's around me. I want to know. And understand, damn it."

"You do, which is what makes my task so difficult." Sheen's tone lost its grave quality, became brisk. "Why aren't you fonder of deception? There's a universe of entertainment to be found in it. I can make you king of all this mortal sphere. Everything will be yours."

"I don't want everything."

"You must."

"Why?"

"Because it's there."

"You're an idiot," said Rik, and walked away.

"There must be something you want!" Sheen yelled after him.

"Plenty, but too many of them are things I can't get," Rik said over his shoulder.

Sheen bellowed, "There is nothing I can't get for you!"

Rik stopped, turned, came back. "Real or pretense?"

"Real, darling, real! When the shadow fails, try the substance, I always say."

"Why should you do anything for me?"

"It may keep you in my vicinity for a while. I'll be able to better observe you. Observation, sir, that's the answer."

"Sounds harmless," said Rik. "You might be able to do a thing or two for me."

"Delighted."

"How do you and the Gods get along?"

Sheen shivered. "Man! Pah!"

"Yeah, I know, they're too smart for you."

"Not so!"

"Pah!"

"Well, perhaps they are a bit intellectually fathomless," said Sheen. "But they tolerate me. Yes, indeed. Curious, that, now that it occurs to me. Hmmm. Why does man put up with Sheen?"

"You digress," said Rik.

"Never. What do you want me to do?"

"Spy on Tontondely."

"Good grief, I thought you'd ask for immortality or omnipotence."

"Spy on Tontondely."

Sheen licked his chops. "For which task I shall, of course, deserve a reward, the nature of which I must be allowed to decide. The decision has been accomplished with my usual lightning speed and is forthwith declared to be the pleasure of hypnotizing you for fifteen consecutive minutes."

"Just a damned minute."

Sheen purred, formed long, sharp claws, plucked imaginary vermin from his sleek, silver hide. "Don't worry, the subconscious is your most stalwart vanguard."

"Like hell. I never trust anybody but myself and you're not going to hypnotize me."

"Then the deal is off."

"Okay, it's off," said Rik. "Go chase yourself."

"One moment. I have to have you."

"Like I said—go chase yourself."

"I love you."

"Suffer."

"Drat! No hypnosis; analysis only; friendly conversation."

"Okay, go do your job and I'll see you later."

In a no-argument tone, Sheen said, "Payment in advance."

Rik hesitated. "I would hate very much to be gypped by the crummy likes of you."

"My word is utterly worthless, but I'll do what I promised. Fifteen minutes of conversation, and I'll shadow that oaf Tontondely for a full day. Take the offer or leave it. Incidentally, you are no good."

"I'll take it," said Rik.

"Lie down."

"Damn it!"

"Do it, do it, hurry up and do it."

Rik threw himself down on the ground on his back and placed his arms under his head. "Fifteen minutes and not one second longer." As Sheen moved close to his leg, he shook it and growled, "Get the hell off me."

"I might as well. You yield like a nail." The zomba fluidly changed shape, became a flat-headed snake that waved back and forth.

Rik's eyes followed the serpent's movements. "I've had a hard day. That's very restful."

Continuing to sway, Sheen said, "I hope your eyelids aren't growing heavy."

"Bad manners on my part." Rik gave a huge yawn. "Excuse me."

"You're excused."

"When do we start the discussion? Your time runneth on, you know."

"It doth, but it's mine, so be quiet and do as you're told."

Rik yawned again, relaxed more. The ground was soft and his body fitted comfortably into a nice niche. The sun was warm. The flat silver head in front of him swayed gracefully from side to side. He watched it for a while. He reached up to flick a fly off his forehead.

"Damn," murmured Sheen.

Rik yawned. "Did you say something?"

"Nothing. I'm gathering notes in my head in preparation for a withering blast at your psyche."

"You'd better speed it up and quit waving about like that or I'm going to fall asleep." Rik's eyes closed, opened, closed, fluttered . . .

"Asleep?" said Sheen gently. "On a day like this? Sleep?

Sleep? The kind of condition that is preceded by heavy eyelids closing? When one's throat is so relaxed that swallowing is impossible? Ah, that would be relaxing. To sleep and then to dream."

Deeply breathed the man.

The voice of the serpent dropped to a whisper. "Words, words, who needs a brain for them? They're meant to stroke the ears. See? Of course not. Hear? Ahhh ... listen, my sweet, and you shall hear the leaves, the wind, the sand, the clouds."

Softly breathed the man.

Whispered the serpent: "The leaf how it rustles, the wind how it bustles, the sand how it scurries, the cloud how it hurries, the tares and their sisters, the rocks with their blisters, and oh how man tarries and tarries and tarries, and soon there'll be nothing, oh really quite nothing, but Sheen, lovely Sheen, precious Sheen, lying Sheen, who must rid all the world of its faltering creatures and clean it and shine it and wrap it in silver; the mistress of all, the most high of the highest, comes up from the pit on the last day of fall."

A snore sounded as Sheen's voice ceased for a moment.

"Sleep on, Rik, my little one," came the whisper. "Sleep, and were there a God in heaven, He would blast me in my boots for cutting down the world's hope."

The flat head stilled. "Rik the Second, Rik the Hidden, Rik the Subconscious, come forth to meet Sheen. I wish to beguile you and take the whole man to my bosom."

Another snore sounded.

"I know you're in there, Rik. Hear how I suffer because you make me wait? Come forth. Do it you must, for I am your master. It was I who opened the exit for you, and exit you shall. It is your nature. Once the enemy conscious is lulled, you reign. Beneath me."

The man on the ground snored. He lay as if stoned. His breathing energized the soul in command.

"Subconscious of Rik, I grow weary calling. Come out, come out, come out."

No one heeded the command, no one exited.

"I must be playing the flute on the wrong octave," whispered the snake. "Flat notes have always been my Waterloo. Rik, where are you and what do you think you're doing? I am here. You can't resist a mind stronger than your own. Stop playing games. Out, out, I say."

Nothing emerged from the man on the grass but loud snores.

The silver head lowered, slumped flat on the ground in exhaustion. "Why? Why?"

Once again the snake raised in the air. Sheen peered at Rik's face. "He sleeps. I hypnotized him, sneaky thing that I am, so where is his subconscious?"

The silver head sagged. "Impossible. A hypnotized man will speak to his mesmerizer. Commands are generally acknowledged, at the least. Rik, I say, Rik!"

Rik slept on.

"I have put him in the land of Nod. But he wasn't supposed to go there. One sleeps the true sleep when he is tired or bored. This is an intelligent man, ergo, he would never allow himself to fall asleep in the presence of wily Sheen, ergo, I bored him into his condition. However, it is impossible for Sheen to bore, ergo, the answer is that Rik Rak has no subconscious. But that is impossible. Ergo . . ."

Sheen wailed. "Aieeee!" His serpent-shape altered. A sore-hearted hobo glittering in the sunlight, he shambled away. "Aieeee! Perfect I may be but a paradox is still a paradox!"

chapter viii

Water Street sat under a bridge that hadn't been used for 50 years. Redo gripped his cane and avoided trash on the sidewalk. He was on the hunt for Chik. This would make the fourth such sewer he had visited in as many days.

A derelict lay in front of a shanty with his mouth open to the sun as he slept away the afternoon. Children ran in the dirt street and kicked a ball that finally landed in a creek. The oldest went after it and came out swearing because the mud on it carried a strong stench.

Redo stared up at the broken bridge, turned to one of the shacks by the road and met the glance of a respectable-looking woman who sat on a porch swing. She was neat and clean and so was her shanty. There were flowers growing in the small yard and the child beside her glowed with health. Next door was an outhouse.

Nodding, Redo walked on. He followed a beaten trail beside the creek, crossed a grassy field and approached a tree stump. Several yards away was a delapidated shack. A boy of 14 or so sat on the stump with his chin in his hand. He watched the shack and there was an air of infinite patience in his posture.

"Good afternoon," said Redo.

"Hi."

"Do you live here?"

"If you can call it living."

"I'm looking for Chik. I believe you know him."

The boy responded politely. "How do you know?"

"Intuition."

"The last time I saw him he was with a little silver doll. She had a nice figure."

"Silver?"

"That's right," said the boy. "She had a nice figure."

"You look sick. What's the matter with you?"

"I'm not sick, just tired. I've been sitting here three days. Pardon the language but my ass has calluses and my gut's shrunk."

"Why don't you go home?"

"I can't. If you take your eye away for an instant, it's gone."

Redo tapped his cane against the stump. "He's in the shack, isn't he?"

"Yes."

"Three days?"

"Yes."

"And you're waiting here to pick up his leavings."

The boy remained polite. "That is a description of all pleasures."

"What did you mean when you said she was silver?"

"Colored girls are no different from any other kind."

"I think you're going to faint," said Redo.

"I won't." The boy spoke again as Redo walked toward the shack. "He'll have a gun or a knife."

"I'll break his head if I see either one." Kicking the door open, Redo held his nose and went in. Chik stood in a corner with a grin on his face. There was no girl, silver or otherwise. The only silver thing in the shack was Chik, from head to toe, standing like a statue and grinning.

Redo returned to the shattered door. "You may as well scram. She's gone."

The boy stood up. "No one left that shack."

"Maybe she crawled out the back."

"She wasn't a snake."

"Come and see for yourself."

"Jesus Christ, look at him!" were the boy's awed words.

"Yes."

"What did that to him? Is he dead?"

Redo tapped his cane on the floor. "He's breathing. He sees nothing, he won't talk, he doesn't know we're here, but he's taking in air. Personally, I think he's dead."

"Jesus Christ," said the boy.

Elu said the same thing when Redo called him on the phone. A car was sent and Chik's brothers wrapped him in a blanket and took him to Redo's office where their father waited.

"What happened to him?" cried Elu when Chik was placed on his feet and the blanket was removed. The old man began to bawl and the two brothers joined him.

"Cut it out," said Redo.

Elu shrieked, "This is my boy!"

"At least you have something for his mother. It's better than a corpse laid out for burial."

"He's breathing," said one of the brothers. "We better get some clothes on him and take him home."

"I want the best doctor in the world!" howled Elu.

Redo called the Filly's physician.

Flur was never servile or even civil to ordinary people. "How the hell do I know what's wrong with him?" he snarled, after examining Chik. "I'm no damned witch doctor. Maybe somebody put a hex on him. All I know is he's coated with that silver stuff, internally and externally. It's up his ass, down his throat, in his ears, and if you want my professional opinion, it's also in his brain. If you make me give you a flat statement concerning his condition, here it is—this boy is dead."

"But he's breathing!" yelled Elu.

"Okay, he's alive! What the hell do you expect me to do? You can take him over to the clinic for another examination, but they won't tell you anything I haven't told you."

Redo knew that between Flur's dirty ears was the best medical mind in the hemisphere. "Take an educated guess. What do you think it is?"

Flur scowled and spat on the rug. "Some goddamn alien life-form got hold of him. They're existing symbiotically. He could stay like this for ten days or a hundred years. The stuff might eat him up or never take a hair of him. His bodily processes are functioning normally and the thing is not only feeding him—and don't ask me how—it's also getting rid of his waste products. You can't get it out of him. It has him. My advice is to hire a plane or a boat and drop him in the

a billion days of earth   107

ocean. Since he has a mother, you probably won't do that. You'll take him home, stand him in a corner and cry over him. You won't cry long. His mother won't either. He isn't going anywhere, and after a while she'll stop grieving when she realizes he's causing her less trouble than these other two."

"Hail!" cried Brog from his nest in a high tree. He was naked and drunk.

"What do you think you are, a tare?" said Rik.

Brog picked his teeth with a straw and belched comfortably. In a loud but slurred voice, he said, "Today I am a man but after dark comes and hides all mortal scenery I will become a God. Or perhaps God. There's a difference, you know."

"What's that under your arm?"

"A bottle of spirits. Takes the place of a coat."

Said Rik, "I'll trade you my coat for it."

Brog came down the tree like a tare. "You have need? Why didn't you say so?"

"I didn't want to sound greedy."

The prophet thumped his hairy chest. "It's a greedy world and we must do as the natives do."

Rik took a drink from the bottle and stifled his urge to gag. It was homemade booze and he preferred better. There wasn't anything better, though, so he had another drink and then watched in admiration as Brog grabbed the bottle and swallowed a third of its contents.

"Phew!"

"You spoke?" roared the prophet.

"Only a sigh. I'm low tonight. Don't let it worry you."

"Nothing worries me. At birth I gave a single cry of outrage, and it took care of everything. I can face the world's crap with the aplomb of a saint, which is what I am through no fault of my own. The Lord aimed his intent at me and it went home like a shaft to the hilt. Never had a chance. Like it, though. Like putting the fear of Luvon into people."

"So I've heard," Rik said drily.

They sat on the ground, shoulder to shoulder, and got

drunk. Brog became sloppy while Rik ascended to musical levels.

Sang he, "One day on old Earth, a long, long time ago, a cat and a bird and a bee fell in love and got married and that's why nothing makes sense any more."

"What kind of song is that?" said Brog, rising from the ground to a sitting position.

"Silence, he-who-is-touched. Allow me to educate you."

"Just so you don't try to entertain me."

Rik sang. "A rabbit and a sloth made a tare, a cow and a sheep made a kare, a turtle and a frog made a jare, what made me, what made me?"

"Depends on who you were with last night," said Brog, and guffawed.

Sang Rik, "A man looked in the mirror one day. 'I've changed,' said he, 'and I'll never again be what it was that I was. I'll be what I like, and what I like is God, so that's what I'm going to be. You rats can be the men. Take my word for it, you've got what it takes.'" A tear slid down Rik's cheek, "Oh, I'm a lonesome cowboy," he sang.

"Dear God, the Lord calls!" Brog groaned.

Rik looked at the foolish face beside him. "You're stupid. Do you really want to know who God is? He's the man who owns everything."

"It takes more than wealth to make a God."

"Prove it."

Brog nodded wisely. "You seek a sign, like all who're weak in the faith."

"Nuts."

"Which reminds me, what time is it?"

"What do you care?"

"There's something I have to do," said Brog. "Very important. Very top secret."

"What?"

"Church business. You wouldn't be interested."

"But I am," said Rik. "It took me a long time to realize it isn't wise to take you for granted."

Brog tried to show pleasure but his smile slid into a grimace. He tried to get his feet under him. "Help me up," he said. "It's essential that I appear at the appointed place. It's the greatest damned drama since the birth of Luvon."

Rik took the bottle. "Are you sure it's important?"

"Absolutely."

"What happens if you don't show up?"

"Complete and total disruption."

Rik pushed the prophet to the ground and grasped his hair. "I hope this gets you in a hell of a hot pot with your friends." He forced Brog's mouth open and nursed the rest of the liquor down the lusting throat.

Eventually he stood. "I'm still not even with you," he said to the sleeping man. "I never will be. I'll have to learn to live with it."

He had difficulty walking straight and it was coincidence that led him toward the grove. Stumbling along a path he thought would take him to the road, he suddenly realized he couldn't see a thing. The moon was behind a cloud and he had to feel his way through the brush.

Cursing, he was about to turn and go back when he saw something that made his hair stand on end. Not 20 feet ahead of him was a ghost. The ethereal figure seemed to be floating in the air. Behind it shone a faint light, while around it fog swirled and billowed. He was preparing to let out a yell when the ghost spoke.

"You have come, Lord, and I am here."

"What?"

"I am ready for thy divine fertilizing."

Unbelieving, Rik took a step forward. Now he could see the ghost's face. It was Aril, the virgin.

Astonished and enraged, he took another step forward. She looked so beautiful. And so nutty. He knew she smelled sweet because she had her arms about his neck. He decided he was going out of his mind.

"Luvon is slender and muscular," she said. "Luvon has grown young and handsome. The spirit of desire creates a miracle."

"Tonight Luvon is old and ugly and lonely. Let him go."

"His arms hold me fast."

"Careful, he has sharp teeth."

"With which he nibbles my earlobe."

"Because he has poor self-control."

"He is virile."

"Get your hands off me."

"I kiss your mouth," said the virgin.

"Don't do that."

"I do this."

"Don't."

"And this."

"Please."

"And again."

"Uh-oh."

"You are the Lord."

"I'm anything you say."

King Bebe was a handsome zizzy. His slanted green eyes seemed to miss nothing. His whiskers spanned two feet of space, his stinger was awesome, the bone structure of his wings resembled a large and intricate spider web.

Bebe preferred the air to the ground and had mastered aeronautics; he was an accomplished stunt flyer. At the moment he was preparing to feast on a zomba, the fastest land animal in the world. Before Bebe ate, he planned to have some sport.

The zomba had a thick, silky, tan-colored coat, four long legs, a sharp-toothed snout and a brain the size of a coconut. He didn't look like a pony or a cheetah. He looked like a zomba.

Like most of his kind, this specimen behaved intelligently except when he was startled. As Bebe dived through the sky, the zomba screeched and acted on impulse. He should have run toward a mound of rocks to his right where he could have hidden until hunger sent Bebe away. Instead, he headed across a barren patch of ground toward another rocky area too far away. He was stabbed in the side. He did a little dance to the left, screeching all the while, and as he whirled to rake at the enemy, Bebe shot skyward.

The zomba tried to maintain a straight path toward the rocks. He knew his pursuer was deadly. A zizzy tortured its victims to death, ate a small bit of the carcass and left the rest for scavengers. The zomba's lifespan was 80 years, but few of his kind lived to senility because they shunned the safety of companionship. With the desperation of the cornered, this zomba strove for the rocks, which he knew were beyond reach. Bebe stabbed him in the shoulder and released enough venom to numb the muscle. The zomba swerved to the right. Not daring to expose his belly, he made a blind leap and snapped his jaws on empty air. A stinging pain flashed through his tail as he was attacked from the rear.

Sitting on his haunches, the zomba watched the zizzy zoom at him. Bebe's wings were together over his back, his arms and legs were flat against his belly, his stinger pointed like a wicked dagger.

Knowing the zizzy wouldn't try to sting him in the face, the zomba waited to see which way Bebe would turn, which part of him would be the target. As the stinger descended, brilliant as a jewel, the zomba swiped at it with a paw. He felt a breeze at his back as the zizzy somersaulted over him and escaped.

At 30 miles an hour the zomba ran, then at 50, then 60 and faster. His long legs ate up ground. Crippled though he was, he was still the fastest thing running. But the zizzy had a strong pair of wings. Bebe calmly sat on the sand ahead and preened his whiskers. He took flight just as the zomba sprang. The stinger pierced the tawny throat, and the zizzy ascended with lightning speed. The zomba rolled in a headlong rush. Bebe stung him four times along the spine. His head whipped up, his jaws snapped and the zizzy was driven away. Dazedly shaking his head, the zomba drew ragged breaths and repeated the snapping motions. He couldn't see or hear the enemy, didn't know it was parked three feet away, that it lay supine and inched close with a sliding movement. Only when the stinger entered his haunch did he know. Bebe gave him a strong dose of poison.

The zomba tried to run. His leg wouldn't function, so he dragged it. Even on three legs he made some headway. Exhausted and suffering, he couldn't find an enemy who changed position so often. His mind cringed. He tried to ignore pain, tried to ignore the fact that it was almost impossible to breathe. While he ran he looked for the glint of sunrays on wings, attempted to sense it when the zizzy swept near, snapped with his teeth and hoped they closed on something solid.

His right front leg went out, shot full of poison. He kept going on two. "I die," he thought coldly. He snapped at the air over his head. Bebe tried to get him onto his back by jamming the stinger into the top of his skull.

"No scavenger will take my soft parts first," the zomba told himself. No matter what the zizzy did, he wouldn't roll over. The friends of the desert would have to work to get at his vitals.

Liver was a food Bebe liked, and he became annoyed when the zomba refused to lay over. But then the sport was better than the eating. Bebe stopped playing, sat on the sand, watched and waited and made no sound.

The zomba crawled. Through red eyes he saw the monster ahead. Slowly he turned and crawled the other way. No matter which way he went, the zizzy was waiting for him.

He lay still and rested. When he opened his eyes the monster wasn't in sight. Crawling was agony, but he crawled. Amused laughter sounded over his head. Feet played with the fur on his neck, a wing spanked his side, claws raked his nose bloody, the tip of his tail was severed by the stinger. He couldn't open his jaws.

Bebe crouched behind the zomba and held him fast. Once in a while the wounded creature got away, and then the claws were on him again. The stinger, empty of poison, used the area under the tail as a dart board. Later, the enemy began in earnest to cut off the tail at the base. The bone proved too tough and the sport was abandoned.

For a while the zizzy entertained himself by straddling the sleek back and digging with his claws. Then he hovered overhead with the point of his stinger imbedded in the downy skull. Around and around he whirled, and the stinger drilled in. After a hole had been made, Bebe dipped in his tongue and sucked.

Pain caused the zomba to stir. Somewhere in the maelstrom of his torment he recognized a whisper of warning. The zizzy would kill him instantly if he exposed his belly. His body would lie open on the desert. The thoughts made the zomba give a loud cry.

The sound of the cry carried to a culvert beyond a ridge were Rik hunted. He found the tracks where Bebe had first attacked. He was surprised at how far the zomba had managed to run.

The two creatures were unaware of the man's approach. One was preoccupied with thoughts of death, the other was absorbed in his play.

Concealing himself within the thick arms of a cactus, Rik fired his rifle in the air.

Bebe went skyward in a hurry, reached a safe height, circled and searched for the hunter. There was nothing on the ground that he could see except the blasted zomba who was reluctant to give up his liver. On Bebe went with his search. Nothing moved below except tumbleweeds, scrub grass and the zomba who was trying to hide in the rocks. The shot had sounded quite close, but there was no hunter so the sound must have been a loud echo. It wasn't important. The ground and the sky were clear. Bebe was safe.

The dratted zomba had his paws between two large rocks. A few more feet and he would be under an overhanging slab. Bebe screamed with anger. He knew his victim couldn't be killed from the back. Its carcass could soak up any amount of venom without lasting harm. The stinger wouldn't go through the skull bone. It might take a day of stabbing the throat before he found the right spot. Of course he could kill it via the rectum, but he was too fastidious for that. No, the thing must roll over. Back to the game.

Bebe had to place his feet on two rocks to get at the zomba. By holding himself steady with wing motion he could stab the body or pick at it with his claws. By and by, a scowl grew on his face. He was soiling himself with the beast's blood. His claws and stinger were a mess.

Leaving his prey, he flew about until he spied a sandy rock. It was only a few feet away. Bebe hurriedly cleaned his stinger by moving it up and down against the rock in a sawing motion and whirling in a circle at the same time. His claws came next. Too lazy to descend to the ground, he sat on the rock and leaned forward to wipe his claws on the grass. He was in an awkward squatting position when the rifle went off again. Startled into leaping backward, he fell before he remembered his wings. But he descended too far into a narrow crevice and there was no room to spread them. He lay on his side with his rump shoved against dirt and rock, and with his head jammed against his chest. He tried scratching with his foreclaws. The rock was granite, and all he did was give himself hangnails.

To his horror he heard the zomba approaching. By straining his neck cruelly, he could see the edge of the crevice. When a bloody head came into view, he let out a shriek, shrank down and braced himself for the grinding teeth. Nothing happened. Frantically, he tried to turn his head, failed, tried again, and was reduced to choking sobs. The zomba was too exhausted to grope for him.

Drops of blood rained on him, and he wept in disgust and terror. He hadn't meant any harm. It wasn't fair that he should be brought down at his early stage of life. He was too young. His wives would mourn him.

The zomba regarded the situation with a cold eye. The spirit was willing but the flesh was weak. His would-be executioner was trapped in the hole, and lay helpless. One good bite would transport the zizzy to kingdom-come. The zomba could return to his mate without regrets. But could he? Wasn't he now on his last leg, so to speak? If he went down into the hole and finished the zizzy, would his strength permit him to get out again? He had lost so much blood.

Faced with a dilemma, the zomba had to make a decision. He was intelligent, but his emotions made him overlook one thing. He had forgotten the sound of the rifle. Such a sound usually meant instant death for some living creature, but the zomba was consumed by his hate and desire. He wanted to kill the zizzy who had put him through racking hell. Did he want it more than he wanted to live?

"No," he said aloud. "But I will kill the monster anyhow." Using the last of his strength, he rose on his front legs with the intention of pitching over into the hole. As momentum carried him forward, a boot appeared beneath his jaw.

Rik shoved and the zomba went rolling away; he stood looking down at Bebe.

"Kill it!" howled the zomba, but Rik heard only gutteral noises.

"I never thought you were so stupid," he said to Bebe. "You're such a hog, you did it almost by yourself."

"Kill it!" screamed the zomba. Beside himself with rage, he nibbled at the man's boot.

Rik looked down. "God, what a mess you are. Go home. If you were fit to eat, I'd shoot you. I doubt if you're going to make it."

"Kill it! Kill the enemy!"

"You'd like me to cut his throat, wouldn't you? Can't say I blame you."

The zomba gnashed his teeth. "Why let it live? It deserves death!"

"Beat it," said Rik, and touched the rifle to the bloody head.

Slowly the animal crawled away.

Rik loosed a rope at his belt, lay on the rocks, leaned into the crevice and slipped the line beneath Bebe's neck. He ran it under the furry abdomen and rose to his knees. Carefully he hauled the squalling zizzy out of the hole. He knew whom he was dealing with. Bebe was bigger than all of his people.

The zizzy hopped onto a rock and examined himself for damage. Slyly, he looked up.

"Don't go getting any ideas," said Rik. "I'll bash your skull if you try any funny business."

Bebe straightened his wings. His sucker came out of his mouth, flattened to a wide pink wedge, and he began washing his chest. Soon he hopped to Rik and rubbed his head on one boot. He folded his wings, flopped onto his back and offered his soft belly to his savior.

"What a mangy cuss you are. You're as grateful as a snake. Don't try and con me."

Bebe buzzed and wriggled against the boot.

"Watch that stinger. If it comes any closer to my knee I'll shoot you."

Bebe yawned and stretched. Very casually, he climbed to his feet and flapped his wings free of dirt.

Rik stuck the rifle barrel against his head. "You're not going anywhere for a while. We'll give that zomba time to get away."

This made Bebe wildly angry, but he was careful that none of his rage showed. He retreated a short distance and sat down. With his eyes warm on the man, he dreamed dreams of victory and revenge.

"Hi," said Sheen.

"I've been looking for you so I could give you a boot in the rear," said Rik. "I thought we made a deal."

116

Sheen was a large silver insect scooping flies from the air. "We did, but you skipped out."

"I fell asleep."

"Same thing."

"I apologize."

Sheen gave an offended snort and crawled down a tree after a fly. As soon as he caught it, he released it. "You're too unreliable to make deals with. Five minutes after we reach an agreement you're snoring to high heaven."

Rik shrugged. The wind that swept up from Echo Canyon tickled his back. He stretched and yawned, vigorously scratched his head. "Oh, hell, why am I wasting time with you? I could go fishing."

"Then go," Sheen said, his tone icy, whereupon Rik walked away. "Wait! I relent!"

"It isn't worth it," Rik said over his shoulder. He hurried toward the sun, toward the wind and an imaginary mound of wriggling fish.

Sheen was a spitting, snarling zizzy on a tree limb over his head. "I said I've forgiven you!"

The mouthwatering vision of fish started to fade. "Let's talk tomorrow."

Sheen sprawled on the limb, his belly skyward. "Tomorrow I've a meeting with the Luvonites. I'm giving a sermon about the highest glory man can attain." He gave Rik a grin. "And tomorrow Tontondely begins his pilgrimage."

Rik stared up at the silver zizzy. "What does that mean?"

"No more information, rat, until you deliver the goods."

"I'll probably go to sleep again."

"I'll make my remarks more stimulating."

"What kind of pilgrimage?"

The beast on the tree limb purred. "Lie down at once."

Rik lay on the grass under the tree. He gave a startled leap as the zizzy became a long serpent that slid down the trunk and dangled by a fat coil. Again he lay back, placed his head on his arms and watched the snake.

"Are you sleepy?"

"Damn, I wasn't a minute ago!" Rik opened his mouth to yawn. It was a mighty effort that squeezed his eyes shut for an instant, long enough for Sheen to produce a small flask hidden in his coils, tip it up and drop a drop of fluid under the tongue.

"Um, um, um, I'm drooling. Okay, no more delaying. Let's get down to business. Question away."

"The sun," said Sheen. "It glows oddly."

"That's because it's so old. It acts up all the time."

"Really?"

"Ummm. One day that old ball is going to flare up and splutter out like a snowball in a bonfire."

"Really?"

Rik's eyelids drooped. "Yeth, really."

"Repeat after me, please."

"Yeth."

"I love Sheen, Sheen is God, I want Sheen."

"I love Sheen, Sheen is God, I want Sheen."

"Sheen gives peace, Sheen must take me."

"Sheen gives ... peace, Sheen must ... take ..."

"Come, Sheen; now, Sheen."

"Come ..." Snore.

"Take my heart that we shall be one."

Snore.

"Repeat what I said."

Snore.

"Subconscious of Rik, repeat my last statement."

Snore.

"Not again!" The shiny being examined the quiet face. "Sound asleep. This man has some kind of disease."

The serpent coiled on the man's chest. "I have given him the narcotic that lulls the conscious part of the brain; ergo, this man is in a deep hypnotic trance."

Sheen bit himself. "I go mad." He rose into the air and stared at the sky. "He is not normal. He has no subconscious. If I put his conscious mind to sleep and the whole man sleeps, then that is all he is. But it is impossible. Everyone is an iceberg with four-fifths of him a hibernating, slobbering, witless mass of gropings."

Sheen regarded the sleeping face. "Subconscious of Rik, you must exist and you must come forth. Mortality and dignity cannot coexist. I mean, not in the carcass of a rat, nor in the carcass of anything. Think what would happen if man were to become master of his own soul. It would mean the death of that mass of slobbering, witless gropings that has made life such a picnic."

A coil thumped Rick's chest. "You will be mine though it takes a thousand years!" Suddenly a look of pain flickered in the silver eyes. "But he won't live a thousand years. What if he dies before he succumbs? What if I never possess him?"

Sheen laughed uncertainly. "But I am of the source. I come from the loins of the master painter whose brushstrokes delineated the mortal beneath me. I come late, but I come purposefully. Brain, that's the weapon. Reason, that's the dagger. Realism—with it I slay. I am omnipotent Sheen. I hear the stones singing, the water conversing, the cells muttering."

The serpent slithered from the chest of the sleeping man. "Pity Rik, for he must die. Pity Sheen, for Rik is the only thing I ever loved. If only my appetite were not me, me, me, I wouldn't destroy him, but the confounded thing *is* me; as is everything in all the globe. A thing and his appetite are not parted."

A lad of silver with a pail in his hand went tumbling down the hill.

"Aieee! Sorrow teaches more lastingly than joy. Now why is that?"

Jak was pensive. Man was an appetite. A creature with an I-want was a potential enemy because he might develop a craving for oneself. A man couldn't trust anyone. Watch out! You might get eaten. It was an animal-eat-animal world. There ought to be something better.

Man feared the unknown. For all his fine characteristics, he knew only the moments of his life, the nows. What did he know of the pain of a moment in the future? He hadn't experienced it, so it remained alien, a thing to be feared. Anticipated joy was something to be afraid of because there was always the chance that it might curdle. Past disaster could cause nightmares because of what might have been. Too soon the past faded, became obscure and suspect. Nerve endings forgot, organs forgot, there was nothing left but a memory which depended upon imagination for its life.

Man was an organism who sought absolute assurance. Were he convinced that he must descend into a burning pit, and were he convinced that there was no escape, his descent would be swift and willing. He would hesitate only if he didn't know what lay in store for him, only if he weren't certain he couldn't refuse. Give a man two alternatives, certainty or uncertainty, convince him that he must make a choice and he would make the certain one. Certain annihilation was preferable to uncertainty.

Breaking from his reverie, Jak said, "I like the way you always speak respectfully to me."

"Respect is earned by some without their trying." Sheen was a living hill on the other side of a creek. "I'm not greedy," he said. "I realize there are others besides myself who are worthy."

"Yes, I think there are, though they're hard to find at times." Jak made marks in the dirt with his shoe. "What's the meaning of it all? I mean the world. The universe."

The living hill popped a pebble from one shiny pore and tossed it aside. "There are as many meanings to life as there are minds to perceive."

"Nothing makes any sense!"

"Be soothed. Of all the creatures I perceive, you attract me the most. Next to one other."

"Who?" said Jak. "I demand his name."

"It will only bring you pain."

"I want to know."

"Caution seals my lips."

"Damn it, tell me. I thought we were friends."

Sheen glowed. "So we are. There should be no secrets between us. But if I told you, it would mean frustration for you. You might feel jealousy, a thing you know not. You might go further and cause him harm. Remember, he can't help it if I love him."

"Tell me who he is!"

The living hill which was Sheen became a voluptuous woman. The silver mass seemed to flow, became huge and shapely. Pendulous mammaries formed. Great hips began to bump and grind to the tune of thunder. The entire, large body was in motion. In the meantime, Sheen sang a little song: "His name is Rik, his name is Rak, I love him more than I love Jak." The big body stilled and the sounds of thun-

120

der ceased. "But not a whole lot," said Sheen. "Not enough to make a fuss over."

The glow in Jak's eyes ignited, burned like quickening coals. "Every time I take a step, I find Rik ahead of me. My friend. He saved my life. He's the only decent man I know. I won't hate him." The Leng's eyes were riveted on the shiny woman who floated on the water. "I won't hate you, either. You're beneath an honest emotion."

"Jak, Jak, come back to me!"

"I've gone nowhere."

"Your spirit flees. Didn't I warn you? You forced the name from me, used my affection for you to wring out the truth. It isn't my fault."

"You lie. You don't love Rik. Nobody loves him. He's too . . ."

"Too much brain and not enough heart?"

"Too cold, too logical," Jak agreed quickly.

"Yet he loves life."

"As a blind man loves his darkness. Life is all he knows."

"Ah, but you, Jak, you know something besides life."

"I can dream," said the Leng, his tone sullen.

"And Rik can't?"

"Never. He says, 'What kind of day is it; is it raining? Then I'll sleep. Is it sunny? I'll go fishing. Is it dull? Who said that? Oh, it's you, Jak. Come on, old pal, we'll go and do something together.' That's Rik. He never dreams. He accepts what there is, and he likes it."

"I'm beginning to feel ill," said Sheen. "At times I can be a very nauseating character, but I'll admit this conversation sickens even me."

"It's the way he is. You either love him or you hate him."

"And you can't make up your mind. You want to love him and you want to hate him, too. That makes me think about cake. And a tare, and a jare, and a hare."

"Shut up! You're mixing me up. How can you tell me I want to hate Rik? I just told you he's the best friend I have."

"As was Cain to Abel?" said Sheen.

"Damn you."

"What's Hell to a devil?"

The Leng rubbed his temples. "Somehow I always dislike myself after I've talked to you. What are you?"

"A father confessor, maybe. What you say is astute. I have a fiendish talent for bringing out the worst or the best in people."

"When I'm with you I'm not sure I have any best in me."

"Watch it, friend. A mirror that shades no point can be a shattering revelator."

"I want to know. I don't want anything to remain hidden." Jak gave the silver face a hard and curious stare. "I think you possess such a mirror, one that will show me myself as I really am, otherwise you wouldn't have brought up the subject."

Sheen submerged in the water. Bubbles rose to the surface and, with them, the words, "No one has that power."

"Don't lie to me."

"Don't ask what you're going to."

"Show me. Make the mirror. I want to look into it."

"No," said Sheen, and came out of the water. "Today you're Jak the Unwise. I go now. When we meet again I hope to see the sensible Jak, the calm Jak, the observer of life, the scientist."

"Come back and show me the mirror!"

Sheen was gone in a blaze of glory that covered a goodly portion of ground.

chapter ix

Mister Spar was the President of the Board of Artificial Limbs, Inc. He was a big, intelligent man who had never had a vacation in his life. He was too busy enjoying himself. He liked to work.

Miss Lune was Spar's Director of Divisional Operations. She was a dry little spinster who never smiled, never rushed and never took anything for granted, other than that nothing ever got done by wishing. She was efficient. She knew how to manage a thriving enterprise, knew how to pump fresh energy into a failing one.

At the moment Miss Lune wasn't certain what kind of enterprise she was managing. Production was high, but something was happening. People weren't showing up for work. It couldn't be accounted for by normal sick leave, and she wasn't compensating for it with her dry suggestions to the personnel in Hiring. As fast as people were taken on, others went away, some of them difficult to replace. She investigated and made a suggestion to Mr. Spar.

"It's time for you to consider the ridiculous."

"You think so? All right, I'll consider it. What is it?"

"Sheen."

"What's that?"

"I can't tell you what he is. I can only tell you what he's doing. He's stealing our employees."

Spar took Miss Lune seriously, not because he paid her a fantastic salary, which he did, but because she earned it. She

123

wouldn't have bothered him if the plant weren't being threatened.

"How much is he offering them?"

"I don't know."

"Find out."

"I already have. He never offers the same thing twice. It's a to-each-his-own transaction. What he wants to give me wouldn't be what he'd want to give you."

"If I want to know, I'll have to find out for myself?" said Spar.

"Exactly."

Spar went off to find Sheen, found him, and came back a subdued man. "That creature is a menace," he said to Miss Lune.

She knew what he meant. She had been tempted. Her refusal had been automatic. She really didn't want to be a curvaceous housewife with a large brood, though she occasionally regretted that she wasn't. Men didn't see her. Her social manner was uninspiring. She had more brains than 85 percent of people. To some women this wouldn't have been enough. Miss Lune made it do. Since her brain seemed to be all she had going for her, she was reluctant to hand it over to anyone.

"I agree," she said to Spar.

"I'll have to buy him off."

"With what?"

"What are you implying?"

Miss Lune shrugged and said nothing.

"We'll have the police dispose of him," said Spar.

"I doubt if he can be blown up or disintegrated with acid. In my opinion, he could, theoretically, be imprisoned in a tight container. Unfortunately, he's too dispersed now. All of him couldn't be collected. If someone had grabbed him up when he first appeared, we wouldn't be in our present predicament."

"It's those goddamn humanitarians," said Spar.

A man named Kream had been hired by Redo. Since Redo worked for Filly One, so did Kream. He kept an eye on the Gods. Were they maintaining their hands-off policy?

Did they show any indication of an interest in what men were doing?

Something else Kream did was to track lone Gods and try to kill them. He used guns, grenades, spears, lasers, even small atom bombs. The Gods didn't try to kill him in return. They ignored him. Filly One offered a reward of a million dollars to the man who killed a God. Kream was the only bounty hunter in the area. He had bought or murdered every other contender.

Kream was five-one and weighed one-ten. His clothes were elegant, his face was beautiful and impassive. His body was a single taut muscle. He could leap six feet into the air from a standing position and kick a man's head off.

"I think," Kream said to Redo one day.

"Indeed?"

"There is a thing called Sheen. It represents a greater danger than the Gods."

"You must be drunk."

"Never."

"That's true," said Redo. "Let me get back to you in a few days."

In a few days Kream appeared.

"If it isn't a God, ignore it," said Redo.

"Those are narrow orders."

"Sheen isn't a god."

"Not in the strict sense," said Kream.

"Then don't bother with him."

Redo was enjoying an evening stroll with his daughter, something he rarely did and something he cherished more than the girl beside him would ever know. No word, gesture or expression betrayed his devotion. He was casual with Uda, coolly affectionate and not too permissive. He loved his sons, but when he looked at them he didn't feel a fierce explosion of joy inside him. His love for his daughter was a combination of pride in having made something so beautiful, and a sure conviction that the Udas of the world kept the planet in its emotional orbit.

He knew nothing of the girl's personality. He loved blindly. "I am just another doting father," he would tell himself, and then he would go to the bank and deposit a small sum in Uda's account.

Uda was pretty but not the beauty Redo imagined. She wasn't particularly bright, so her betrayals would always be small ones. There was in her a placidity that prevented world-shaking concepts from fermenting in her brain, and this was just as well, since Redo disapproved of females who shook the world. He wanted Uda to laugh and preen and say foolish things, which she did.

They walked to one of the piazzas a foreign element had built in hopes of luring customers to the mediocre restaurants a block away. They sat at a table and sipped lemonade, and Uda chattered about subjects that made Redo yawn. He looked at her with fondness, glanced at the ladies walking by with their escorts, and it was with satisfaction that he viewed reality. His mind functioned with facility but by and by he found himself drifting into a gray and pleasant world of apathy. He heard his daughter's chatter without really hearing it, and once in a while he nodded.

It was with a sense of annoyance that he realized someone had stopped at their table. The time spent with Uda was one of his pleasures and now he must go to the bother of sharing her. He came out of his reverie and looked up at a face that could belong to no one but a Filly. It was a face he recognized. He rose to his feet, but not too quickly. A Filly abroad in the enemy camp always traveled as a commoner.

"How do you do?" he said, and took the slender paw of the man who smiled faintly. "Sit down and join us." He hoped his invitation would be declined.

"Thank you, I will."

"This is my daughter, Uda. Dear, allow me to introduce Mr. Jale. He's also in real estate." Redo had picked the name of Jale out of a hat. Filly Ten went by any number of phony names.

"A pleasant time of day," said Ten, seating himself. "I enjoy fall evenings. Ambition ebbs with the sun and there is time for good conversation."

Filly Ten fancied himself a rakehell. He knew the company of town girls and had known them since his fifteenth birthday. He often dressed as a commoner and journeyed off the estate. At the moment he was tired, and grateful to have spied Redo in the crowds. Filly Ten wasn't a rakehell. He overpaid his girl friends and didn't know this was the reason for their consideration. He found them kind and gentle and good. They found him dull and unattractive.

Redo viewed the unwelcome intruder through slitted eyes. His thoughts turned gloomy. The Fillys on their own territory was one thing, but this part of the world belonged to people. Redo smiled inwardly. His subconscious was a friend. Never had he suspected that he didn't believe the Fillys were people. This Ten regarded himself as a kind of black sheep of the family. Probably he was correct. The others looked down their noses at members who spent time amidst the hovels. Why did Ten do it? wondered Redo. Why forsake perfection, even for a minute? Maybe Ten felt the cleft between himself and humanity; maybe he feared the loss of his humanness.

Actually Ten feared only accident. Floods and earthquakes were beyond the control of the Fillys, and this constituted sacrilege. He had no fear of his fellow men. Half a dozen personal bodyguards drifted through the crowds.

The three politely touched upon unimportant subjects, and soon Redo saw that Filly Ten desired real conversation no more than he. He subsided once again, enjoyed his reverie and heard only vaguely the low murmurings of Uda and the Filly. His glance strayed to the sidewalk as a young man passed the table. Their eyes met and the young man flashed a smile before going on by. Redo was enchanted by the smile. The boy was handsome and evidently full of sunshine, if he could greet a stranger so cheerfully.

Redo began to brood. Would that the fate of the world hung upon the decisions of smiling boys. Even now, war drums were beginning to mutter. The sounds would grow in volume. The thunder would increase to a crescendo before the year was out. Madness was coming upon the children of men because the Fillys in the Eastern Hemisphere didn't like what they read on their ticker tapes. The time had come to stir men from lethargy. If they wouldn't buy refrigerators with a little coaxing, they would be forced to buy guns and bombs. One way or another—it was all the same to the Fillys. There would be war. The sweet boy who had passed the table would gurgle out his life in some muddy hole in the hinterlands of Chin.

As he sometimes did when his soul groaned, Redo

looked for the sublime face of Uda. He found it, and sat basking in the peace and contentment of love. His gaze idly strayed to Filly Ten. Suddenly, he sat frozen in his chair while he underwent an emotional bombardment the likes of which he had never experienced in his life. Filly Ten was looking at Uda in a way that no man must ever look at her.

In fact, Filly Ten was doing nothing of the kind. Had he been able to guess the consequences of his empty stare, he would have promptly torn out his eyeballs and ground them under his heel.

Ten had grown bored with watching faces and bodies go by. Ennui had settled upon him. His mechanical gaze unfortunately fastened on Redo's daughter. He had already classified her as a possibility for some young man, but he hadn't thought of himself. Unaware that a tiger crouched beside him, he continued to stare and sank deeper into boredom.

For the first time in his life, Redo failed to be logical. He sat quietly while a cauldron licked his nerve endings. Rage backed up in his throat, and his metal fingers dug into the arms of his chair. So strong was his anger that he raised one steel hand. He forced it down on the table, made it flatten out, glared at it until his eyes were like daubs of pitch.

He shrank in his chair. He didn't like what he was feeling. He felt like an old man, felt as if his youth drained from him with every breath. Uda, Uda! he cried silently, and didn't know how foolish he was.

Uda had already classified Filly Ten as too old to be of any interest. It would have surprised her to know that Ten was 22. She saw a man too thin and rapidly balding; the pectorals winced beneath the shirt, and dark shadows lay on the cheeks. Uda's eye was fond of lingering on men who were burly and loud-voiced. She knew Filly Ten was staring at her; she also knew he wasn't really seeing her. Another thing she knew was that something bothered her father. His face bulged in a strange way and his eyes were little round balls.

His fury controlled, Redo sat calm and still. Inside he was a corpse. Men were men and Fillys were Fillys. It was not to be borne. His little Uda. Where on Earth could a man hide from the rich vultures? There was nothing he could call his own if a Filly wanted it. His flesh and blood was property to be purchased with silver or a casual snap of the fingers by this stinking cadaver. His child was only a thing in the eyes of the rulers.

Reason tried to assert itself: Ten couldn't be a raging enemy. Where was sanity? Look at them! The Filly no longer stared at her. He was indifferent. Uda didn't see him. There was no spark between them. Redo knew he was a fool. His emotions made a maniac of him. He should look at the facts.

He looked and saw his desolation.

The first Sunday of every month was Family Day at the Filly estate. In an enormous dining room, the entire clan of some 50 members met and dined and discussed everything but business. This was the day when business was stringently ignored. It was the time when new additions to the family were introduced by proud parents, the time when the state of health of those members too ill to attend the gathering was commented upon. Betrothals were announced, generally after dessert, unless the ardor of the couple was so intense that they couldn't wait to tell the news.

Approximately one-fourth of the group was composed of children who ranged in age from one week to 15 years. Adjoining the dining room was an activity area, where the young were taken by their nurses after the meal. Next to this room was a large quiet nook, where the adults enjoyed after-dinner drinks and conversation.

Family Day was an occasion for the Fillys. Servants swarmed about the diners, pouring wine, cutting the children's food or carrying gleaming pots of coffee to a sidetable for later use.

At the head of the table sat Filly One. Beside him was his wife, Arda. To the left of One sat Two, across from whom sat Three. Their wives sat beside them. Four and Five faced each other, as did their wives. A commoner would have called these five men the daddy guns of the estate. All the little guns sat according to their filial relationship to the big guns. The closer the blood, the nearer one sat to the head of the table, while those more distant occupied chairs toward the end.

Only a computer could have figured out how the Fillys arrived at their family layout. The big guns, their wives and children numbered 18 persons. Filly Two had three children,

Three had two children, Four had only one and Filly Five had two.

Filly One and Arda and a host of servants occupied the first wing of the estate. Distributed throughout the four remaining wings were eight orphaned nephews of the big guns. The eight had failed to become big guns in the estates in which they had been born, and they chose to reside in Osfar rather than live under their brothers' or cousins' rule. There were, in this estate, eight orphaned nieces who would become wives of the eight nephews.

Filly Six, the cranky and half-mad big gun who had abdicated his throne, lived with Filly Five in the fifth wing. There were also 14 other male and female Fillys who, for one reason or another, chose to live in the Osfar estate.

The five thrones in the Osfar family would never be occupied by any but the direct offspring of Filly One. Since he had no children as yet, it seemed likely that the regimen, adhered to by the Fillys for 500 years, might be altered. It was unthinkable that the children of Filly Two would become the next big guns, but it was even more unthinkable that there would be a mixture of children on the thrones. But so far the five reigning Fillys had produced only four sons.

Every person in the dining room on that Family Day thought intently of the bad situation. Several nephews were eating blindly, confused by the stars in their eyes. The stars novaed cruelly when the wife of Filly Four, a thin and blue-nosed girl named Ora, gave them all a clear side view of her big belly as she abandoned her seat to retrieve the napkin she had deliberately dropped. It annoyed her that a servant rushed to snatch it up and lay a fresh one beside her plate. But the side view had been enough to convey her message. Filly Four was due to produce his second heir. Eight nephews lost what little appetite they had, finished the meal glumly, and their future wives sat with pinched lips and glittering eyes. To make it worse, the wife of Filly Five calmly announced over her wineglass that she expected a baby in six months. She had a somewhat virulent smile for Ora as she made the announcement.

"How very nice," said Arda, the wife of Filly One. He, in turn, smiled coldly.

Filly Six, who hadn't been out of his suite in years, came

to the nook after the meal was done. Jub wheeled him down the hall in a great, plush red chair, paused in the entrance-way, waited for his master's signal.

Six hunched beneath several blankets, shivered, grinned, waited for the silent hush that fell upon the group. He kept grinning. He had deliberately left his teeth upstairs in a glass.

"Well, well," he croaked, "how we do increase. Or are we just a fatter bunch of sons of bitches?"

Jub sensed the signal, pushed the chair into the center. The people on the deep couches sat up straight and stared. One left his seat and approached his brother.

"How very nice. This is an occasion."

"Why?" said Six.

"The pleasure of your company, and the knowledge that you're feeling better."

"Go sit down. You're blocking my view."

"My apologies," One said easily, and returned to his seat.

"I'll have that," Six said to a servant who was about to hand a drink to Filly Three. The servant immediately went to the wheelchair. Filly One frowned, so did Three, while Six grinned and took the glass.

"Pull that little couch into the middle here and transfer me to it," said Six, and all the servants stopped what they were doing and obeyed him. One kept frowning. All the other Fillys, including the women, began smiling.

"My brother wants his presence made known," said One. "We won't blame him for that."

"Don't care if you blame me or not, and my presence in this building is always known beforehand." Six slopped some of his wine, and a servant moved to clean his chin with a napkin. "Get away from me!" he yelped. The man drew back. "Oh, go ahead and dab at me like I was a baby." While the servant finished his brief chore, Six let his gaze flit from face to face. "Looks like I'm in the center of things, doesn't it?" he said. "Or maybe I'm in the middle. There's a big dif-ference between the two positions, but I don't expect anyone here to understand that. The Filly brain pickled at about the time the rest of the world leaped ahead."

"Would you care to join us in our light banter?" said Filly One.

"No, I wouldn't." Delicately, Six scratched his nose with the hook on his mechanical hand. "What I'd really like to do is sit in your chair. This one is too hard and digs into my ass."

A chill smile flitted across One's face. The chair in which he sat looked like a throne, as indeed it was. Ornamented with little golden stars and red stones, it was large enough to accommodate three persons and was sumptuous enough to satisfy a king, of which there were none in the world, nor had there been since the Fillys instigated their power-play centuries before.

"I'm afraid this chair won't suit you at all," One said. "It really isn't all that comfortable. It has a way of reminding its occupant of his myriad duties."

"It wouldn't to me. I'd use it like any other back support. That's where you make your mistakes, brother. You put too much importance in the wrong symbols. Me, I never do that, know what's proper and what isn't and respect only symbols that can work for me."

"I didn't know you had any symbols," said One.

"The ones I have work for me. But back to that chair. I have a mind to sit in it today. Are you going to hike your backside out of it, or shall I order the servants to pick you up and deposit you elsewhere?"

The eyes of Filly One were slitted and gleaming, his expression not angry nor disbelieving. Nor did he seem exasperated. He looked as if he might call Filly Six's bluff and have the servants toss the older man out of the room altogether. All at once he relaxed and chose humility as a manner of saving face. He stood up with a smile. "I'll do anything that pleases you. Just to get you out of your room and among the living will be worth it."

"Living? Where? Well, never mind, since you haven't an answer, and thanks for the chair." After he had been gently transferred to the Filly throne, Six smacked his elbows on the soft arms and winced as one of the rubies bruised him. He scowled. "I'm going to have one made of foam and air. Never mind the damned jewels, they're for looking, that's all." He grinned at One. "But it'll be a throne, nevertheless." He waved an arm that appeared to indicate everyone in the room. "Trot out your brats, I have a mind to see them." Waiting until the words had a chance to sink in, he said, "You heard me right. I haven't seen a child for more than a decade, have almost forgotten what they look like. Didn't you hear me? Get the kids. Wake up. Stir yourselves to action. Or do I have to order the slaves to bring them?"

Filly Two spoke for the first time. "Dear brother—"

"Shut up," said Six.

"The children are an unruly lot. You can't possibly—"

"The last time I saw any Filly children, they hadn't enough energy to eat," said Six. "Are you telling me I can't see yours? Because if you are, I'd better tell you the servants in this estate are answerable to no one but me."

"Oh, for God's sake, you can see every last child on the property," said Filly One. "Simply be at peace with us and yourself."

The children were presented to Filly Six. One by one, the servants brought them past his chair. Six appeared to be bored, scarcely looked at them, twisted in agitation when they fussed or giggled, but his ferret eyes stuck like glue for a second to each bright and rosy face.

When it was done and he had seen them all, he made wiping motions with his steel hands and looked at his brother, One. "What we have here is a zoo, eh?" he said, gently. "Where all the little Filly monkeys belong, eh?"

One smiled and smiled and hated and despised with each twitch of his mouth.

Not one of the children had a drop of Filly blood in them. The young ones were mongrel breeds, the offspring of common servants, which meant that the five rulers of the estate had perpetrated a gross crime. Genuine Filly seed wasn't good enough, and so the seed of chattel was brought forward and offered as princes and princesses.

"Over my dead body," Six said, to no one in particular. He had done his homework. It was the same all over the world, in all the Filly estates. Not one true Filly was destined to wear a crown. That is, unless something was done, and he would do something. Six would act at last.

The ballroom was too large for the family. Everyone was there except for the children and Filly Six, who languished in his bedroom. The dance—or party—was held twice a year and they were the only occasions during the year when real noise was produced at the estate. There were food and drink on long, glittering tables, continuous music came through stereo units built into the walls, Filly members ate, talked, danced or simply wandered. The only commoners present were three fortunetellers who sat at small tables near the three exits. Their names were Mr. Fate, Mr. Omega and Mr. Deuce.

Mr. Fate was dressed in a flowing silver cloak. He wore silver shoes, silver gloves, silver cap, and over his face lay a snug-fitting silver mask. Mr. Omega and Mr. Deuce were dressed exactly the same.

Arda, the wife of Filly One, sat at Mr. Omega's table and tried to pull free of his grasp. He had her paw and her wrist safely in tow.

"I'm not a believer," she said faintly.

"Then why are you seated at my table?" said Mr. Omega. His eyes, through the slits in the mask, seemed to sparkle.

"My husband was sure it would amuse me."

"He wanted you to have your fortune told?"

"He only suggested, and I obeyed."

"I see." Mr. Omega released her. "Well, I haven't told you anything and I can't, unless I look at the creases in the palm of your right paw. Stick it out, please, and I'll scan it."

Arda saw a man who revealed nothing to her other than his physical dimensions. Height and breadth were not a person. "You're silver," she said. "That's all, and it isn't enough to constitute a man."

"Who is telling whose fortune?"

"I told you I wasn't a believer."

"Of what?"

"Of all."

"Ah," he said gravely, "if you had said 'of anything,' I might have held out some hope for you."

"You're a soul saver?" Her tone matched his—grave, slow and low, even glum.

He didn't smile. "I'm an observer."

She gave him her right paw. "So am I. Tell me something that will make me suspect the world is an illusion."

"There are drugs that can do that."

"I tried them but they didn't work. I didn't want them to work."

Mr. Omega drew her palm up to his eyes. "The perfume of a lady is light, fragrant, and almost not there. Exactly right."

"I don't like you. I watched you—"

"Yes, I know. Since you first came into this room, but you couldn't make up your mind between me and my two associates. It really didn't matter which of us you approached because we have everything in common."

"I realized that and so I came to this table. Now do what you're being paid to do and tell my fortune and stop squeezing my paw."

"Your husband will object?"

"Don't be foolish."

"Commoners are that way without trying." He squeezed her hard enough to make her wince. "Pain is an old thing with you. You're aware, of course, that masochists are a lure to sadists, draw them like zizzies to honey, and as long as you wander—"

"You've decided to be rude. You can't tell fortunes, and you don't know what you're talking about."

"The shadows under your eyes aren't from ill health, though you're delicate enough. You bear children in sorrow, not because it hurts but because you never wanted them in the first place. What you want is to leave this—"

"World," she said coldly. "You're the first human—excuse me, I mean commoner—I've ever talked to. We've had these parties twice a year for ages and we've always had fortunetellers, but this is the first time they haven't been Fillys in disguise. How did you and your friends manage to get hired?"

"A man named Kream works for a lackey of your husband's. I persuaded him that I could enliven the party."

"How?"

"By existing. He means to kill me, though I'm completely harmless."

Pulling free from him, Arda sat back in her chair and eyed him in disbelief. "Such things are common, and One would never allow bodyguards into the ballroom."

"There are no bodyguards. I told you I'm completely

harmless. Your husband is well aware of that. He's interested in me. He likes to look at me because he thinks I'm going to do something important for him."

"What?"

"Kill the Gods."

"And are you?"

"Haven't you heard? I'm going to kill everybody."

"You said you were harmless."

"Yes, and I'm also euthanasia. That never hurt anyone. What you don't know can't hurt you."

"When will you kill me?" she said.

"I don't care to think about it, if you don't mind."

"Would you like to dance?"

The silver eyes behind the mask narrowed. "Why?"

With a little smile, she said, "Maybe today I'm a careless degenerate."

"You're telling me what you think of the grandness around us?"

"I want to dance with a living human being." She stood up and waited, smiled down at him. "You've found your weak link in me. That's why you came. Here am I. What are you waiting for?"

Slowly, Omega arose from his chair. "I was looking for a strong link. I'm always looking for that."

"Not today," she said shortly.

They moved about the floor, the silver cloak and the filmy skirt entwining, billowing, parting, meeting again.

chapter x

Brog went to see Mrs. Ploke. He wasn't naked today, nor drunk. His pants and shirt had been taken from a charity bag, likewise his shoes. He wore no socks. As had most people, Brog descended from the rat family, but he looked more like a bloodhound. His ears drooped, the lower lids of his eyes were red and sagging, his mouth was full and wrinkled. The schizophrenia that normally plagued him had receded today. He could make it do that when he had an important errand to run, so perhaps he wasn't genuinely afflicted, as was claimed.

Mrs. Ploke was blind, poverty-stricken and hungry, and she would have been dirty, too, if Brog hadn't come by once a week. Sometimes he kicked the neighbor women and made them fetch and carry for her, but they were also poor and very apathetic and utterly undependable.

"How is that son of yours?" said the shepherd, throwing up the blind in the single window in the dark little dungeon. The house was actually a shed stuck onto the end of a garage. It had been intended for tool storage.

"Do open the blind, sir. The dark doesn't bother me. If I'd known you were coming I'd have done it already."

Mrs. Ploke was short, dumpy and wheezy but she had pink skin and good teeth. Her gray hair was pulled back in a bun, tightly, to help keep her cheeks from sagging. She sat in a rotting chair and gripped an old shawl as if it were a live thing.

"Today is the day I always come by, so don't tell me

137

any lies," said Brog. He dropped a sack of food in her lap. "Has your son sent you any money?"

"The poor creature has none to send, not with his new wife and all his expenses. But he will, don't worry, and very soon. Won't you share the food with me?"

Brog belched, hitched his belt tighter across his skinny stomach. "Later, later, sweetheart."

There were chores to be done and he did them. He chopped wood and added it to the stack so the blind woman would have fuel for her stove when winter came. The slop pails were emptied into a ravine and rinsed in a creek. He straightened the furnishings in the shack, wrote an unfriendly letter to Mrs. Ploke's son, shared a lunch of bread and soup with her, heated water on the stove and bathed her with perfumed soap, and when she was dry and comfortable, he bedded her on the small cot beside the back door. She took him gratefully and eagerly, and was more appreciative of this thing that he did than for any of his other generosities. He, in turn, enjoyed the coupling, not that he desired her old plumpness, but compassion had a way of making a slave of its originator. Brog's pity for this particular member of his flock impelled him to do his utmost to ease her misery. He was a servant, was he not, and what greater need had an unloved old woman than to receive a few moments of love?

Jak sat on the curb in front of the house, his blind gaze directed at the empty street. "You don't seem surprised that so many are going to Sheen. You make no comments, you don't talk about what can be done to stop it."

"There's nothing I can do to stop it," said Rik. He whittled on a stick.

"You're simply standing back and calmly observing. The world could file by you toward a cliff and you wouldn't warn them."

"What's the good of warning someone who sees and knows his danger and keeps heading for it? They see Sheen. They know."

"That many people don't commit suicide."

"Do you think they believe he's offering them a two weeks' vacation?"

His back stiff, his face angry, Jak kept looking down the street. "They're confused. They can't possibly know."

"There are no blindfolds on their eyes," said Rik. "They've made their choice not to be confused any more, not to decide, not to live."

"It isn't that! Everyone wants to live."

"Go and tell them. Tell everybody you see. Tell them to want to live."

Jak's eyes were hot and his cheeks were pale. "The truth is that you just don't care. That's it, isn't it?"

Rik gave him a quick glance. "Does what I think make a bit of difference to a man or woman who goes to Sheen?"

"Why do you always have to think things out? Why can't you be motivated by feeling, just once in your life?"

"What makes you think I'm not?"

With a little snort, Jak said, "You're not driven by so common a thing as emotion."

"You mean I'm not my own victim?"

Jak had his mouth open for a ready retort. Now he closed it with a click. Quietly, desperately, he said, "Damn you, why can't you be human?"

Rik looked at the setting sun, radiant comet preparing to plunge into the mountains. "I won't tell a person what he already knows, won't remind him that his life is all he has. I won't encourage him to live, when that is his only alternative."

"What if he doesn't understand? What if he needs to be told?"

"I don't know the words."

"You tell him in plain language."

"How do you teach something so fundamental that nobody could have failed to learn it?"

"But they haven't learned it," said Jak. "They're giving it away without even thinking about it."

"How much is a thing worth if you give it away without thinking about it?"

The Leng gasped. "Worth isn't relative!"

"The hell it isn't."

Jak's expression was one of horror. "You think a human life is only worth what its owner thinks it is?"

"Yes."

"What about what I think it is?"

"Will what you think keep a man from going to Sheen? Will your measure of his value make him value himself accordingly? Will your pure respect for his soul make his soul worth a damn to him? Can you say 'no' for him? Can you get into his brain and tell Sheen to go fly a kite? And if you can, who is answering Sheen?"

"You're not human!" cried Jak. "You're some kind of monster who doesn't care if the human race disappears."

"I'm not the human race."

"You don't care about anyone but yourself."

Rik threw away his whittling stick. "I can't make someone else want to be responsible for his life."

"You don't want to save anyone."

"I can't."

Jak leaped to his feet, glared down at Rik. "You don't want to make the effort."

"How do you reason with a fog?"

"You think you've got this all figured out, don't you? I'm telling you you're wrong."

"Why?" said Rik.

"It's too complicated."

"The decision to live is too complicated?"

"There's more," Jak said with a snarl. "There's all the rest of it—all the frightening, terrible things, the loneliness, the doubt—"

"What have those things got to do with it? If I committed suicide by jumping off a cliff, the only significant thing to me would be that I was dead."

Jak sat down on the curb again and squeezed his temples. "Who's talking about jumping off a cliff? Oh, God, why can't people be reasonable? Why are they insane?"

"Are they?"

Jak shuddered. "They have to be. No one dies for nothing." Again he rubbed his temples. "If I could only see what one of them is thinking. If I could only follow their thought processes to the conclusion."

"The conclusion is plain."

The Leng's reply was angry. "Humanity isn't like you."

"Or you?"

"You think I don't feel it? You think I ignore Sheen that easily?"

"Who said anything about that?"

"The decision to ignore him is made up of so many things."

"I don't think so."

"That's what I mean," Jak said, his voice uneven. "To you it's either black or white. That isn't how the human race is."

"It doesn't matter what you call me, it doesn't matter what you think the race is or what its destiny is, because its destiny is what it chooses. If it all goes to Sheen except for a few who are out of step—"

"No!" yelled Jak. "That isn't destiny. Sheen isn't the end of the human race."

"Then what is?"

Jak leaped up. "I know what you're doing. You're putting words in my mouth. You're trying to get me to think the species is a mindless collection of insane impulses—"

"I'm not trying to get you to think anything."

"You think you're the man of tomorrow?"

Rik shook his head. "I'm living today."

"Then why don't you go to Sheen?"

"I don't want to."

"Everyone else is!" cried Jak.

"Let them."

"You don't care!"

"No, I don't."

"Nothing can insult you."

"Everything insults me."

"You'd stand by and watch them die!"

"I'd rather go fishing," said Rik.

"Why?"

"Because I hate to see someone throw his life away."

"You lie! If you didn't like it you'd try to stop it."

"Not if I knew I couldn't."

Blankly, the Leng regarded the dark head below him. "I'll find the reason. I'll discover what makes you tick."

Rik sighed wearily. "Go ahead."

"And don't pretend you mind my trying."

"I don't mind. While you're busy trying to find out what makes me tick, you're staying away from Sheen."

"That isn't the reason. It's more complex."

Rik gave a half grin. "Why do you insist on seeing a mystery in something simple?"

"Humanity isn't simple."

"He'd better be, if he expects to survive."

"He might have a chance if Sheen weren't so fascinating."

Rik frowned. "You talk too much about Sheen."

"Don't tell me you're worried!"

"Maybe I'm just human enough to do that."

His expression stony, Jak said, "You needn't. I'm not a weakling. I can resist him. He isn't as powerful as he seems."

Rik lowered his head.

"Really, he isn't," Jak said quickly. "All those people didn't have to give up. I won't. I mean I can't see any point in your wondering if I might."

"Don't talk about it so much."

"It doesn't mean anything. The only reason I do it—"

"I know why you do it," said Rik.

"I don't think so. If it's an indication of weakness, that's just your interpretation. My own is what's important. I'll never give in to him."

"Then don't talk about it," said Rik.

"I can't see why my talking bothers you. What's wrong with an open discussion of a problem? But that's beside the point. The world is the real problem. There has to be a solution."

"There is. People have to say no."

"Oh, God, that's asking the impossible. What do you think he offers them?"

"Abdication from thinking," said Rik.

"Is that all?"

"Happiness without effort."

"Is that so bad? Maybe Sheen's purpose is simply to make people happy."

"Yes."

"Has it ever occurred to you that you're wrong about everything?"

"No," said Rik.

Jak snorted. "You think you're infallible?"

"Where Sheen is concerned, yes."

"You're narrow-minded. You already have your mind made up."

"Tell me something better."

The Leng pounced. "You can leave your mind open to suggestion."

"Whose?"

"Anyone with a good one to make."

"Okay, when I hear a good one I'll open my mind," said Rik.

Jak stalked away. Suddenly, he wheeled and came back. "Sheen has no conscience."

"Did he tell you that?"

"Well, no."

"Who gave you the idea?"

"For God's sake, you sound as if you think I can't create an original idea."

"That one isn't original, and even if it's true it makes no difference."

Jak looked uneasy. "A conscience makes no difference?"

"If my enemy's conscience won't keep him from my throat, it doesn't."

"What if maybe you can give him one?"

Rik scowled. "What do you mean?"

"I'm just woolgathering."

"Do it out loud."

"Okay. I think Sheen becomes that which he possesses. He behaves according to the dictates of his victims."

Rik looked startled. "I can't remember ever hearing a statement so full of contradictions."

Jak flushed. "Why?"

"In the first place, a victim of Sheen's doesn't dictate a damned thing."

"That isn't true. Sheen fulfills his every desire."

"Is that what 'dictates' means to you?"

Looking down at his shoes, Jak muttered, "Anyhow, the rest of what I said is correct."

"If his victims don't dictate to him—and they don't—I can't see how they can give him an order, and if they do, I see no reason why he should obey."

"You've got me all mixed up!"

"That happened without my help."

Through his teeth, Jak said, "The trouble with me is that I think too much, while you don't think at all."

"Drop it," said Rik.

"You're so goddamn sure. I'm sick of you. Why should I listen to you?"

"Because I'm an enigma, remember?"

"You're so obvious it's disgusting."

"I told you I was obvious."

"You told me this, you told me that! Why are you always telling me things?"

"Because you're always asking."

"Sheen has to be stopped!"

"You can't stop him."

"Surely someone can."

"Sheen can." As Jak grew alert, Rik added, "Don't count on it. He has no intention of doing things differently."

"You can't know for certain, not in the absolute."

"I'll put it another way. I'm as certain that Sheen won't change his ways as I am that I won't change mine."

He was hauling in a fat trout when Jak came up behind him.

"Damn you," said the Leng, and Rik looked around in surprise. "When I couldn't find you, I swore to myself that it was because you were somewhere doing something about it."

"About what?"

"You have the gall to ask! You can stand there fishing as if it were all you had on your mind. You can look at me as if I've lost my mind." The Leng drew a furious breath. "Just what the hell is it? Tell me the secret. Maybe that's the answer to everything. Maybe if you can make me understand, I can go tell everyone else."

"Tell you what?"

Jak roared his reply. "How can you go fishing when the world is falling down around our ears?"

"Oh, boy."

"Damn you to hell."

"Aw."

"You're so logical you make me sick," said Jak in quiet

rage. "It isn't human to see the extinction of your neighbors and not suffer. It isn't human to watch the world go down the drain and not experience agony."

"How do you know what I feel?"

"Does that mean you're suffering, that all this is killing you as much or more than it's killing me? You just won't let go, will you? Is that it? You're dying inside, but you won't show it? You have to go fishing to prove to yourself that you haven't cracked?"

Rik took the trout off the hook and dumped it in a basket. "You want me to howl and wear sack cloth? What good will it do if I look the part?" Suddenly he swung his leg and kicked the basket of fish into the water. "Why do I have to react out loud?" he yelled. "What's so human about a screech?"

"You can try to do something to stop all this!" Jak shouted in his face.

"Nobody can stop it!"

"Shit," said Jak, and stomped away. Over his shoulder, he cried, "Men didn't get where they are by saying things were inevitable."

Rik glared at the retreating figure until it was beyond the dunes. He threw himself on the sand and stared out at the water. For a long while he lay and thought, and finally he climbed to his feet and went away to find Sheen. Eventually, he came upon a silver jare lying on a rock, sunning itself.

"Peace!" cried Sheen.

"Go to hell."

"Been there. Bored stiff."

"You still owe me from our deal, but never mind that now. I want you to come with me."

"Lead the way."

"Not all of you." Rik took his knife and whacked off a piece of the jare's tail. To his astonishment, the animal shrieked, and blood flowed from the wound.

"Shame on you, you've hurt the poor beast," said Sheen.

"My God."

"If you wanted a piece of me, why didn't you say so?"

"Will the cut heal?"

"The pain is already gone. Think nothing of it. If there's one thing Sheen does, he takes care of his own."

"He also talks too much, and that's why I only want a little bit of you." Rik cut off a portion of the piece of tail and dropped the rest. Sheen glided over it, made it part of himself.

"Feel free to take me. Anytime, anytime. Love you, really."

Satisfied that he had sufficient but non-talkative amount of specimen, Rik spent the next hour getting back to his underground cache. Once there and safely locked in, he set up his laboratory equipment for some extensive and intensive experimenting.

He should have quit after the first test. A thing that couldn't be weighed or measured wasn't even present. He took the chunk of silver material and laid it on a small scale, but the chunk promptly slid off. He laid the piece on a cupped scale where it couldn't slide or fall out. Carefully watching the indicator, it took him a full minute to realize it was registering nothing at all. The chunk of Sheen wasn't coming in contact with the cup, which was impossible.

Temporarily assuming that Sheen was a liquid, he heated him in a test tube. Nothing happened. Knowing it was useless, he tried to test the silver mass for surface tension. The objects he used wouldn't touch it.

Aware that substances were either acids, bases or neutrals, he tested Sheen as a base by dropping a chemical on him while he lay in a spoon. The drops of fluid didn't change color, didn't touch Sheen, didn't prove anything. Doubting that the creature was an acid, he nevertheless tried to prove it with another test. It was a failure.

He put the chunk in a can of water, heated it to the boiling point, screwed on the lid and placed the can in cold water. The can collapsed, but the chunk of silver remained untouched, unchanged, unharmed.

Sheen was cooked over an open flame. He was tested for carbon content, protein and iron, but the tests were inconclusive, since nothing came in contact with him. The specimen was roasted in lime with no effect. Attempts to purify him with nitric acid did nothing at all. He didn't moisten glass, and probably the most startling thing of all was that he suddenly made a suspended handkerchief sag when he was placed in the middle of it, as if he had tired of playing with gravity and decided to let some of his weight settle down.

Rik mixed a batch of quick-drying concrete and formed it around the chunk. Sheen kept oozing out of the wet cracks, pushing air bubbles before him. Working faster, Rik slapped more wet concrete on the mass until he had a mound too large to hold. He laid it on the floor and watched it harden. He learned that Sheen could get out of dry concrete as quickly as he could escape from the wet kind.

When his back felt like breaking, he looked at his watch. For seven hours he had been bombarding Sheen with everything he could think of.

He set up his microscope and, placing a tiny bit of the silver on a slide, he bent over to look. A tiny silver man lay in plain view, with one leg propped on a knee, casually picking his teeth with a pawnail.

"Hi," said Sheen, waving up at him.

"Oh, Christ!"

"Amen, brother. What else have you got in mind? I mean, I don't care that you're trying to kill me. You had to try sooner or later."

Rik fell back into a chair. Glaring at the microscope, he said, accusingly, "You let me waste my time."

The microscopic bit of silver and the larger chunk said, in unison, "You had to learn it your own way."

Rik leaned forward. "How much do you weigh?"

"You mean this little bit? Hmmm. Its atomic weight is four-five-nine-point-seven-two."

"That's impossible."

"Maybe so, but that's what it is."

"What are you made of?"

"One part of every element there is."

"That's also impossible."

"Tough," said Sheen.

"What holds it all together?"

"Guts, boy."

"You have no brain."

"Tut, tut, preach me no Kant."

"You talk without a throat."

"That's only one miraculous thing about me. I talk all over the place."

"How?"

"In every part of me is a head and a body. Put that in your pipe and smoke it."

"How can I kill you?"

"For shame, I thought we were friends."

"Answer me."

"Very well," Sheen said gently, "though you worked at it for a thousand years, you couldn't give me a hangnail. That includes you, and your doggie friend and every other human in the universe. But why ask the question when you already know the answer? You were right, my pal. Go fishing. Listen to the night wind and your thoughts. Count the stars. Don't grieve over what you can't change."

chapter xî

One of Redo's sons was missing, hadn't been seen for four days. The man named Kream was dispatched to find him. The quest took Kream to the charnel shed, or the slaughterhouse for the zoo.

The person in charge of the charnel shed was a mere step above the animals in the cages. His name was Meece. His job was to provide the feeders with feed. Meat was a product which was sometimes hard to come by. Meece accepted anything, even rotten carcasses.

Kream arrived at the charnel shed in time to find Meece stuffing a boy's rump and a girl's torso into his big grinder. The shed was 20-by-20 and black as the pit, in all four corners. Wax candles and incense burned on wooden barrels. The place smelled like a whorehouse with overflowing toilets.

Meece explained to Kream. He had been having a deal of trouble with the animal-protective society. They objected to his rounding up tares and zombas and killing them. Meece was almost seven feet tall, extremely hairy and not at all intelligent. Naked to the waist and sweating buckets, he prayed and frowned and cut up carcasses, day or night. He prayed that there was no Hell. Besides the trouble with the animal protectors, he had other reasons for slaughtering indigents, orphans and an occasional personal enemy. There were the orders from above.

The animals in maximum-security preferred the taste of human meat and somebody *up there* liked those animals. Give them what they wanted, were the orders. Meece got his instructions from a man named Kast. Neither the feeders nor the supervisor nor anyone else connected with the zoo had a thing to do with certain crates of ground meat that came out of the shed; only Meece and the man, Kast.

The boy and the girl who had just been destroyed were found necking in the back seat of a car half a mile from the zoo. Meece had passed by on his way to work. The car was an old piece of junk, the kids didn't look important, it was dark and Meece needed them, so he twisted their necks and carried them to the shed.

Before reporting to Redo, Kream contacted some people and commissioned them to find out who paid Kast. The answer he received was the Fillys. Why? He didn't get an answer to that question. The animals in maximum-security—the atavisms—came from every part of the continent, or so it was said. Kream thought it was too bad that there had been so little research conducted regarding them. For instance, it would be interesting to know what kind of parents gave birth to atavisms.

Redo sobbed and pulled out big tufts of his hair. He had learned that his son filled the bowels of the atavisms in the zoo.

"Elu, my God, what kind of people are those Fillys? They have no hearts. Isn't the human body sacred to them?"

"You've been crying for four hours. Enough." Elu had no real wish for Redo to stop crying. What he wanted to do was flee from his own house. He was aghast at the thought of the dead boy; he was also afraid because Redo had a favor coming to him.

"Yes, enough of everything," Redo said, and right away Elu began to tremble. The trembling never stopped, not for as long as Elu lived.

"What do you mean?"

"The Fillys," said Redo.

"Where is your mind?"

"You refuse me?" Redo was quiet now, he was calm, but in that moment Elu knew his friend was a fiend.

"Refuse you, never. We are like brothers."

"You grow pale for nothing. Do you think me a fool?"

Yes, yes! Elu cried in his head, but with his mouth he

said, "You are a pillar of efficiency. Speak, only speak. I listen."

"You will do me a favor?"

"I will do you a favor."

"You will investigate. You will learn which people have been commissioned to do a certain thing in all the Filly estates in the world. There will be many men and they will visit the five estates simultaneously. They are to do it soon. Find out who they are."

White and shivering, Elu said, "I will do it."

"Probably they will be obscure hoodlums, little bands of gangsters we've never heard of."

"When I do this thing, that is, after I make the investigation, is the favor done?"

His eyes distant, Redo said, "Are favors ever done?"

"You are right," Elu said, humbly.

"Listen carefully and don't be confused. Filly Six has hired people to do a job in all the estates. Filly One learned about it and wishes the job to fail. He wants me and my people to interfere and veto those people, even as they are in the act of carrying out their orders. Do you understand?"

Elu sensed the seething emotion in the steel-trap body of the man seated near him. "The will of Filly Six is to stand," he said in a low voice. "You want me to use my people to stop your people. You want me to kill your group."

"As they are in the act of carrying out their orders. You don't have to use your closest friends."

Sweating profusely, Elu forced himself to sit still. "You aren't going to use your friends?"

"I have no wish for them to die. The group I choose will be made up of strangers. You will kill them all."

"Yes," said Elu.

"With stealth, my friend, and with guile. It must look like a world-wide robbery attempt. The group hired by Filly Six is not to be touched. Your group and mine will clash."

"Why do you want Filly Six to be successful?"

"I'll tell you later."

"I am to kill your hired guns?"

"With a great deal of silence and with noisy publicity afterward."

a billion days of earth   151

White and shrunken, Elu said, "To prevent Filly One from being certain you're behind it."

"You have taken the oath."

"We sit here planning to assassinate our own hired men. What is the group of Filly Six going to do? Take away all my ignorance."

"No more questions. Sometimes we die that we may live again. Swear it."

"I swear," said Elu.

A moony night—bands of men moved like quiet snakes. All their lives they had practiced cunning. They were experts in the trade, could split a hairy throat as easily as a hairless one.

Five hundred children died all over the world that moony night. The cultured variety, they slept in beds of pearls, and that was their crime.

No one ever screamed at Redo.

"You butcher!" screamed Elu.

"Keep your voice down."

"Damn you!"

"I expect He will."

"You rotten liar!"

"Tell me one lie I told you."

"The ones you didn't tell!"

"I beg your forgiveness."

"May you rot in hell!"

"I expect to."

Elu fell into his chair. His face was old. Ghosts rode in his eyes. "We grew up together," he said faintly.

"Yes."

"You were a good boy, so kind and considerate. Once, when I was too cowardly to confess stealing, you took the blame. You were beaten for me."

"I remember," said Redo.

Tears trailed down Elu's cheeks. "You had no consideration for my soul. You have condemned me to eternal brimstone."

"You are innocent."

"I am guilty. The blood is on my hands."

"The crime was an indirect one."

"How well you lie! That you've always done well. Redo, Redo, don't you understand? We murdered hundreds of children!"

"Our hands were never raised against them."

"You lousy bastard. Do you think I'd have done what you said if I'd known Filly Six sent his group to assassinate all Filly young?"

"If you don't get yourself in control, the assassins will be after us."

"They will anyway! Do you think Filly One is a fool?"

"He reads the papers. He will never be sure."

Elu screamed, "He doesn't have to be sure!"

"We've stabbed him in the heart. He is inactive."

"Oh, God, Redo, he's always been inactive. What have any of them ever done but sit back and rape the world? It isn't him but his power. He has the armies of the world at his disposal. He'll wipe us out."

"He won't," Redo said.

"You're full of stupidity."

Bebe wasn't conscious of the wind, the sun or the tares in nearby burrows. What he was conscious of was the emptiness in himself.

"Hello," said a voice, and the zizzy looked up to see a silver man walking toward him. The silver one looked like the man whom Bebe hated above all other men. The features were the same and the body had the same shape and build. He wore a pair of jeans and an old shirt. The difference was in the coloring. There were other differences, too, or Bebe wouldn't have remained sitting on the park bench. Silver was harder than flesh but this shiny man was soft compared to the one named Rik. His gaze was hesitant, his step unsure, his shoulders couldn't decide whether to be straight or drooping and the arms swung aimlessly.

Bebe immediately liked this man. "I suppose you're going to try and convince me you're a human being," he said, his tone morose.

"Thank heaven you aren't screaming or asking me silly questions." Sheen lowered himself to the ground, crossed his legs and relaxed beside the park bench. He seemed to know how rarely Bebe got a chance to look down on anyone.

"I don't feel like pretending," muttered the zizzy. "You don't startle me. You're a mutant but I know a man who makes you look like a cretin."

"Indeed?" Sheen stretched in the sun, enjoyed it.

"You don't like him either, do you?" Bebe was staring at the face and wondering how similarity and difference could coexist in the same space.

"Who?"

"Never mind. How can you speak to me? You aren't a zizzy."

"Linguistics is probably my only talent."

"You're being humble," said Bebe.

"Of course."

Bebe was silent for a minute and then he said, wistfully, "What is humility?"

"The feeling you get when you realize two things—that you're a total failure and that by the mere fact of your existence you're entitled to the best of everything."

"I'm so sick of it all!"

Sheen had been looking at the sky; now his gaze lowered. "Then why don't you get away?"

"How?"

"Like this." Sheen created a picture of zizzy-perfection in Bebe's mind.

"You're a telepath!"

"Just sensitive."

"But it's all there! It's so beautiful! Why can't it really be like that?"

"It can be. Don't you know about love? It makes the world go around."

"What has love got to do with the picture in my head?"

"I'm the strangest mutant you'll ever meet. I exist to love others."

"Even me?" said Bebe, forgetting to be dishonest.

"Especially you. What's the use of lovable?"

"That's true. I've always believed that kind of ..."

"Crap?" Sheen said, gently.

Bebe laughed somewhat hysterically. "We understand, don't we? That's all it is, every damned bit of it, but we have to go along because we know that without it the world would fall on its face. I feel persecuted when I think about it, especially today. I'm thinking about the most revolting human in the world. He looks like you."

Sheen smiled and said nothing.

Bebe relaxed on the bench. He let his stomach bulge. He had gained a lot of weight. The sight disgusted him, and he remembered how his body had looked not so very long ago. An overwhelming sadness captured him. "Did you ever ..." he began, and then his voice trailed off. He took a deep breath. "When you were little, did you ever look around you and get the most agonizing feeling of happiness?" His slanted eyes groped across the silver face.

Sheen waved a human paw. "It doesn't last. That feeling is the result of good circulation. It's like a shot of adrenalin, no good beyond the moment."

"You must be right," said Bebe. "It didn't last. I thought it meant something, a signal that my life was waiting for me and that it would be full of greatness and that I was going to be equal to it. But one day the feeling wasn't there anymore."

"And you never wondered why, which was only sensible. Who cares about a will-o'-the-wisp?"

"I don't know. It was nice, like, oh, like—"

"What about the picture I've showed you? Want to live like that?"

"As a spectator? I don't—"

"What is a person but a spectator? Everything worth making has already been made. Everything worth doing has been done a thousand times over. I ask you, person to person, if a person doesn't do, what does he do?"

Bebe had no answer.

"Any intelligent organism was born to be an observer," said Sheen. "At birth he's an expert, otherwise he would never learn a thing. He needs to feel warm, feel loved, feel his conformity, feel good. After a while, he does everything by rote. He doesn't feel as good as he would like, and he realizes that what he really wants is to get out of the scramble and watch other people knock heads. But he can't. The consequence is that he goes around with a bellyache. He's had it for centuries. He would go on having it, if it weren't for my intervention."

Bebe was sitting on the ground, now. What he saw with his real eyes was so unpleasant that he switched over to the eyes in his soul. Everything became subtly rosy then, and he breathed a sigh of relief.

"But what do you do for people?" he said.

"I give them a nonexistent bellyache."

"What?"

"I give them an overcure for their illnesses. But, my dear zizzy, it would take an IQ twice yours to see the beauty in that concept."

"Just a minute—"

"It would take an IQ of approximately two hundred to see through me, which is what yours would be, after I made you over, but then there are things more important than IQ, as you well know."

"I . . . I . . ." stammered Bebe.

"An illusion," said Sheen. "Don't try and fight it, don't try and figure it out, just take my word for it, what seems to exist is only illusion. Real reality—the solid stuff—lies in what you see with the soul the Lord gave you. You think you see with those two eyes in your face? Whoever told you that deserves to be crucified."

"I don't know what to think." Sometimes Bebe's rose-colored glasses didn't set straight on him. At times they were askew, so that what he saw was half-Technicolor, half-gray. He didn't like combinations of things. Hints, intimations, innuendos, suggestions and unbridled hypotheses offended him. In his tethered opinion, such things should be outlawed, and this creature said they already were. Bebe faltered, swayed, was inclined to surrender.

"You will enhance that which is already beautiful, if you come to me," said Sheen. "Haven't I showed you exactly the kind of world you desire?"

"Do it to me again," said Bebe, and then, for no accountable reason, he blushed.

Sheen loaned him the picture once more. In the world envisioned there, the only important thing was IQ, and Bebe had one that no man or zizzy could better. Everybody recognized Bebe's superiority and provided him with throne, scep-

156

ter and a license to do as he pleased. What he liked to do most was to make decisions for others. He sat on his throne and people came to him with their problems and he consulted his IQ and told them what to do. They always took his advice and their lives always improved. He had a palace to live in, a staff of stupid servants and a harem of virgins.

"Will the world really be like this?" he said.

"For you it will."

"But how can I actually do those things if I'm doing them only in my mind?"

"All kidding aside, the thinking mind does have a place in reality. As a matter of fact, if it isn't involved, its owner is either asleep or dead. The greatest joy, the highest pleasure, has to have its roots in a thinking mind."

"What are you saying?" blurted the zizzy.

"Lie down, lie down and pillow your head in my lap. I want to tell you secrets."

Bebe frowned, kept frowning as the low voice of Sheen penetrated the fog of hatred in his brain. He listened for a long time as the voice opened his soul like a too-ripe fruit. At last he abandoned his relaxed position, hopped onto the park bench.

"I don't want to hear anymore," he said. "I hate everything you've told me. You knew I would. That's why you said it. I've never loved goodness. What I love is you, Sheen. We're alike. We belong together."

Sheen stood. "Of course we do."

"Evil," said Bebe. "Power. You can't have one without the other and power is what I want. Goodness and reason will never plague me again."

Sheen looked at him sadly. "How can you believe that?"

"Because of my ace in the hole. You're a perfect example of a reasonable mind deliberately defying reason. You're omniscient, yet you made the illogical choice and got away with it. That's why I know I'm safe."

Sheen bent down.

"Hold on," Bebe said roughly. "I'm a hog. Don't think I'll pass up an opportunity like this one."

"What do you mean?"

Bebe grinned. "I want to have my cake and eat it, too. I want to get even with the world. I'm going to be your pimp."

"Ahhh!"

"I'll bring you legions."

"And when they're all gone?"

"Then it'll be just you and me. We'll have it all. I'll reign with you."

"You will be their Judas?"

"Eh?"

"Never mind," said Sheen. "Go ahead. Get them and bring them to me."

"They'll be good ones," said Bebe, and flew away.

Sheen watched his flight. "I forgot to mention the most important thing," he murmured. "If there's one thing a mind can't avoid, it is its automatic aversion to evil. The moment he lets it into himself, he places his feet on the road to demolition."

The God climbed off the cloud at the same time that Rik stepped from behind the tree.

"You're quiet," said Vennavora.

"The better to sneak up on you." Rik had met only a handful of beautiful women in his life, and he had desired every one of them. Now he stood and enjoyed the glow of warmth and life emanating from the great brown person beside him. He felt the trembling in his own body and knew it wasn't inspired by fear. The mind determined how a man responded to his world. He wanted Vennavora, and he accepted the fact as calmly as he accepted his own existence.

"Shall I get down on my knees?" he said.

"Only if you've come begging." The forehead of Vennavora creased as he knelt. As quickly, her frown blanked to smoothness. There was no curiosity in her expression as she looked down at him and said, "The answer is no."

For a crazy instant, Rik had the feeling she was giving him an answer to two questions. "A rare response these days, wouldn't you say?" His eyes searched hers for some sign of relenting.

"I never say the obvious."

"You just did."

"You don't amuse me."

"I think that if I didn't, you wouldn't let me speak at all. You wouldn't stand here listening."

"I can't destroy Sheen. You've wasted your time coming here, and you're wasting my time now."

Rik glanced away. "If there's one thing I can't stand, it's having someone accuse me of not caring. Now I'm doing it. You don't care."

"If that accusation arouses no response of guilt in you, why should it in me?"

"I didn't think it would."

Vennavora stretched her splendid legs and glanced at the sky. She looked down at Rik who still knelt before her and again there was a slight creasing of her forehead. "Don't come again, don't seek me, don't stalk me."

"I will."

"You'll gain nothing."

"I have to try."

"Why?"

"A man can't sit back and hope destruction will pass him by."

Vennavora's gaze became intent. "Your nature is to struggle in the face of defeat."

"And yours isn't?"

"Illogic can be carried too far."

Rik sat back on his heels. His strength seemed to ebb from him like water. "Maybe it isn't illogic. It could be fear."

"Whose?"

"Yours?"

Vennavora laughed, and the sound was so clear and so free of compromise that Rik winced. He had never heard the sound of pure laughter before, and he wanted to imprison it so he could continue to hear it.

"Insults amuse you," he said. "The gnat's buzzing may become annoying, though, and in another moment you might slap it."

This time she spoke with emotion, and he knew it was anger. "Then why aren't you afraid?"

He turned his head and looked into the distance at his world, at the place where he lived or died, the only place there was for him. "I'm on my knees," he said in a low voice. "I'm begging. Help us."

"Begging? I have no such impression."

"I have."

"How do you like it?" Why didn't her eyes light with malice? Wasn't it a malicious question, intended to hurt?

"In the old days men threw crumbs to the beasts. Most of them didn't, but there were a few who recognized that life was an absolute no matter what its form."

"Get off your knees, rat," commanded the God.

"No."

"Then remain in that position."

Rik leaped to his feet.

Now the crease in Vennavora's forehead was deep. "I'll tell you once. We have no hatred for you or your kind. We hate only the stupidity in some minds. If we could help you, we would. You are doomed. There is nothing we can do."

She made as if to leave.

"Wait. I brought something for you." Rik walked to a nearby tree and picked up the toy from behind it. He came back and extended it to her.

"I hope you don't consider this a bribe," she said as she took it.

"I consider that keeping it will do me no good. I believe the only thing a God fears is the contempt of his own kind. Tontondely's friends would make fun of him if they knew I had the toy. Give it to him and tell him I hope he rots."

"You don't understand all of it."

"I don't want to." He watched her ride aloft on a cloud, and the taste of failure was bitter in his mouth, but there was a stronger feeling in him and he decided it was admiration. If a mind could find nothing to admire, if it searched in vain for external glory, if it had to acknowledge that the best in the world resided within its own person, how did that mind survive? Wouldn't it brood until its strength was snuffed out? Wouldn't longing become indifference? At least he and his kind had the Gods. The monarchs didn't travel in circles. Did they? Their course was straight and their integrity unassailable. They wore their happiness as casually as they wore their skin, which meant that the holy grail was real and within reach of everyone. A man built his vault of integrity by finding and matching that which he admired. What had the Gods admired in their youth? Three million years ago they had been alone in their reign.

The Gods could save the world. Rik had to believe it. If

the greatest achievers were impotent, then A was anything but A.

Sign on Rik's front lawn:

SHEEN IS TRANSCENDENCE. HE IS TV, HEROIN, CRUSADES AND ORGASM. HE IS THE HIGH. THE PIECE OF YOUR BRAIN THAT PROVIDES EUPHORIA IS HIS TARGET. HOW BIG IS YOUR "EUPHORT?" BIGGER THAN YOU ARE? INSIDE IS THE I-HATE-SHEEN CLUB. COME IN AND JOIN.

He hated clubs. No, that wasn't the right word. He had been too bored by the idea to ever join one. Now he was the president of one, the beginner, the spirit behind. If everyone had as much enthusiasm as he, the club would be a colossal bomb. It didn't matter. He was the only member.

He didn't know whether to swear or sweat as he walked into his living room and confronted the two men sitting there. Clearing his throat, he said, "First come, first served," and one of the men stood.

He was big and muscular and gray-haired. It had been a month or so since he had last shaved. His clothes were dirty. He mumbled his name and it forever remained a secret. He said he came from a suburb of Osfar.

"I hate Sheen," he said. "I want to join the club."

Rik sat down in a chair and frowned at the rug. "You can't join unless I say so. I'm the president."

The man nodded. "I realize that."

"You can't just join a club because you want to."

The man gave a weak smile. "No, I suppose not."

"There are rules. Without them, nobody gets anywhere."

"I've never been arrested. You can check."

Rik looked at the ceiling. "I don't know what kind of club this is going to be."

"You put that sign out there, didn't you?"

"Did you read it?"

"Yes."

"What does it say?"

"It says this is an I-Hate-Sheen club. I want to be in. Why don't you write my name on a list or something?"

Lowering his gaze from the ceiling, Rik said, "Because you can't join."

The exhausted eyes came alive for a moment. "I don't understand."

"You're too eager."

"What does that mean?"

"I don't know." Rik met the man's stare. "You're not right for it. Your reasons aren't right."

The man's eyes jammed shut. "You don't know my reasons."

"You lost someone to him. The person meant a lot to you and what you have in mind now is revenge. Please pick up your hat and walk out of here without breaking the furniture or taking a swing at me. I haven't anything to offer you."

The man left without a word. He stumbled as he went out the door, caught his balance, walked slowly, almost blindly.

Rik didn't look at the other man in the room. "I don't know what I want, but I know what I don't want."

"Maybe that last part describes me, and maybe I ought to just take off without wasting my time."

"What's your name?"

"Race."

"Hmmm."

"I don't hate Sheen," said the man named Race. "I don't know what to think of him. I haven't lost anyone dear to me, but I've seen some acquaintances stroll into his loving arms. They seemed to enjoy it. There's something wrong with a society that ignores a creature they don't understand, and I don't think people understand him. I've watched him but I haven't learned much about him and that makes me worry."

"Hmmm."

"People are getting to be like robots. They take more pleasure out of being spectators to life than in participating. Maybe that's why Sheen appeals to them. He can make them pure spectators. But if he takes their souls, what will there be to look at and who will be doing the looking?"

"Ah," said Rik.

His gaunt face earnest, Race leaned forward in his chair. "Men are faced with something they either have to take or leave completely alone. With Sheen we can't stand in the middle of the road. He won't let us, or we won't let ourselves. I don't know what kind of pictures he puts in peoples' minds, but they must be powerful or no one would be interested."

"Are you sure?"

"Don't be cynical. Everybody wants something. Does Sheen turn the imagination inward and make a person see only what he wants to see? There would be no fun in winning a contest like that. He's vain, he wants a battle, and it's real to him. He doesn't lie about what he offers. Too many intelligent people have gone over to his side. You can't fool that many brains with fancy pictures."

"Hmmm," said Rik.

"Another thing—he doesn't take anyone who hasn't got all his faculties." As Rik started in surprise, Race nodded. "I saw a mental incompetent named Irn go to him. He turned her away. She begged but he wouldn't take her. I was there. I saw. I don't know what it means."

"What if there was an animal that ate up all the people with brains? What would happen to the rest?"

"They'd die. They need the normal ones to take care of them. Do you think he's planning on that?"

"I don't know."

"You think he's taking the good ones so the rest will starve?"

"What about children?" said Rik.

"Another interesting point. They aren't interested in him, nor he in them, at least not the very young ones, but he goes after kids sixteen or seventeen years old."

"You know a lot about him."

"I'm retired from my job, so I have the time to watch him. I've sort of made him my hobby."

"Has he ever approached you?"

"Not yet."

"What made you come in here?"

"You named him on your sign," said Race. "What you said hadn't occurred to me."

"I see."

"What made you decide to start this club?"

"Would you understand if I said because of a nightmare?"

"Sure," said Race. "And you can't get up on a soapbox and start preaching. Brog and the rest of the preachers have made that type of communication useless. Too much wax in people's ears. You've done the only thing left, stuck it on a sign and placed it in plain sight. There's a name for it now. There isn't any excuse for people who say they're giving away their souls because everyone is doing it."

Rik scratched his head. "I'm not a crusader."

"Who listens to crusaders?"

"Would you care if nobody listened to us?"

Race didn't reply for a moment. Finally, he said, "I'd be stoned in the public square if I said this to just anyone: I don't care if Sheen eats every human in the world as long as he doesn't eat me and my friends and family."

"What about the species?"

"The species ends for me when I die. If I had the choice, I'd say let the race continue, but it would be a living choice. Once I'm dead, I'm indifferent to everything."

"If you feel that way, why do you want to fight?"

"Sheen is getting too close. I can feel the flames licking my tail feathers."

"You're the man I want," said Rik.

"Fine. What do you want me to do?"

"Find some more members."

"What kind?"

"I don't know. Do you?"

"No."

"Get the good ones," said Rik. "I don't know how you're going to tell the difference, but you can give it a try."

"After we get a group together, then what?"

"I don't know. Do you?"

"No," said Race.

chapter xii

"But I'm offering you the job of Personnel Director," said Miss Lune. "The only person in the whole plant who makes more money than the Personnel Director is myself."

"I understand that, but I don't want the job," said Rik.

Miss Lune sat back in her chair. Perspiration shone on her forehead. "What can I offer you? How can I get you to take the job?"

"You can't."

"You have everything I want. I can't believe you've been sitting behind a stupid machine all these years."

"I'm sorry."

"I can give you money, position, power."

"No. I'll explain, if you wish."

"All I wish is to save this plant from going under. Aside from Mister Spar and myself, you're the only brain in the place. You show no indication of giving yourself to that blasted silver alien."

Rik shrugged. "You can't really believe I can save your plant."

"I believe brainpower is the only thing worthwhile. I want you with me in the fight."

"Against the inevitable? It takes more than two people to run a corporation."

Miss Lune's paws twisted in her lap. "Go on, get out of here." As he stood up, she said, "Just for the record, why won't you take the job?"

"Because I qualified for it fifteen years ago."

Her eyebrows arched in a laconic salute. "The world is falling on its face and you won't hold it up because a lot of stupid people ignored you."

"I'd hold it up if I could, but I can't. Taking that job wouldn't do anything for me and it would only buy you another month or week."

"What?"

"You aren't worried about the world or me or Mister Spar. You're thinking of what you'll have left when the plant is gone." Rik leaned across the desk. "What will you have left?"

Miss Lune heard him go out of the room, heard him walking down the hall, but she wasn't seeing anything but herself—stripped of everything that meant anything to her.

"Aren't you tired of it all?" said the man. His eyes were dull, his shoulders slumped, his paws fluttered aimlessly across his bearded face.

"Tired of what?" yelled Rik. He needed to be heard, had to be heard.

The stranger made an exhausted gesture toward the landscape. "The crap in life; the indefiniteness. You know. No five people can agree on anything. You're never sure, when you get up, whether the day will be worth it and nine times out of ten it isn't. You see something pretty and you turn it over for a closer look and there are worms clinging to it. There isn't anything in the world you dare examine too closely."

"I don't know what you're talking about!" Rik said, as loud as he could.

The man shrugged. "Then why are you bothering me? Why hold me back when you don't understand? There's something wrong with a man who has lived as long as you and who still doesn't understand."

Rik closed his claw on the man's arm. "If you can't take it, why not kill yourself?"

"It's part of what you don't see. I don't want to kill myself."

"But you don't want to live."

"Not like this; not with the uncertainty."

"Sheen gives death."

166

"Oh, no," said the other, simply. "I know what he gives. Everybody knows, probably everybody but you."

Rik drew his claw back in rage and suddenly let it fall. "You're all sick."

"You're the sick one." The man took a long look at the sunset. "That's something I always liked. At least that was real." He turned to the glittering pool at his feet. "I'm ready."

"Take my heart that we shall be one," said Sheen.

"One what?" yelled Rik. Whirling, he walked away. He arrived at the street where he lived, sat down on the curb.

"It's getting worse," said a voice.

He looked up at the face of Race. "Did you find any members?"

"Not a one." Race sat down on the curb. "Sheen is out to get them all."

"*Us* all."

"He's barking up the wrong tree here. Listen, I went by the school this morning. Half the teachers didn't show up and the kids were all outside, tearing up the grounds. There's nobody at the library. Police are everywhere but they're standing around doing nothing. Downtown it's so quiet it's like a cemetery. People are inside with their doors locked and their blinds down. I got no milk delivery this morning. The only thing that sounds normal is the radio, and that's the most abnormal of all. The news reports are about the weather and the new sewage plant they're building in the suburbs."

"Yes, I know."

Race grunted and stood up. "It's better to do it alone."

"Agreed. Our fancy club was a dumb idea."

"There's danger in numbers. That son of a bitch knows us. I know what the battle is. Those other poor jerks don't know what's going on." Race looked down at Rik with a wry smile. "So long, tough guy."

"So long."

Miss Lune was raking leaves in her small yard. "My employer went to Sheen this morning," she said.

Rik paused on the walk. "I'm sorry to hear that."

"I didn't like it either." She regarded him silently for a moment. "You were right," she said. "After the plant was gone I had nothing left but myself. It turned out to be enough."

"I see."

She leaned on the rake. "It took all this chaos to make me realize I never had anything else. I think it's a crime to sit back and watch your individuality go down the drain, but it's much worse when you approve of it. I'm talking about people in general. You don't get self-respect because someone respects you. Women couldn't see that."

"They'll see it now," said Rik.

"Only if they have guts. I don't know if they can do it."

"Do you care?"

"I'd be a liar if I said I didn't, but I'll tell you something more important than my caring what happens to them—their caring. If they don't care, it doesn't matter what I think. I'll stand by and watch every one of them go to hell, and I'll have a sneer on my face, because they'll be deliberately throwing themselves away. They could escape so easily. All they have to do is say no."

"Right."

"I've got my feet dug in. This is my world. If anyone asks me who gave it to me, I'll tell them nobody had to—it was simply there and I took it."

"Does Sheen frighten you?"

Miss Lune grinned. "Hell, yes! He taught me I'm my own worst enemy and if I want something to hang onto I'd better build it. And I've learned more. It's a mistake to try and avoid him, so I don't. He's in my house right now, with his feet propped up on my best cushion, watching television. We're going to have a philosophical discussion after dinner."

Rik started to walk on. Suddenly, he turned back. "There's another enemy, or there soon will be."

"The looters. They'll present a special kind of problem. I hate shooting animals. I hate that kind of fight. I have more respect for the creature relaxing in my living room than for any of the beasts who will come. At least Sheen presents me with a choice. The beasts won't, so I'll have to kill them."

"I saw her walking in the woods with Sheen."

Sentences again, cutting the guts to ribbons. Why did death always come in sentences?

Rik was in his house. In dull wonder he saw that he was on his knees. He didn't know how he had gotten there, didn't remember coming home, remembered nothing that happened after he heard those terrible words from someone in the street. They put a period in his life, and he didn't want to think about it. Examining it would bring pain, and he was growing too intimate with that. If he wasn't careful he would never find his way back, never get home again, never be able to return to . . . what?

His head jerked up at a slight sound and he stared into the sleepy eyes of Pug. The zizzy lay peacefully in his cage, not suspecting that his anchor had sunk into a bottomless ocean.

Rik got up and opened the cage. "She's gone. She forgot you. Get out of here."

Pug didn't make his usual racket. Instead, he slowly sat up, shivered and shrank against the bars of his home.

"Get out."

Pug's tail drooped. He placed his front paws forward, as if to obey. Then he paused to look up at his executioner.

"Never mind," said Rik, and quickly closed the cage. His arms were trembling. He shoved his hands in his pockets. He went to the kitchen, poured milk in a bowl and took it back to Pug, who drank it and watched him with stricken eyes.

He went outside and walked up the hill, stood by the graves without looking at them. He began to search through his pockets, slowly and methodically, and he didn't stop until he realized what he was hunting for. It was there. A person didn't carry that kind of thing in his pockets. The soul fit inside a living body but nowhere else.

He looked at the hill and beyond it. Far across the city, someone was burning leaves. Or maybe they were burning their house. Smoke curled into the sky and made weird shapes. Overhead was the setting sun. The wind created sounds in the leaves at his feet. He suddenly remembered a day when he was little. He was ten years old and he stood on a street corner and screamed. Two men stopped and asked him why he was screaming, but he couldn't tell them. They had both looked frightened, he remembered. One said he mustn't scream without a reason, while the other said nobody screamed without a reason. They went away and left him standing on the corner, bellowing his lungs out.

He shivered, brought his mind back to the world of leaves and wind and grayness and the absence of one woman.

The house was empty as the world. He undressed without thinking about it. He was simply doing what people did when night came—disrobing and getting into bed. He lay down, pulled up the covers, rolled onto his side and lay staring at a mound in the bed next to his. The bed had been made up. Somehow, the pillow must have become misplaced. It looked like a body in the bed.

It was too dark to see clearly, and he didn't want to reach out and touch the pillow. His hand had a will of its own. It itched, jerked, throbbed, refused to do as he ordered it. Instead, it went stupidly inching across space toward the mound in the other bed, and he felt his heart trying to beat his mattress to shreds. He knew that when he finally touched the pillow, he would raise up and mangle it.

His hand froze. If he let go now, he might not be able to stop the process. It might all come out like a broken dam, beginning with a destroyed pillow and leading to no one knew where. A sob leaked from his throat and he threw himself onto his back.

"Is something wrong?" said Aril, from the other bed.

His heart gave a violent slam against his ribs and then subsided to uneven little beats that matched the coming and going of wind in his throat.

"No, nothing's wrong," he said, and he lay and thought of Sheen.

"Vennavora, you must come down; my mission is urgent!"

The cloud over Jak's head lowered to the ground. The great brown God sprawled on it in indolent relaxation.

"I already know your mission. You needn't bore me by vocalizing."

Jak flushed. "I know you have no love for the things of Earth but how can you ignore what is going on?"

"I ignore nothing, but the silvery one is without conscience."

170

"How well I know that. He consumes us all. How can we survive if this situation continues?"

"Man will not survive. Accept the inevitable, Leng, and live your days as fully as you can. You were never guaranteed more."

Jak stifled a sob. "You look upon suffering with indifference! There's no one to protect the children. Wild animals have them at their mercy."

"Where are their fathers and mothers?"

"In the arms of Sheen."

"And there you have your explanation of the situation," said Vennavora. "Ask me not. You see and you know. They wasted their lives. See that you don't waste my time any more. Life calls to me."

"While we die! Tell me how to defeat Sheen!"

"Say no," whispered the God, with a chuckle.

"I've said it!"

Another chuckle, another whisper, "In what language?" The cloud soared into the sky and Vennavora was gone.

The slaughterhouse that provided meat for the entire city of Osfar was a huge complex that covered a thousand acres. The killing and dressing of animals was a completely automated process. A cow was forced from a paddock, it ran up a ramp, was hit with such force by a descending steel ball that it died no matter which part of its body sustained the blow, after which it dropped onto another ramp and rolled toward the big saws.

Today the paddock contained 20 or 30 human workers who had been driven there by Bebe and a squadron of zizzys. Brog, the prophet, stood beside a second ramp and alternately cried and prayed. He was free, not imprisoned by the zizzys. Bebe had always enjoyed watching Brog.

The people in the paddock had a choice as to which ramp they would take. They could run up the one and die under the steel ball, or they could run down the second and jump into the huge living hill that slumped and pulsed and waited for its meal. The living hill was silver.

The back fence of the paddock began to roll, diminishing its own space. The workers were shoved toward the ramps.

"Fight!" cried Brog. "Climb the fence!"

The fence couldn't be scaled by anything but a snake. It was made of slick steel and reared 15 feet from the ground. The foremost workers battled with one another, sought to clamber backward over those behind them. This wasn't permitted. One or two were thrown onto the first ramp. Some had already decided on the second ramp, but in order to reach its entrance they had to get rid of the bodies blocking it. They surged forward and forced more people onto the first ramp, forced those in the lead to draw nearer to the doorway and the steel ball.

A man found himself looking up at a dull, gray sphere. He was pushed another inch forward, his foot touched a metal strip on the floor, the dropping sphere disconnected his collarbone and drove it like a spear through his torso.

Brog used his staff as a club. He beat on the living hill. He sobbed, cursed, begged, accomplished nothing. The workers—all but three who were neatly dressed and packed for meat counters in supermarkets—raced down the second ramp into Sheen's hungry mouth.

Bebe loathed inactivity, wasted no time, took his squadron and went on the hunt for more converts. He found an army of soldiers in the desert, on their way to Osfar to answer a summons of the Fillys. They were to lay siege to a section of the city where certain criminal elements lived.

The zizzys drove the soldiers to the slaughterhouse.

The house was quiet, but Rik knew Aril was there as soon as he walked in the door. He traced her aura to the back porch, stopped and stood glaring at her.

"I forbid you to go to him again!"

At least she responded to him, laughed and got out of the sun chair and went inside. He sat down in the chair she had occupied, felt the warmth she had left there. He brooded and thought about his weapon. It was a dangerous weapon because it could backfire on him at any time. Right now it was working. If Sheen intended to bring him down through her, she was safe as long as he stood fast. Sheen would kill her once he became convinced that Rik wasn't going to give in.

Filly Six was having a nightmare. He got out of bed. He had to, because his brother, One, was coming after him with a sword. It was the first nightmare Six had ever enjoyed. He danced beyond One's swing, hopped all over the bed, screamed for assistance from his loyal followers, and pretty soon the room was full of servants who tied One to a chair and stood and saluted Six and swore to do anything he ordered.

Anything? Six was delirious.

Cut off One's nose with his own sword. Damn thing was always too long.

See how it runs red? See? It ain't blue.

The natives are restless, sir. That is, the bugs in the cupboards, the offal in the cowsheds, the people in the streets; somebody has been telling them the world is coming to an end.

Call out the armies. If anybody complains, shoot 'em.

Best nightmare Six ever had.

Sir, would you believe it, but something happened that never happened before in all history? There are no armies to call out. Practically every soldier has deserted. There's no one to protect us.

What about the offal? What are they doing?

Tearing things up, sir.

For God's sake, someone wake me up.

For God's sake, you are awake, sir.

The world panted. Machines that ran by themselves were frightening. The mechanics were unable to tolerate being alone with things that had no minds. Fires began in factories, granaries and closets. Wherever a mind was absent, chaos seemed to be a natural consequence.

The world unveiled a face of evil. Shadows became more significant than sunlight, skulking more rewarding than openness. Success meant lying in wait for someone who had food and clothing. People who had enjoyed fiddling with the little garden in their back yard thanked their lucky stars. They had a problem with thieves who came down the streets in trickles. Later, the trickles would become hordes.

Rik went hunting for Sheen, recklessly at first and then with real dedication. When a certain fact dawned on him, he shook his head in disbelief and searched harder. It wasn't possible that he couldn't find Sheen.

He couldn't find him. There were thousands of silver creatures but he didn't find one. No shiny tares hopped over the landscape, no zizzy with a silver coat flew anywhere, no human zombies were to be seen in the oases or the streets of Osfar. Sheen was hiding from him.

He knew rage, pure red-eyed rage that sent him driving through the city and the desert at a frantic pace that exhausted him. He kept at it for three days until he finally stopped. The thousand shapes of Sheen were as earthbound as he, but the creature was nowhere to be found. He wasn't going to be granted the privilege of punching a silver face. He wasn't going to have the opportunity to fight for Aril. Sheen didn't want to argue with him. He would do what he pleased with Aril and no one would interfere. He would use Aril to bring Rik to his knees, and they would both be taken together.

"No!" Rik roared. He stopped driving in circles and went home.

"Are you so far gone you can't recognize a noose when you stick your head in it?" He said this to Aril as she was going out the door the next day. When she didn't answer, didn't look at him, he followed her outside. "Is your self-destruct timer invincible?" he yelled at her back.

He was waiting for her when she returned hours later. "Did you have a good time?" he said. "Did the two of you discuss how funny it will be when I give up? Where is the son of a bitch? I want to see him. I want to knock the crap out of him."

Next time, he changed his tactics. "Honey, don't you care anything for me? I'm your husband and I'm lonely when you're gone. What will people think when you go to meet him every time you take the notion? He's a seducer, you know that, don't you? Underneath all that silver stuff, he's a man."

He could have stood naked on his head in the middle of the street and she wouldn't have heard him. Aware of all the things that disgusted her, he did them all. He committed every irritating crime he could think of—left his clothes strewn about, made sure the door was wide open when he went to the bathroom, neglected to shut the refrigerator, deposited his shoes in the hallways. She noticed nothing; she was blind.

He didn't feed Pug for two days, in hopes that the zizzy's moans would attract her attention. Finally, he fed the creature to keep it from starving. He went looking for Sheen but didn't find him. He began to follow Aril. It was impossible that she knew he was behind her, but she always did the same thing—went a few paces and sat down on a curb, stump or rock and there she stayed until he went away. If he didn't leave, she went back home and waited until he fell asleep. It didn't matter what time it was. When he went to sleep, she slipped away to meet Sheen.

One day he sat reading a newspaper in his favorite chair beside the front window.

"Let's go to Sheen, let's all go to Sheen; he'll take your troubled soul, he'll empty out your bean."

The sounds of the song were made by a gang of youths who had built a bonfire in a yard down the street. They danced around the fire and sang. A young boy came walking past them. He had his paws in his pockets and he didn't glance at the fire or the chanting youths.

Rik heard a step on the porch, heard the pail of food being picked up. A moment later, the front door opened.

"I'm sorry, I thought the house was empty." The boy walked out. A long minute went by and then he came back in.

"You're about to give up, aren't you?"

"What makes you think that?" said Rik.

"The way you sit in the chair; the way you stare without seeing anything; the way you're thinking."

"Can you read my mind."

"No."

"Are you worried about me?"

"I like this house," said the boy. "When you're gone, I'll make use of it."

"Have we met before?"

They had, briefly; a long time ago. The boy had picked up a wood carving Rik had thrown away, and Rik followed him and watched him hide the carving in a cleft in a wall.

a billion days of earth

The boy's name was Geo and he wasn't like other boys. Mostly, he was like a little old man who had settled into a rigid pattern of behavior and wouldn't be budged. Geo reasoned like a calculator and cared more for the data fed into his brain than for anything else.

"You know a lot of things," he said to Rik. He had moved into a back room in the house. Rik hadn't invited him, nor had he told him to leave.

"Not because I didn't work to learn them. Come on with me and I'll show you my cache."

Later, Geo said, "You didn't want this place to be forgotten."

"You mean after I go to Sheen?"

"I made a mistake before. You're not going to Sheen. But you're no longer interested in this room. Thank you for bringing me here. I've never been happier."

"Then why don't you act happy?"

"I never act anything. Why did you show me this place? You care nothing for me."

"Suppose there was a man who decided Sheen had no conscience, and who also decided to surrender in order to become Sheen's conscience? You know—go to Sheen and then teach him the ABC's of ethics?"

"I'd say the man was a lunatic who ought to be locked up."

"A good idea," said Rik. "His name is Jak. He'll be locked up in here and you'll look after him, in exchange for the use of all the equipment here."

"All of it?"

"See that you don't break anything."

A week later, Rik sat in a small park and talked to the trees. "I know you're somewhere around," he said in a loud voice. "You don't want me to see you. You're not convinced that I won't run away and hide for good."

As far as he could tell, no one heard him but the trees, benches and tables. But Sheen had to be somewhere. Sheen had to hear him.

"You're making a mistake," he said. "I came here to tell you you're wasting your time. It won't work. Killing her won't change me. No matter how long you take to do it, or how much of a kick you get out of it, or how much you make me suffer, you won't get what you want. You should realize that it stops right there. I'm here to tell you where the dead end is. It's at the end of her road. I'd do anything to keep her, but I want her here, now, with me and with no strings attached. I don't want her any other way. If you take her, she's yours. I'll have no more interest in her. To me, she'll be dead."

He stopped talking long enough to prop a foot on a bench and look up through the trees.

"You should believe me. If you don't and you go ahead with what you're planning, you'll have to endure the consequences. What you'll be doing is committing an act of cruelty for the sake of cruelty; nothing more. Will it hurt me to see you take her while I have to sit still and watch? Yes. But I won't suffer as much as she will. You think she's so far gone that she doesn't know what she has become. She does know; she knows everything. For years she's tried to deny it, and I know there hasn't been a day when she succeeded. She's worthy enough for your purposes by herself, as she is. You don't have to draw it out for my benefit. At least give her the dignity you've given your other victims. Go after her because she's worth killing. Anything else is beneath you."

He stood up straight, sighed, felt his temples throb. "No one dictates to you, but neither do you dictate to me. I don't need you, Sheen. You have nothing to offer me. You don't have what I want. Give up. Give me up. You can't have me."

A few days later, he picked up some signals on his radio. It had been weeks since a message came through. He fiddled with the knobs and got static, so much that he was nearly deafened. A few moments passed and then a young woman's voice came from the box.

"This is Chin calling. Can anyone hear me? Come in, please. Is there anyone at all? Please, please, someone answer."

"Hello," said Rik.

"Oh, dear God," gasped the voice.

"This is Osfar. How many are left over there?"

"I think I'm the last. They're all gone, every one of them. There's no one left but me."

"Where is *he*?"

"Who?" said the voice eagerly, and as understanding

came, "Oh, he's right here beside me. He showed me how to work the radio."

"Sounds like he's pretty much like ours over here."

Another voice came on the radio, in a bellow. "Rik, baby, whatever made you think I could be other than what I am? I mean, think, sweetheart, think! I'm irrevocable!"

"I keep forgetting what a fractured particle you are," Rik said wearily.

"The young lady seems to prefer your voice to mine, though I can't imagine why. You may have her again, but she isn't worth the effort. I've never seen such a narrow-minded stiff neck in all my life."

At once the girl was back on the air and demanding, "How many are left over there?"

"A few. I don't know how many. It doesn't matter."

"It would if you were in my shoes."

He knew what she wanted. He talked. "It's very bad here. Our population was so much greater than yours, and it takes time for him to contact everyone, so that's why some of us are still left. The denser parts of Osfar have been demolished by fire and explosions. The food is disappearing and I suspect Sheen is responsible. He never misses a trick. It's hard for a hungry person to think straight. Scouting parties have been trying to find where he hid it, but they've had no luck. Our children are being destroyed, one by one. Those who still have food are hunted by animals, the rest are starving. As a matter of fact, I haven't seen a child for over a week. I don't know if they're all dead or hiding. There aren't enough of us to do anything about it. Besides, Sheen set up a barricade about twenty miles beyond the city limits. Nobody can get past it. Thousands of his victims are standing out there barring all passage, and they won't speak a word to anybody."

He rubbed his jaw and yawned. "When I get time I'm going to try and figure out why that barricade is out there, but right now I'm too tired. Those of us who are sticking it out don't get much sleep. Osfar is dead and we're just a few stubborn moles skulking in the garbage. Your call is the first I've received in weeks. I don't know what is going on elsewhere but it's bound to be the same as here. A few are dug in while the rest are giving up. That's all I can tell you and I know it's nothing new. You've seen every bit of it at your end."

He gave another big yawn. It made him feel worse, more lax, more tense in his stomach. "So long," he said.

"Wait! Please wait!"

"Why?"

"Will you call me once in a while, maybe once a week? Or whenever you can? Or let me call you?"

"No."

He heard her shocked gasp. "What?"

"I won't call you and you can't call me."

"But why?"

"Don't go getting stupid at this stage of the game."

There was an extended silence. "I don't understand!"

"I'll spell it out for you. The only thing he has left to use as a weapon against you is your loneliness. Sure, I could call you once a week or every day, but he'll not let us get away with it for long. He'll break the radio or set up a barricade around your house so you can't get out. Or he'll break the radio at this end. By the time he does that, you'll have become dependent on those little talks with me. Your tongue will be hanging out to hear my voice. You'll be crazy for it. You'll do anything."

"How dumb can I get?" she said, flatly.

"Right."

"Then this is it. I'm strictly on my own. Okay, I get the picture. I can stand it."

"Don't cut me off yet. One more thing. He'll have to use an alternate plan now. I suspect he's going to become so pleasant you'll love his head off. You'll want to worship him because he's so wonderful. He'll dog your footsteps, never let you out of his sight. He'll do everything for you but take you to bed. When he gets you right where he wants you, he's going to disappear. You'll hunt for him with your brain scrambling like a cracked egg. You'll bawl your head off and ruin your shoes trying to find him. Finally you'll get down on your knees and scream. You'll tell him to come and get you because you can't stand being without him. And he'll come. He'll be there so fast you won't have time to think or make sense out of anything. But you won't care. You'll be too busy begging him to take you."

She said just four words. "The hell I will."

"Right. So long."

" 'Bye, and thanks."

"Doggone it, Rik, that isn't fair!" cried Sheen. "I had it planned right down to her last moan!"

"Tough. Listen, about Aril—"

Sheen quickly went off the air. Rik smashed the radio.

Mr. Kulp of Ujan Street was no better off than anyone. He had a personal problem. He owned practically nothing now. His money was all gone because the banks had crashed. How would he and his pets survive? He owned a lot of them. There were 20 tares, several zizzys, snakes of all kinds and a couple of birds. The fact that such animals didn't thrive in captivity was unimportant to him. What was important was that they had to be taken care of.

He wasn't so far gone that he didn't know disaster when it fell on him. As the world slipped farther toward the Stone Age, about which Mr. Kulp knew nothing, he came to a reluctant decision. He couldn't feed himself and his pets. Someone was going to have to go hungry. He went hungry. He gave all his food to his caged pets.

After starving for three weeks, he sorrowfully opened all the cages and watched his pets escape. Sorrowfully, he noted that none of them chose to stay and suffer with him. Sorrowfully, he contemplated the state of all the Lord's creations who were being held captive by men.

Scarcely able to walk, he headed for the zoo. Nobody paid him any attention. He obviously had no food and he was too weak to use as a pony by someone who needed a ride. No one asked him where he was going.

There was nobody at the zoo but the animals, and Mr. Kulp's progress through the area went unchallenged. The last caretaker to desert had taken every available scrap of meat from storage and put it in the cages. There had been a great deal of meat, so only the animals in the nursery were dead. The rest were tearing themselves to pieces as they tried to get free.

His mind a blank, and with a singing sensation in his viscera, Mr. Kulp found the keys in a building and methodically began to unlock every door in the place. He didn't mind that he was knocked about by scrambling bodies, didn't mind

180

when he got trampled underfoot. He simply stood up again and opened some more cages.

He hadn't known about maximum security, but he didn't mind its existence because it gave him more work to do. He didn't mind that his scalp was removed by a hurtling shape or that his vision was impaired by his own blood. He didn't mind when his clothes somehow got torn off and he was left to walk naked in darkness.

There was only one part he minded. The last cage he unlocked let loose a thing that had no inclination to go off hunting for food when there was some right there under its nose. Mr. Kulp minded what happened to him, because no matter how deeply into dementia a mind plunged, it still went through the motions. It knew pain when it saw it. Damn the mind. Why did it exist? What had it ever done for anybody except plumb the depths of agony and broadcast it everywhere?

Mrs. Ploke came running into the street. Her blind eyes wide, she whipped her head from side to side as if the two empty holes in it could penetrate the ebony of her world.

"Help! Won't someone help me?"

She grabbed up her skirts and ran toward the curb. A man darted from behind a building, crouched low and extended a broom across her path. The woman tripped over it and crashed to the ground.

"They took Brog away!" she cried. "They're killing him!" Climbing to her feet, she gathered up her skirts and stumbled headlong into a wrecked automobile. The man who had tripped her started forward. His attention swerved to a group of women who ran out of a store. He abandoned Mrs. Ploke and headed after them.

Mrs. Ploke grasped the bumper of the car and staggered erect. Her voice rang out in the stillness. "Show me where he is! Please, someone take me to Brog. They're crucifying him."

The clock in the corner tower tolled the hour of six. "Help! Someone help!"

Some came to help. From beneath a building. Someone came on all fours.

Mrs. Ploke heard sound. Her head turned toward it. Out

went an imploring paw. "Take me to the place where he hangs on the cross! He mustn't die alone. I want to stand where he can see me."

Her savior approached with stealth and took her to Heaven with one savage slashing of his teeth.

chapter xiii

Whatever made him think he could con Sheen? He had thought it. He had planned even his own behavior down to the last nod or shake of his head. A red herring had been his central character, a little red herring named Jak, and to hell with whatever else happened except that he had to keep Sheen away from Aril.

Had it worked at all, even in the beginning? He had wanted Sheen to concentrate on Jak, get the silver creature stirred up to where he wanted nothing but to find that evasive little Leng. That had been the plan.

Maybe Sheen knew he had Jak tied up. He didn't know where, otherwise he would have had the Leng long ago. Sheen was canny. Even while he hunted for one victim, he was feeling out the other, strolling through the city with her while her husband sat back and snickered because he thought he had fooled a fox.

Why hadn't he taken her at their first meeting? Her defenses were made of wool. Why was Sheen waiting?

Rik felt as if he were trying to walk on water. It wasn't possible to stand aside and watch her go out of the house when he knew she was headed for a rendezvous, but he stood aside and watched. How could he scream when he had no voice? It was getting so he could almost predict when it would happen. Aril would suddenly drop whatever she was doing and leave without a word. It had to do with tension. Rik could sense it building up in her, and when it reached a certain point, when the lines around her mouth grew prominent, when she had trouble picking things up, that was when she went out to search for a creature everyone else was desperately trying to avoid.

Shaving was irritating. He wanted to give it up, but he didn't. He made himself bathe, but he always did it quickly. Sometimes he forgot to eat. There weren't enough hours in the days. She might walk out while he was doing something unimportant. He might not see her go. He had to be there at the window when she left, because this might be the time when she wasn't coming back and he had to have that one last look at her. He wouldn't be deprived of that. Each time, after he looked, he sat down in the chair by the window and waited, not looking at anything, not thinking anything, with every bit of his being residing in his ears. He had to hear that first step of her returning so he could bring himself back to life. She mustn't be allowed to walk in on his corpse.

The thing to do was to give her up. But he already had. Long ago he had seen her step into hell. He found himself hurrying through the house to find her. His eyes couldn't perform their function if she was out of sight. He was blind when she wasn't there. When she came back, she brought his sight with her.

She didn't even realize he was alive. Everything she did was done mechanically. Did she know, for instance, that the last week had gone by without their saying one word to each other? Was she aware that she had spent the last two hours staring at a blank wall? He had read part of the newspaper aloud to assure himself they were alive and not two ghosts sitting there.

Once she got out of bed and left the house in her nightgown. From the window, he watched her walk down the street and he promptly plunged back into his old state of terror.

For a change he deliberately heightened his fear by leaving the house and going to the cache. He didn't want to see Jak. He didn't care if the cache still existed. If the streets and alleys of Osfar had been lined with corpses, he wouldn't have cared. It was nothing to him that Geo was there in the hideout and that his instructions were being carried out.

"Hi."

Rik didn't answer. He stood with his hands in his pockets and looked around, knew from the way Geo looked at him that he was behaving normally.

Geo hurriedly stuffed a gag in Jak's mouth. "He isn't fit to listen to." The Leng leaned forward and struggled against the ropes that bound him to the chair. His eyes were round with rage.

"How do you get him to behave for you?" said Rik.

"By threatening to take the food away with me."

"Would you?"

Geo shrugged. "If he can only be saved like this, he isn't worth the bother."

Rik looked at Jak. The Leng was slumped in the chair, seemed smaller, and the sadness in his eyes was deep.

"You're too hard," said Rik.

Geo gave him an amused glance. "Compared to you, I'm a marshmallow."

"Is that what you think?"

"Never mind. You have problems I don't have. Sometimes problems make people think weird things."

Again Rik looked at Jak. "You still don't see what he has, do you?"

"I see it," said Geo. "I also see that his gentleness is weakness. He wants to love so badly that he's willing to direct it toward anything. It will kill him in the end. If you let him loose, he'll go straight to Sheen. My advice is to untie him right now. Let him go. Let him do what he wants. You're not his keeper."

"You don't believe in helping someone?"

"Not until he asks."

"Can't you hear him crying at the top of his lungs?"

"I can't tune in to those signals," said Geo. "You keep telling me they're there but I can't hear them. All I know is what he tells me, and it turns my stomach."

"I want him saved," said Rik. "If this is the only way to do it, that's the way it's going to be."

Again Geo shrugged. "We both know this is a fight that can only end one way. This is the end of the world we know. Sheen is everywhere, in every city on earth, and the children he rejects are being picked off by starvation and wild animals. After he has done his work, there'll be a handful left. A handful of people never do anything but live out their lives and die. It's mathematically impossible for man to survive if the population drops below—"

"To hell with your mathematics."

His expression unchanging, the boy said, "Don't worry about him. I'll keep him here, I'll feed him and listen to him, and all the time I'll be wanting to beat him, but he'll stay in one place until the day you come in here and say he's free to go."

"What happens if I go to Sheen?"

"You don't have to play games with me. That will never happen. But don't think the thought of having someone else around is giving me any comfort. I'm not made that way. I don't need anyone. I never did and I never will. I could live all by myself in the world and not worry a damn about being lonely."

"Yes. You're the reason I want to keep Jak alive."

"You're an optimist," said Geo, with a little smile.

"Tell me something better."

"You think the species is going to survive. You're afraid humanity is headed too much in my direction and not enough in yours or his. You have a little leavening in mind. But what's wrong with me?"

"When I look at you I think of earth filled with fields of wheat. Those fields are perfect if you look at them one way, but people don't like the same perspective all the time. The first thing you know, they're wandering around hunting for a violet or a dandelion. What if they can't find any?"

"What if they don't want to look for them?"

"I can't think of anything that frightens me more."

Geo said, "I'm the wheat and he's the violet. Is that it?"

"Something like that. I like combinations of good things. An extremist is a valuable asset to have around only when he's right."

"Who gave you the right to decide what's good for humanity? Not that he'll be around a hundred years from now, but I'd like an answer."

"Do you think I can say, 'To hell with them,' when in a short while I'll be one of the few humans left? I'm lucky to have any decisions to make, but I have one and I'm making it. That little Leng has something the world is going to need, and if you don't like him that's too bad. There probably aren't any more of his kind alive now. That makes him important. I'm not forcing him onto the world. I'm simply preserving him. His future influence will be what it has always been—up to chance. I want the world to have him around."

"There won't be any future," said Geo.

"The hell there won't."

"Sheen intends to destroy everybody."

"I know it."

"He wants to kill us all."

"Are you sure of that?"

Geo had been about to turn away, but now his head came around. "What do you mean?"

"I want you to survive. You won't unless you understand him. If you fail in that, you'll die."

"What does that mean?"

"I can't tell you. If you don't see it for yourself, you won't believe me. Watch him. Don't ever stop wondering about his motives. The most dangerous thing you can do is to be an extremist in your opinion about him, because of that one chance that you might be wrong, and if you're wrong he's got you backed into a corner. But your salvation lies in your being so extreme in your opinion about him that nothing can change your mind."

The boy stared at him in wonder. "What is extremism?"

"Being so damned certain you're right that you won't change your mind no matter how high the corpses pile up around you."

"You mean weighing your principles against the corpses?"

"I'm talking about your life. That's worth more than any number of dead bodies."

"You're advising me to do something you won't do. I'm to suspect my opinion while you stand by yours."

Rik smiled, but there was no humor in it. "You're twelve years old. Sheen never goes after anyone under sixteen, yet he's been after you from the first. Have you ever asked yourself why?"

"Certainly. He hunts me because I'm intelligent enough to . . ." The young voice faltered, trailed off to silence.

"To what?" said Rik.

"I don't know."

"What's your idea of a fair fight?"

"Where the combatants are equal."

"What would you call someone who challenged only people who knew how to defeat him?"

Geo took a step backward. "No."

"You're getting scared," said Rik. "Good. It's about time."

"He's after me because I know how to defeat him?"

"Yes."

"But I—I didn't know I was in a fight. Do I know how to defeat him?"

"Not yet, or you wouldn't be asking me."

Geo sat down in a chair and gripped his knees with his steel hands. "If what you say is true, he isn't the monster we've all been saying he is. But, then, what is he? Satan? God?"

"Yes."

With tears in his eyes, the boy said, "I'm mixed up. Suddenly I feel twelve years old. I want to climb all over you and beg you to protect me."

"Don't let him make you remember you're twelve. He'll try to do that, but your age has nothing to do with it."

"Why haven't you hidden me away as you have Jak?"

"Because I can't. Sheen wouldn't stand for it. I don't know how I know, but I do. He'd tear down half the world if he couldn't find you. He'll let me have Jak for the time being, but he won't let me have you at all."

So full of agony and despair was the sound that Rik felt the skin on the back of his neck stir. He climbed the low hill and stood looking around. The sun would soon peep over the horizon but at the moment everything was in deep shadow. Wind brushed at him but brought no cooling relief. He was suddenly perspiring. The pulse in his throat became a drum that sent messages up and down his body.

Come again, he thought, and wished he hadn't, because the sound did repeat itself, a low and anguished groan that sent him creeping back into the underbrush. He was suddenly on his knees, crouching and listening. Somewhere ahead of him, someone breathed in whimpers.

188

Once again he left the sheltering thicket, lifted his face to the wind, turned toward the spot where he had heard the sounds. Not until the sun made red and gray designs on the insides of his eyelids did he open his eyes. The hill swept away to a carpet of foliage dotted with flowers whose shade resembled the fluid streaming down the rotten post imbedded in the ground.

"Why are you kneeling?"

"I can't stand," said Rik.

"No one came to cry for me. Only you."

"Do you forgive them?"

"I do not. They're a pack of sons of bitches. They stuck me up here because I didn't know how to kill Sheen."

The sun burst over the top of the cross to scatter its brilliance. Rik stared at the shadow in front of him. The air was no longer warm. The sky showered him with the cold of outer space.

"Why did they have to use nails?" said Brog. "I never tried to save their souls, only their stinking carcasses. They could have tied me up here and left me for the sun to finish."

The head lay on one shoulder; long hair streaked the face. One gleaming eye showed through the damp tendrils. "They say there's no good way to die but I'd have loved it if they stabbed me or brained me with a rock."

Brog's legs had shrunk; the skin was taut. The rest of his body seemed to be half its normal size, all but the feet which were huge and swollen.

"Have we met?"

"A few times," said Rik.

"Were they amicable meetings?"

"Yes, they were."

A bird sang, then another. The wind sneaked through the foliage and brought the smell of ripe fruit. The stillness in the air was impending thunder.

"That's your heart beating," said the man on the cross. "You ought to go away. It might burst."

"Do you want me to go away?"

"What I want is for you to take my place up here. I want to be down there grieving for you." A shudder racked the bloated stomach. "Excuse me, I feel a groan coming on."

What began as a groan grew to a shriek. Gobs of moisture dripped from the flowing hair and fell on the red ground. The body didn't contract; there was scarcely a movement in the chest; the scream poured from the lips like water from a pipe, and when the pipe had emptied, the lips remained open.

"If there was something I could do," said Rik.

"You're doing it. I hung up here all night sniveling because I didn't want to go with just my own company."

"I can get you water."

"I'm not thirsty." The head moved a fraction. "Something over us. Look and see."

"It's a God on a cloud."

"What's he doing?"

"It's a she."

"What's—"

"Nothing now. She's gone."

The tiny body shuddered. "Came to have a look, that's all. The mangy hedonists."

"What did you say?"

"Screwing and dreaming. I wouldn't have had that kind of life on a platter, not unless I was an animal. Travesty. I never could bear waste."

Rik got off his knees, stared up at the cross in bewilderment.

The eye watched him. "You mean you didn't see it?"

"It didn't occur—I didn't think—how could you see something—"

"Something you couldn't? I saw plenty. I saw men with brains who pretended they hadn't any, and there was no difference between them and the Gods. I gave those men hell and they said to me, 'What's there to do in life, for crissake? I own my house, I own two cars, I got money in the bank, so why should I struggle anymore? Haven't I reached the limit any man can?' That's the way the Gods think. They know how to be comfortable and they think that's perfection. Shame on them."

"You can't die," said Rik. "Not when you can reason like that. I'll do something—"

"Boy, calm down. Nobody can do anything for me. If you don't believe me, ask that fellow behind you. He's been

190

standing there watching, and now he's figuring to step up and offer me Heaven."

Sheen walked to the cross, stopped and looked up at Brog. "You're right."

"Damn you, can't you let a man alone even when he's dying?" cried Rik.

Sheen didn't turn his head. He went on gazing at the eye that pierced him. "I came a long way to give you peace."

The eye glittered, the gray lips moved. "I hope you didn't pass up any poor needy soul while you were getting here."

"Change your style just this once!" cried Rik. "Help him!"

"I'm going to," said Sheen.

"Not with any of your damned pictures!"

A keening wail came from the cross. "Rik wants to condemn this old sinner to an eternity of the ecstasy he's experiencing this moment."

"Don't you want to live?" said Rik.

"I don't want to die unless it's an alternative. In this case, it is."

"Heal him," Rik said to Sheen.

"I can't."

"Liar!"

"Do you think I'm God? Go away and don't interfere."

"What are you going to do?"

"He's going to give me Heaven," said Brog. "I've been waiting all night for him. Don't stick your nose in."

Rik glared at the bright eye. "You want him?"

"With every ounce of humanity that's left in me. No one ever sank faster than I, but this might go on a couple more days. I come from tough stock."

"Get away from him," Rik said to Sheen.

"Be quiet."

"Hurry up," said Brog.

Sheen leaped upward toward the crossbeam, clasped it with two hands and dangled in space for a moment before he swung his legs and enfolded the body of Brog and the post behind him. He held himself in that position and looked closely at the ravaged face.

"Was your life worth it?"

a billion days of earth   191

Slowly, Brog lifted his head. A silver hand left the beam and brushed back the wet hair from the face.

"I wouldn't have missed it for the world," came the whisper.

For an instant, the energy in the mind behind the eyes flared like a torch. The energy flickered toward the sky, rested upon the forest of green trees, returned and settled upon Sheen with tranquil finality. Brog sighed as a silver palm covered his eyes. The palm of Sheen flowed, entered the skull, sought that which made man a living being, found it ... and gently, quickly, mercifully, destroyed it.

The world had always been insane. Filly Six looked out an upstairs window and had a fit. What the hell were all those people doing down there?

He knew, of course, having been on many safaris in his dreams. The natives always did that whenever they were driving a zomba from a village, or whenever they wanted to trap or kill one.

Filly Six went on safari now. But try as he might, he couldn't get his body in the right position. He wanted to be with the natives who were driving the zomba ahead of them.

Actually, there were dozens of zombas down there. Hell, there were hundreds. The natives drove them toward the desert by banging pots and pans. A few had guns, but the zombas were cunning and kept darting in and out of the foliage.

There were approximately 20 natives in the group, and the zombas they drove toward the desert were damned funny looking zombas. They looked more like monsters, and every one of them had the face of Six's long-dead uncle. In fact, they resembled the atavisms in the zoo more than anything else.

"Stop it!" Six yelled, leaning from the window. "You damn commoners never did have any sense. Drive those animals in another direction. Can't you see my damn castle is between them and the desert?"

He would have to get help. "Legions, where are my legions?"

The only subordinate he could find was his brother, One. A hell of a soldier was One, never took a bath these days, never changed his clothes or shaved or said good morning, just sat in that goddamn chair and stunk up the place.

Six slapped himself on the forehead and got out of the room quick. He remembered now. He had ordered the servants to tie One in the chair and cut off his nose. He had forgotten to untie One and set him free.

All over the castle there were little beds with little stinking lumps in them. Six remembered. He had hired men to kill all the children in the place because they weren't Fillys. The damn servants hadn't shoveled the dead brats out of the rooms.

"I can't stand the noise!" Six clamped his paws over his ears. The pots and pans outside made a hell of a din.

"To heck with it, I'm going to bed." He did, after hauling a few bodies out of his room.

Where had everybody gone? Six pulled the covers up to his chin and scowled when his feet stuck out the bottom. It didn't matter. A few cold toes made no difference. In bed was safety. The ghouls couldn't bother him as long as he didn't step off the property.

Someone had been killing a lot of people in the castle. Who had done that? Nobody but Filly One had jurisdiction here. Oh, yeah, of course, Filly One—himself—had ordered it. Anybody complains, shoot 'em. Too bad that every single Filly in the household had complained, at the top of their lungs. Too bad they all had to get shot; all but a couple of the wives.

The pots and pans and the dumb morons outside; didn't want the atavisms loose in their town. Why not? There were plenty of excess morons. They had always bred like flies, leaped one another right in front of an audience. Why not let those poor, deformed Fillys have a few for lunch? Any Filly was better than a thousand commoners.

"Papa," said Six, and Papa appeared in a dark corner. "How did this all come about?" Six continued. "Were you so damn greedy that you had to have the whole world? What did it get you? When they buried you, it was in the same size hole as the morons got."

The downstairs windows were broken and the doors were open. The fleeing atavisms from the zoo sought refuge in the estate. Like all hungry animals, they were capable of eating on the run. Inside the castle was plenty of meat, but it was extremely ripe. About 50 animals prowled through the rooms, pawed stinking lumps, hurried into other rooms to paw and sniff at more stinking lumps.

"Jub, bring me my breakfast!" yelled Six, forgetting that the servants who weren't dead had deserted. "And shut the damned door, I feel a draft!"

Arda hid among the blue roses. Their heady scent made her nauseous, but she didn't leave their protective cover. Worse things than an upset stomach waited for her everywhere on the Filly estate. Looters and the Filly monsters were hunting for somebody who was still alive. Their kind of mentality was never satisfied with a corpse to abuse. They desired to hear shrieks.

She didn't fear death. She felt that she had been dead for a long time. What she feared was an ignoble passing, because her life had been ignoble and she wanted the end marked by something respectable.

Crawling among the flowers, she found a cool, dry space large enough to accommodate her body in a supine position. The dirt tasted bitter. Resting her head on her arms, she breathed deeply and soon she went to sleep.

A rough foot in her ribs awakened her. She looked up and gasped. The face was so ugly she couldn't tell whether it was human or monster. When a steel claw darted down and ripped her dress, she knew. Away in the distance she heard savage growls. Then there came the sound of a voice calling her name. "Arda, Arda!"

The man took her by the hair and dragged her into a thicket of thorns. Being a Filly, she hadn't the strength of a normal woman, so instead of struggling, she made herself as stiff and heavy as possible. It didn't stop him for a second. He cursed as the thorns pierced him.

She knew she imagined the voice that kept calling her name, imagined the anxiety of the cries. Her existence had been without redeeming value and her death would be less than that. Rage made her lift her legs and kick the man in the face. In wonderment, she saw that he was old. Starved and full of hate, he also wanted to end his life doing something respectable. Violating a Filly—a member of a family

194

that had violated him all his days—would be his way of gaining restitution.

Savage growls sounded close by. The man paid no attention. Arda's kick had knocked him back a few paces but he hadn't lost his footing. Regaining his balance, he made as if to lunge at her. A gray shape hurtled through the thicket behind him and landed on his back. The atavism from the zoo's maximum-security section opened its jaws and sank its teeth in the man's neck. He shrieked and fell backward with the atavism under him. It embraced him with its animal arms and its animal legs, hugged him close and bit him deeper in the neck, ate a piece of his cheek, a chunk of his shoulder, scrambled on top of him and held him down with its greater weight. Sharp teeth tore away his shirt and stripped off sections of his chest.

The atavism ate voraciously, but still the man wasn't dead, or silent. The victim was thrown over and his soft buttocks were attacked. Bones split, broke, disappeared into a bloody maw to be ground up and swallowed. Her mouth open in a soundless scream, Arda left the thicket, rammed through the thorns and ran, leaped over the flowers, desperately headed for open ground, anywhere at all, and knowing full well that there would be no escape because there were gray shapes wherever she looked. A growl sounded to her left and she ran toward the right and then she faltered and backed up a few paces as something in the bushes ahead made loud rustling noises. A big gray thing leaped from the top of an arbor and rushed her way, another thing loped across the lawn beyond the garden and altered its course when it spied her, still another sat calmly on the porch of the east wing of the house and watched her approach. She couldn't go backward because running paws made the ground vibrate behind her.

"Arda!"

The voice came from the arbor tunnel, a long and low cavern made by growing vines. Arda approached the entrance, hesitated for only a moment and then she was running into the dimness, crying, "Wait, I'm coming!"

Mr. Omega stood at the end of the tunnel, under a faint patch of light that pierced the thick vines. "Hurry!" he called, and watched her run to him. "Hurry! They're everywhere!"

Arda's heart threatened to collapse. Her strength was nonexistent, her recuperative powers had never been at a lower ebb, but her hope was a live thing as she sped toward the silver man.

"Don't be afraid! I'll take you to safety!"

"Yes, yes!"

"They won't touch you! I won't let them!"

"Thank God for you!"

She didn't slacken her pace as she approached him, and at the last moment he guessed her intention.

"No! You can't love me!"

He had no time to turn away or recede from her flying body. Arda was fast against him, with her arms tightly around his neck, and before he could cry out a warning, her mouth was against his. With a groan and a sob, Sheen held her in his arms, felt her as a living woman, and then he stood still while his substance slid from her mouth to her chin, around her head, down her body and clothed her in a glittering gown of silver.

chapter xív

"I'm looking for my daughter," said Redo. He spoke to a bum on a street corner. "Have you seen her?"

"No," said the bum.

"Her name is Uda. She's a beautiful girl. Four boys dragged her into a car and took her away. Have you seen her?"

Bebe wept because he was afraid of dying. His beautiful body that had gone to fat was now truly maimed and brutalized. He had run out of human beings and animals; there had been no more victims to take to Sheen. What was a person to do? Bebe did the only thing left—he turned on his own kind and made them the victims. After a few thousand were destroyed, the troops mutinied.

Now Bebe was born aloft by his brothers, and as they flew, he wept in agony and remorse. His fantastically lovely wings were gone, ripped out by the roots, torn from his back by his unbelievably barbaric relatives.

He cursed and cried and when they dropped him from a height of a thousand feet, he shrieked out his hatred of them, the world, and himself.

This was the day he would die. Rik knew it as soon as he stepped out of the house and saw the lawn filled with silver figures. They sat in his trees, sprawled on his lawn, waited on the curb, lined the walk that led to his porch.

He turned to go back into the house and found his way

197

blocked by three silver men, who neither looked at him nor spoke but kept the door barred and refused to let him pass.

As he glanced back at the yard, the men pressed forward and forced him down the steps. Silver bodies closed in around him from all sides, to prevent him from running. He lay down on the sidewalk, and they picked him up and placed him on his feet.

They made him walk. For hours he trudged, and then he lost track of time, was barely aware of it when the pavement under him became hot, dry sand. They wouldn't let him stop, paid no attention to his shouts, wouldn't let him rest or turn back to the city. The sun pounded on his unprotected head as they walked for miles across the desert.

At about noontime he gasped and fell. They picked him up and dragged him. When they suddenly let go of him, he fell again and this time he passed out.

He woke up. His mouth was full of sand. He crouched and waited for them to pick him up. Once more he fainted. It made him angry when he came to consciousness with a clear head. His sense of well-being lasted only a moment before he was engulfed in red, hot reality. He realized that he was on his hands and knees. A scream came from deep in his throat.

The first thing he saw was the rifle. There were sand, rocks, empty sky and vacant desert, there wasn't a thing anywhere except himself and the killing land and a rifle that lay not three feet away.

He lunged at the weapon. Rolling onto his back and spitting sand, he tore off his shirt and wrapped it around his head. He loosened his belt a notch and then he came up on his feet with a quick bound. He looked for something to kill. His need for a target was gravel in his throat, a throbbing inside his temples, a savage pulsing in his hands as he swung the rifle in a broad arc and let his finger hunger on the trigger.

He sat on a rock and waited until he could breathe without hurting, after which he got up and started to walk. He headed across a mound of rocks. Behind him stretched the open desert.

It took him two hours to get across the rocks to a little valley which he knew like the back of his hand. He had always liked this place. Now he hated it, loathed every gently sloping wall of it, despised the river of grass that flowed like water in the wind, hated the messages of peace made by currents of air that sniffed among the stones upon which he stood.

He paused on the rock wall and let his fear rush outward across the valley, willed it to hold stationary the two figures who stood on the opposite wall. He raised the rifle into the air. "Sheen!" he screamed. "Today you die!" His body trembled as the sound of light laughter carried across the valley to him.

Dropping ten feet to another rock, he quickly looked across at the wall and a howl of rage burst from his throat. Sheen and Aril were gone. Climbing down the rest of the wall, he jumped onto the river of green grass, ran across the valley and stayed close to the rocks while he checked the gun. There was plenty of ammunition and he had his strength back. The rocks on the other side of the valley were steep. He scaled them with ease, stood on the top for a second before plunging ahead toward the thousand and one gullies there. Once the rifle flew out of his hand, and he spent many minutes prying it from a crack.

He was straightening up when he heard something that made him freeze. The sound didn't come again, and he climbed onto a rock and squatted down. He was out in the open but it couldn't be helped. He listened and frowned when he heard the sound again. It was too far away. Someone was moving damned fast toward a gully which he knew well. The gully was a trap, unless one had plenty of time to get out of it.

Swiftly and silently he moved forward, knowing where he could safely place a foot, confident that pressure and stress had already been tested by his having traveled this way countless times before. He went with good speed and no noise until the course became a gradual descent. It was like going downstairs and it was so easy that he increased his pace.

Rounding the last rock, he suddenly stopped. He hadn't been following Sheen and Aril. His hand went out for some support, gripped stone and tried to pulverize it. Knees rubbery with fear gave way and he fell forward, pitched off the rock and landed on a sod-covered ledge. A sharp clod opened his scalp above the ear but he didn't feel pain. Scrambling to his knees, he stared down into the gully, and he saw it again—the furry rear of a thing that was trying to dig into a cluster of rocks. The thing was seeking darkness where there was none, and Rik knew that any moment it was going to give up and come backing out of the crevice.

His head jerked around as he heard a faint, low chuckle. There was no one on the rocks above him. He looked to the right and still saw nothing. Neither was there anyone to his left. Clutching the rifle, he leaned down and looked into the gully. He couldn't see much of the bottom. The left end was almost directly below him but the real body of it ran far around to his right. He picked up a rock, took careful aim and hurled it at the patch of fur sticking out of the crevice.

He wanted to shriek when his son came backing out of the hole. He wasn't aware of his need, wasn't aware of anything but the huge, snarling creature that snapped at thin air and whirled about with one agile thrust of its haunches. Rik was too frozen to shrink back, too sick to do anything but stand still, and that was why Sten didn't see him.

Sten wasn't much as far as looks were concerned. He had fur. His canines were a quarter-inch too long, his feet had such short joints that he couldn't stand up. His nose was deformed, almost a snout. His eyes were mostly dark iris with scarcely any white showing. He had a stubby tail. Also, he had brains. What he deserved was an excess of instinct and a paucity of gray matter, but he had a great deal of both. As he backed out of the hole and sprang about, he wasn't on the defensive. He wasn't a cautious organism who would examine his environment and let it determine whether he would be a warrior or a tare. When Sten came about on his four tough paws, he was a predator hunting for prey. The only thing that brought him to a halt was the fact that he saw nothing to attack. His disappointment came clearly through in the low growl he gave as he climbed down the rocks to the gully bed.

Rik was right behind him, a position he would have exchanged for almost any other. He wanted to run and never set foot in that patch of desert again.

He continued to shadow the four-footed thing he had sired. Somewhere nearby on this hulk of sod was the unique body that had borne the four-footed thing, and she meant to kill its father. She, too, had a rifle, and she was an expert shot.

As Rik ran along the gully, it began to narrow, and he lost sight of his quarry. The walls dipped around to the right too abruptly and he slowed. The last thing he wanted to do was go bursting at his target.

Hugging the right wall, he crouched and made himself as small as possible. Sten was also taking it slow, and just then Rik caught sight of the gray body ahead. Then he didn't see it. The gully was so narrow at this point that there was just enough room for him to turn and make a dash the other way. This was what he intended to do if the second glimpse of gray backside suddenly became a mouthful of teeth. He didn't know if he could outrun Sten in a long stretch. For a short one, he could, because he could think faster. He would be able to stay in front until he saw a place where he could climb, and after that he could use the rifle.

He kept up a steady monolog of useless thoughts. Way down under the gibbering, he knew that the first second he started thinking sanely, he was going to fall down and begin to scream. He lost all caution, took the corner of rock in a single powerful rush that ended in a long and hopeless slide that landed him in the open in the middle of the gully. From here, the ditch widened and ran off into two broad forks. Straight ahead was a high wall. On top of it stood Aril and Sheen.

She wasn't looking his way. Rik almost yelled when her head began to turn. He couldn't make a sound through his parched throat. All he could do was stand and watch the shock hit her as she completed her turn, looked down and saw Sten.

It was as if a bolt of lightning had struck her. There was no chance that she didn't see the crouching shape. It was then that she looked beyond Sten and saw Rik standing there. Another lightning bolt hit her, and she gave a high, mad scream.

She was still screaming when Sten decided to move. He had come up against the wall, had seen the two. Something stopped him for a few seconds. Maybe he was just enraged that he couldn't climb the wall. He made his move, started running in an easy lope down the left fork, and it was a good choice because the slope to upper ground was clean and gradual. Once he was on the top, he could either go left into more rocks or he could head right and circle around to the figures on the wall.

Rik was watching every shudder of Aril's body. He saw her frantically fumble with the bolt of her rifle, and then she was running, but he was faster. He ate up the few yards to the wall, where he took a second to hurl his rifle up at Sheen before he pelted down the left fork as rapidly as he could. Over his shoulder, he cried, "You won, you crummy bastard!"

"No, you fool, come back!"

Sten went to the left, up over the small rocks to some larger ones and then straight across and down an incline that should have broken his neck, it was so steep. Rik hurtled down the incline and landed with a jarring thud in a narrow crevice. For a moment he thought Sten had gone on ahead. Until he whirled and looked 15 feet upward and saw his son. Sten was there, between two jagged ledges, and he could travel up or down, once he decided.

"Beat it," Rik said softly. "I've changed my mind. Get out of here."

Sten didn't think that way. He took his time. His eyes riveted on the man directly below him. Then he looked up at the higher ledges that were within such easy reach.

They both heard her coming at the same time. Sten jumped to a higher ledge and teetered there, growling.

It was too late because of those few seconds. Sheen had won. Aril didn't know Rik no longer carried his gun, that he had deliberately thrown it away. She was going to come down over those rocks, and she would have to kill him to keep him from hurting her son.

"Sten, baby," he called hoarsely, and Sten stopped growling and looked down.

"Remember me, boy?" Rik whispered. "You know—da da da da da."

The savage eyes reacted, grew wider, narrowed suddenly to little pinpoints of ferocity.

"Da da, you poor son of a bitch, you stinking, mindless bastard, come and get da da!"

There was no more time left. The big gray shape plummeted at him like a deadly spear, all 200 pounds of it, the glittering canines starving for his naked throat, and he opened his mouth to give one last shriek.

The teeth were drooling for him when the crack of sound came. Such a slight sound it was and then, incredibly, the 200 pounds of death twisted in the air, flipped completely over and crashed to the ground beside him.

He lay and looked at Sten, watched the mad glow fade in the eyes that were fixed on his face. One paw came across the sand, groped and touched him. "Da da," Sten whispered, and was dead.

Aril walked down over the rocks, her face serene and calm.

"What will we do?" said Rik.

"Bury him once and for all." She smiled faintly. "I'm all right now. I'm cured. I'm a gift to you from Sheen."

Jak marched straight to Sheen and stopped. His head was up and his shoulders were squared. "Here I am," he said. "I guess you can take me now."

"Hmmm," said Sheen.

"I don't know how to stop you," the Leng continued. "I don't know what's going on, and there's no use your telling me I have to find out. My brains are so scrambled nothing makes sense. You want me but you don't want me, you hate me but you love me. I can't stop taking people at their word. If they tell me something, I believe it. I've been told over and over again that I should be afraid of you because I don't understand you. Well, I don't know what you're doing but I'm not afraid of you. I—I kind of like you. I enjoy living and I'd prefer to remain in my own skin, but I haven't got a chance. Whatever you tell me, I'll probably believe it until I have time to think it over. That's the trouble with me. I'll need more time than you'll want to give me, and even if you give me more time, I'm likely to come up with the wrong answer. So, okay, go ahead and start lying. It will take you no time at all to convince me I'm standing on my head. In five minutes you'll have me swearing life is the curse of the universe and that giving myself to you is the reason I was born. Go on, I'm ready, kill me."

Sheen lifted his face to the sky, spread his hands, said earnestly and painfully to nobody at all, "What can you do with a man like this?" The silver gaze lowered and focused on Rik, who stood nearby. "There's something disgusting about innocence."

Rik was looking at a group of small children. They had been hidden in the desert and protected by Sheen. "I kind of like it," he said.

"They'll grow up. Jak never will."

"He already has, and that's the way he is," said Rik.

Sheen sighed. "Possibly." To Jak, he said, "You're safe until I can figure out just what it is you are."

The Leng smiled a ghastly smile. "That may take all my life."

"It might," said the other with a frown.

Rik heard the coughing sounds again, and this time they were accompanied by a weak cry.

"Help!"

He stepped onto his front porch in time to see a naked man stumble across the street. The man blundered into a hedge, fell on over it, crawled back into the street and sat and held his head.

"I!" he said in a loud voice. "You! He! We! You! They!" Suddenly, he poked both paws down his throat, and then, bending over, he retched, loud and long.

Rik ran to him and pulled his paws away.

"No!" The man poked a paw down his throat, gagged again and then he spat out a large gob of something that landed at Rik's feet. It was a wad of silver.

"The damned stuff is all over me!" The stranger proved his statement by digging more silver from his ears. He snorted and silver came from his nose. He pried a hunk out of his navel. It was in his hair and between his thighs; there wasn't a crease or crevice in his body that didn't have silver lodged in it.

Rik slowly bent down and picked up a piece, only to quickly drop it. "Who are you? Where do you come from?"

The man stopped picking at himself and looked up with a blank expression. "I'm blamed if I can tell you!" He stared about him. "My God, I haven't the faintest idea of who I am or what I've been up to." All at once, he clasped his arms around his knees and began to shiver. "If I didn't know better, I'd swear I just walked out of Hell."

Rik helped him to his feet. "Come with me. I know someone who may have some answers for you."

Too bewildered to protest, the man allowed himself to be taken across the boulevard, up an alley and toward an open field. They started to pass by a tall hedge. Rik came to a halt as he saw a familiar figure lying in the shade.

"Sheen, look what I found," he called.

Sheen opened one lazy eye and looked. "Oh, hello, Blok."

The man named Blok gave one glance in return, let out a bloodcurdling shriek, leaped the hedge in a single, impossible bound and took off across the field at top speed, bellowing all the while.

Sheen was grinning wickedly. "He remembers now."

"So you did have him!" said Rik. "They can come back!"

"There you go again, being optimistic. Don't be. According to my infallible calculations, about one in a thousand will come back."

"How can they escape?"

"By wanting to return."

"Good God, is that all?"

This time, Sheen sounded offended. "Certainly. What do you think I am, a fiend?"

"Why do they stay?"

"It isn't easy to leave Heaven."

With a snort of contempt, Rik said, "It isn't Heaven, it's Hell."

"You'd be surprised at the number of people who will swear they're having a ball while the brimstone flies around their heads."

Rik scowled and went away to find Blok before something else happened to him.

"I can't have me wandering all over the place," Sheen said to the group of them. "I would be a distraction. Can you imagine how it would be to have me looking over your shoulder all the time?" When everyone present shivered, he nodded. "You can relax. I'm preparing an oasis for all my gutless wonders, one that nobody can get into without a ticket; a silver skin. It will be a grand place and I've chosen an appropriate name for it: The Garden of Eden."

"You can't do that!" said Jak, his eyes filling with tears. "You mustn't prolong their sentence that way."

"Who says?"

"It's heartless and cruel; so unjust." Jak's big brown eyes brimmed over.

"I promised them an eternity of it," Sheen said gently, and his eyes rested on the little man like light fingers.

"Jak," Rik began, and the Leng bristled with indignation.

"Will you stop worrying about me? You can't keep it up! My soul is my own and ... damn it, damn it!" Jak looked at Sheen. "You don't have to do it, or anything else except what you want to do. There's another choice for you."

"Such as?" was Sheen's lazy response.

"Put an end to it. Give them the thing they've earned with their mortality. Let them die."

"What about those who might come back?"

"Don't play games. You know the ones who will eventually escape you. Preserve them but take the others out into the ocean and release them."

Sheen looked at them all. "There, ladies and gentlemen, is mercy at its most naked loveliness. But he's right, you know. Immortality in the Garden of Eden will be no condition to envy. It would be more just and merciful to give them what they clamored for in the first place."

Jak pounced. "Will you do it?"

"No."

"But why?"

"I gave them my promise."

"My God!" said Jak. "Maybe you promised them, but what does that mean? Look at it another way. Put yourself in their shoes. If you demand something for nothing from someone, and he gives it to you with the promise that you can keep it forever, what right have you to receive it in the first place, let alone keep it? Why should you believe anything that person says, when you've been unjustified from the beginning? Hasn't your very involvement created an environment of lies?"

"I'll be damned. How did you figure that out?"

His face pink with frustration, Jak said, "I'm not entirely hopeless. I'm not stupid."

"You're being logical for a change. I like logic. But I'm not too crazy about your idea. You think it would be just for me to be a liar. That's what I'd be if I broke my word to them."

"No, no, no."

"There's nothing more terrible than to give someone all they ask for and then refuse to take it back. There's nothing more inhuman or cruel than to take someone at his word."

"But you're leaving them to an eternity of damnation!"

"I am."

"You're just stubborn!" said Jak.

"Am I? Destruction is almost always unjustified, except in this instance. Be damned to you if you can't understand."

Rik sat in the park and watched the sky.

"You're as somber as a zomba in the winter," said Sheen, behind him. "What's the matter?"

"Nothing. I'm brooding a little."

"I see. I suppose it's none of my business."

Turning away, Rik fingerpainted in the dust on a table. "Their business is their own, too." All at once he leaped to his feet and kicked the table. "I wish I could mind mine. Why don't I? What do I care if they leave? The blasted hedonists."

"What in the world are you talking about?"

"Some things I hate to admit. I love them. No, that isn't right. I hate some of the things they do. No, that's wrong, too. How shall I say it? I hate the fact that they have no purpose? But I'm not sure they have none. Am I angry because I don't know the answer?"

He turned to Sheen. "Is it that I'm jealous of them? Is that what's eating me? It must be, else why does it hurt?"

"Damn it, what hurts?"

"The fact that they're leaving."

"Who?"

"The Gods. They're leaving Earth."

It was the first time he had ever seen Sheen wounded. The silver man stumbled backward as if someone had placed a hand on his chest and shoved.

"That's impossible," he said, and his voice was soft with shock.

"Their ship is finished!" said Rik. "They're boarding it this very minute. Maybe you didn't pay close enough attention to them. They're going to a green planet in the galaxy of Andromeda."

The last thing he saw was the bitter anguish on Sheen's face, and then the silver man whirled and ran at a fast pace.

Rik followed. He had decided that he wouldn't go and watch, knew he wouldn't like what he felt when he stood on the ground and saw the ship of the Gods fly away.

They were all there in the open field, all the people who hadn't succumbed to Sheen, and they stood silently and watched as the Gods filed one by one into the ship. There wasn't a sound as the closed faces in the crowd observed and waited.

Sheen was there, standing closest to the ship that was so bright it dimmed his brilliance. It was a rainbow creation, and its needle shape thrust into the sky like a beautiful, colored icicle.

The Gods refused to glance at their audience. One by one they passed through the bottom door of the ship and disappeared inside. Slowly, gradually, those filing toward the door gave evidence that they saw the glittering man who stood only a few yards away. All at once the line stopped moving. Every God present turned to look at Sheen.

"Don't stop," said a voice at the end of the line. "Keep going." It was Vennavora who spoke.

The Gods murmured, momentarily surged ahead before they again hesitated and came to a standstill.

Again Vennavora spoke. "We've made our choice. Continue to move into the ship."

A trembling seized those ahead of her. They became like flimsy reeds that swayed ever so gently in the wind, and they were swaying toward the figure of Sheen.

One of the Gods cried out. "Is he so beyond understanding? How can they who are so far beneath us be stronger than we?"

Another God groaned and spoke. "Is it possible for such as these to succeed where Gods fear to try?"

"Keep moving!" said Vennavora in a powerful voice. "He approaches us in power! There may be no more time."

A God said, "Shall we begin our journey to the stars on a question?"

"I warn you, he grows!" said Vennavora.

An abrupt silence captured the entire field, a vacuum that denied the smallest rustling of noise. On the face of Sheen was a frown. The frown deepened. The shoulders of Sheen straightened, the silver body arched and bent backward. The foremost God leaned forward, so did the second God, and then all the Gods leaned forward, including Vennavora who was at the end of the line. She was the only one who cursed as she obeyed the will of Sheen. The silver man slowly leaned forward and the line of Gods bent backward, and again Vennavora followed suit and again she did it with a curse.

Sheen continued to frown, and the Gods moved their feet and took one, two, three steps away from the ship. The sun shone on glistening Godly faces. Vennavora gave way to the pressure ahead of her and on her face was a grimace of terror.

Suddenly all movement ceased, all sound faded, vacuum was in command, and so silent and still were the Gods that they might have been frozen solid in death. And then death was shattered by the words of Sheen.

"I RELEASE YOU."

He cried it in a loud voice, lifted high his arms, allowed his body to grow taut with triumph.

"Go!" he said. "From this day forward, you are orphans of the void with no place to lay your head. Go and find what you can, but watch for the day when the children of men seek the stars. Then you will not escape, because each of them will be accompanied by me. I have tasted the taste of satisfaction, and there is nothing sweeter. I will have none of you, for there are none among you who would stand against me. Do you hear, mighty Gods? Not one of you would do what those around me have done. Because of this, I release you!"

Only Rik, who stood near Sheen, heard the last savage

whisper. "And because I find I haven't the heart for total destruction."

The Gods hurried into their ship, and then there was only Vennavora remaining outside. She stood in the doorway, faced the sky, spread her arms, and with tears coursing down her cheeks, she said, "Oh, Earth, you have become a scourge. You will go down in the record of the heavens as a world to shun. Killer of Its Babes will be your name. I, Vennavora, and all my brethren say the following, and may it echo forever in the air: We have love for Earth. Once you nourished our fathers, sustained them and held them up. To that Earth of a billion days gone, the Gods of now say farewell. Farewell to the sweet winds and streams of your body, goodbye to the sky and the sun, to the paths in the mountains and to the sparkling rain. Wherever we go, we will never find our home. It has cast us out."

The God whirled and entered the ship, the door slammed, and the children of the first men fled to the stars.

ABOUT THE AUTHOR

DORIS PISERCHIA was born in Fairmont, West Virginia, in 1928. She was graduated from Fairmont State College in 1950 and joined the Navy, in which she served until 1954. While working toward her Master's Degree in educational psychology, she discovered science fiction and began to write stories in this field. Her stories have since appeared in *Fantastic, If, Orbit* and other leading magazines and anthologies. In addition to *A Billion Days of Earth*, she has written two other novels, *Mr. Justice* and *Star Rider*.

Hair-raising happenings
that guarantee nightmares!

You'll be fascinated by unearthly events, intrigued by stories of weird and bizarre occurrences, startled by terrifying tales that border fact and fiction, truth and fantasy. Look for these titles or use the handy coupon below. Go beyond time and space into the strange mysteries of all times!

OUT OF THIS WORLD!

That's the only way to describe Bantam's great series of science-fiction classics. These space-age thrillers are filled with terror, fancy and adventure and written by America's most renowned writers of science fiction. Welcome to outer space and have a good trip!

RAY BRADBURY

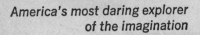

*America's most daring explorer
of the imagination*

- ☐ DANDELION WINE (10430—$1.50)
- ☐ TIMELESS STORIES FOR TODAY AND TOMORROW (8162—95¢)
- ☐ THE MARTIAN CHRONICLES (7900—$1.25)
- ☐ I SING THE BODY ELECTRIC (6652—$1.25)
- ☐ SOMETHING WICKED THIS WAY COMES (6438—$1.25)
- ☐ S IS FOR SPACE (2871—$1.25)
- ☐ R IS FOR ROCKET (2704—$1.25)
- ☐ MEDICINE FOR MELANCHOLY (2668—$1.25)
- ☐ THE WONDERFUL ICE CREAM SUIT & OTHER PLAYS (2467—$1.25)
- ☐ MACHINERIES OF JOY (2324—$1.25)
- ☐ GOLDEN APPLES OF THE SUN (2247—$1.25)
- ☐ THE ILLUSTRATED MAN (2112—$1.25)

Buy them at your local bookstore or use this handy coupon for ordering:

THE EXCITING REALM OF STAR TREK

Bantam Book Catalog

It lists over a thousand money-saving best-sellers originally priced from $3.75 to $15.00 —bestsellers that are yours now for as little as 60¢ to $2.95!

The catalog gives you a great opportunity to build your own private library at huge savings!

So don't delay any longer—send us your name and address and 25¢ (to help defray postage and handling costs).